VIENNA

VIENNA

Audition for Cold War

JIM MILLER

iUniverse, Inc.
Bloomington

Vienna
Audition for Cold War

This is a work of fiction. All of the characters, names, incidents, organizations, and dialogue in this novel are either the products of the author's imagination or are used fictitiously.

iUniverse books may be ordered through booksellers or by contacting:

iUniverse
1663 Liberty Drive
Bloomington, IN 47403
www.iuniverse.com
1-800-Authors (1-800-288-4677)

ISBN: 978-1475-93526-4 (sc)
ISBN: 978-1475-93525-7 (e)

Printed in the United States of America

iUniverse rev. date: 7/27/2012

1945 MILITARY
GUIDE TO TERMS

Americans:

CIC: The US Army Counter Intelligence Corps was created in 1942 to monitor "loyalty" of our troops and prevent enemy espionage. The organization went through constant reorganization throughout the war. Agents were alternately assigned to front line commanders or distant staffs with no clearly defined mission. As a result, they became fiercely independent, sometimes operating without the guidance or coordination of their chain of command, often working with or under the OSS.

OSS: The Office of Strategic Services, forerunner of the CIA, was a loose collection of soldiers of fortune and bureaucrats who conducted undercover operations worldwide. Deactivated by President Truman in September 1945 without an immediate successor, the US was left without a functioning national intelligence agency.

Army G-2: Staff organizations in the US Army were identified by a G designation when headed by a general officer and S for staffs commanded by a major through colonel. G-2 included human intelligence (spying), signals intelligence (radio, electronic eavesdropping,) propaganda, interrogation and analysis.

Examples of staff designations:

G-1, S-1 Personnel/Administration	G-5, S-5 Plans
G-2, S-2 Intelligence/Security	G-6. S-6 Communications
G-3, S-3 Operations	G-7, S-7 Training
G-4, S-4 Logistics	G-8, S-8 Finance

USFA: United States Forces Austria occupied part of the

country in the four way partition after the Nazi defeat in 1945 until it gained independence in 1955. American controlled cities included Salzburg, Linz and Graz. The capital city of Vienna, which lay deep inside the Soviet Zone, was similarly subdivided among the four occupying Allied powers with the Americans controlling the northern section. The inner city (Innere Stadt) was an international zone administered on a rotating basis by each of the four powers, British, French, American and Russian.

The Russians:

NKVD and KGB: The People's Commissariat for Internal Affairs (NKVD) included ordinary police, border guards, prisons (including the Gulags) and the Directorate of State Security which spawned two secret police organizations, the NKGB and MVD. During World War II the NKGB, or just KGB, which included both civilian and military members, briefly separated from the NKVD but was officially reunited shortly thereafter. In fact, it never really merged. The KGB and NKVD kept separate identities with deep distrust. The two organizations often duplicated efforts and spied on each other.

MVD: The Ministry of Internal Affairs, it was often shown as overseer of other intelligence agencies, NKVD, NKGB, GUGB, and SMERSH, but it exercised lax and sporadic control.

GRU: This Main Intelligence Directorate is still the Russian military foreign intelligence agency. Completely independent of the more political NKVD, KGB and MVD, it concentrated on military matters with far more emphasis on "signal intelligence," intercepting radio and telephone transmissions, and careful documentation and analysis. Highly secretive, its activities were seldom known by the other agencies which actively spied on and were, in turn, spied on by the GRU.

The British:

MI-6: Special Intelligence Service performed primarily overseas. It had branches devoted to imagery and document analysis, black propaganda, cipher (Bletchley Park,) and most notoriously, covert operations. The fictional James Bond was MI-6.

MI-5: This national Counter Intelligence agency was similar to the FBI but included Special Branch which conducted aggressive spy operations. MI-5 was infiltrated by several Communist spies including Kim Philby and the Cambridge Five.

The French:

Beset by internal friction, French Intelligence was disorganized and ineffective. Conservative and liberal, colonial and nationalist, isolationist and globalist interests vied for power as the country struggled to recreate itself at war's end. France had a confused and vacillating relationship with Russia, the Austrians and even its British and American allies.

The Austrians:

Despite occupations by Nazi and then Allied armies, the Austrians remained doggedly determined to control their own affairs. They formed a provisional government and reestablished government functions just weeks after German defeat. Their relationship with the Allied forces was always tentative and poorly defined.

The post war Austrian flag (on this book's cover) shows the traditional Austrian Eagle but with shackles broken to symbolize liberation from the Nazis. Its talons hold a hammer and sickle symbolizing solidarity with working people and a traditional, if disputed, acceptance of communist philosophy.

Photography by JoAnn Luecke   Edited by Judy Wegenast

CHAPTER ONE-1945

September 10, 1245 Hours

It was an impressive limousine. Long and black, it had a chrome grill like a submarine's prow and sleek flowing lines that made it look both fast and somehow sinister. Originally built for a Nazi general, the oversized car reeked of power and dominance. Fender posts that once held small Nazi flags were broken and all swastika insignia removed. Now it was a humble motor pool car for use by American staff officers like Major James Cole.

A lanky man, Cole was a full head taller than the average of that time with arms and legs that just never fit quite right, even in this huge vehicle. He sat alone in the expanse of back seat uncomfortably shifting and crossing his legs, aware that his uniform of olive drab wool smelled of the damp. Worse, his soggy clothes released odors long stored in the car's shaved lambskin seats. There were lingering scents of Nazi officers' cigarettes, sour liquor, whiffs of perfumes, and an acrid odor that might be urine or maybe even stale blood. The huge car was a rolling library of olfactory horrors.

Outside the window, the passing world was shrouded in mist and rain. Cole muttered, "They think the war is over."

"How's that, Sir?" The driver had to shout over his shoulder to be heard above pounding rain.

Cole hadn't meant to start a conversation. He hadn't really even meant to say the words aloud, but it was done. He crossed his cramped legs and, with a sigh, did what he always did. He assumed a role. Why not entertain the young man for a while? As he did so, his expression, his posture and his voice changed to resemble the suave actor, Stewart Granger.

"I said the war isn't really over. Look at those women. *Trummerfrauen* they're called. Rubble women, they push their wheelbarrows and hand carts endlessly, even in this rain they try to rebuild their precious city one brick at a time. They're like ghosts, digging and hauling and digging some more." He hesitated for effect. "But they remember. They remember that Vienna was once capital and crown jewel of the Austro-Hungarian Empire. They remember the greatness and they aren't giving up."

The driver flashed an overly friendly smile. "Well, we did defeat them, Sir. Kicked their asses pretty good I'd say."

"Yes," Cole unwrapped a damp cigar. "That toppled statue we just passed was of one of their Nazi blonde supermen. Now it's scrap. They were the Aryan master race, supposed to rule the world. Now, look at them."

"Yes Sir."

Cole rolled the cigar between his palms and continued in his role. "Things are changing fast. We can lead this country into real democracy or watch it degenerate into a morass of ideological clans at war with each other."

The cheerful young soldier turned to look back at his mysterious passenger. "You sound like quite the philosopher, Sir."

James Cole shrugged as he hunched over to light his soggy cigar. "Not really. Victors become heroes. Losers become philosophers. This is a ruined place and a ruined people with fear in every face. Let's just hope that fear doesn't rule them. And driver, keep your eyes on the road, there's debris everywhere and this rain's getting heavier."

2

Cole was bored with the conversation. Chastened, the driver turned back forward and continued into the storm as he mumbled beneath his breath, "Well, we won, damn it. There's no need for *us* to be philosophers."

For a long time, there was no sound but the monotonous smack of the wipers and the occasional thump of a pothole. They passed emaciated women in dark scarves and dripping, tattered coats struggling with loads of brick and stone. There were no men. As the car passed, every sullen eye turned to watch the only vehicle on the street.

After a time, Cole decided to continue his lecture, "If you look at these people you would say they were too docile to be a threat." Still playing Stewart Granger, his voice deepened dramatically. "But there are still Nazis among them. They aren't giving up and they aren't becoming docile." Cole made a sly effort at a smile and proclaimed, "I am here to wipe the Swastika's stain from the soul of this nation."

His smile widened into a grin. He knew that people tend to remember really outrageous statements and the people who made them. This driver would probably remember him, Major James Cole.

"Sounds like you have some really big plans, Sir." Then changing his tone, the driver became a salesman pitching a potential customer. "You know Sir, Vienna can be a pretty tough place to operate. If you need anything, I just might be able to help you."

Cole puffed. "Need anything? Do you mean the black market?"

"Oh, no Sir, that's against the law. It's just that I know some people who know some people who can get almost anything for a price. I'm sure it's all quite legit."

"Quite legit, Corporal? Just what can you get?"

The driver shrugged, "Most anything you want, Major. And, by the way, I'm back to private. I just haven't had my stripes changed yet, had to take a demotion to stay in the Army after President Truman's cutbacks. I know it sounds crazy but I like this place and I see a lot of opportunity here."

"All quite legit?" Cole smirked and continued, "Okay son, get me some Reichsmarks. I'll pay with greenbacks so there is no record."

Now the driver was all business. "How much do you want?"

"Two thousand US dollars' worth."

The driver whistled low. His voice was reserved, cautious. "If we're going to do that kind of business you might as well call me Billy. Everybody calls me Billy, Billy Connors. Major, $2,000 is big money. You could buy a nice house for that much and I could go to Leavenworth for dealing that much."

"Son, I'm in Intelligence. In fact, I'm a new detachment commander. You won't be going to any prison. Help me and I'll take care of you. I'm going to need a lot of help during my time here and you could profit handsomely. Think it over while you wait for me outside Colonel Mather's office."

Billy Connors grinned. "You bet I will, and while you're there, give my regards to that cute little Fraulein Gint."

His bravado done, Cole slipped out of his role, sat back and faced his own uncertainty. He had been a successful intelligence agent during the war but always working alone or on a small team. Now, he was going to be a commander. How would he handle it? He hated groups. The bigger they were the more he hated them. He stretched his neck to calm a facial tic as they arrived at the headquarters.

1300 Hours

Once a virtual palace, the huge Gothic mansion of gray stone had been gutted and converted to mundane office space as a temporary USFA Army Occupation Headquarters. Billy Connors pulled as close as he could to the entrance just as the rain slackened.

Cole fumbled with a door handle that worked opposite American cars. Then, stepping out into foggy damp, he shook off the chill and took a deep breath. It was time to put on a show, to assume another role. He straightened his coat, puffed himself up and imagined a forceful persona, like the actor Randolph Scott. Then, cigar clenched in his teeth, he marched up wide entrance stairs flanked on either side by rows of flagpoles sodden and sagging from the rain.

Inside, a marble floor echoed every footstep and sound in the reception hall. Everything was oversized; the doors, the stairs, the windows, as though giants had once lived there. At the reception desk, he was greeted by the bright and, as advertised, very attractive Fraulein Gint. Probably no more than nineteen, she had Betty Grable's hair style and smile. The girl rose smartly and stood shoulders back, youthful breasts forward.

"Good day, Sir," she bubbled. "Colonel Mather is expecting you. Please follow." She spun and led him through a labyrinth of desks. Typewriters and teletype machines clattered. The air smelled of cigarette smoke, paper and duplicating fluid. Cole fought to keep his eyes off the cotton print dress that clung as she swiveled her way through the warren to arrive at an enclosed office with a massive etched glass door. Without knocking, she entered and announced, "Major Cole to see you."

Then, with a cheery nod, she disappeared. Cole inventoried the room. Faded bare walls held nothing but three framed pictures; one of an angry looking Colonel Mather, one of General Mark Clark, the American Occupation Commander, and one of President Truman.

The colonel looked up from his paperwork. He was an intense, sharp featured man with suspicious eyes and thin lips. Cole waited patiently as the colonel took pains to clean the bowl of his pipe. Finally, he leaned back in his chair and bit down on the unlit pipe.

"Frankly, I expected you to be a little more impressive. Instead, you remind me of an Ichabod Crane impersonator." Mather wrinkled his nose and his glasses bobbed. "They say you're quite an operator, quite an operator."

Cole straightened. "I do my job, Sir."

Colonel Mather seemed irritated. "And just what exactly is your job?" He scowled. "You are officially commander of Counter Intelligence Corps, Detachment Eight. Frankly, I see no need for counter intelligence in the post war world. We are at peace and must put aside old rivalries. "

Cole considered his words. "As chief of the Vienna task force for Denazification under your G-2 section I will report to you." He pressed his lips together and continued carefully. "I will, as you know, have other responsibilities through other channels but I will not allow these duties to interfere with my work for you."

Colonel Mather pointed the stem of his pipe at the beanpole major. "Other channels, you mean you'll be working behind my back, doing things I know nothing about. Your friend, Colonel Robert Brown, told me to keep my nose out of your business and yet, when the shit hits the fan, I am certain it will be all over my face, not yours."

Cole scowled and came back a little louder than he should have. "Sir, my job is to make sure that when the shit hits the fan you *won't* be getting hit. And Sir, I do my job."

Colonel Mather glared. "You had better be right. I will not tolerate your CIC detachment cowboys running wild. Now, get out of my office. Stay out of my sight and don't waste my money. The budget has *no* money for your secret little enterprises. Do you understand?"

Cole saluted and left, pausing to exhale outside the glass door. He heard the colonel mutter "Asshole" as the huge door closed.

Fraulein Gint was waiting, all smiles and a bit of harsh German perfume. She pressed a manila folder into his hand allowing her fingers to brush. "Here are directions to your office, a list of people assigned to you and some other information. If you need *anything*, call me. My number is on the folder."

Cole smiled back. Here was a potential war bride looking for an American husband to take her out of this place. She might be useful in the future.

1330 Hours

Sergei Iliych Zelenkov watched out the train's window feeling more and more excitement as Vienna's fancy buildings with their elaborate facades flashed by. Despite Allied bomb damage, this remained an elegant, enchanted city, a grand place with history in every brick. He had grown up in Orusk, a mean, muddy frontier town of raw wood buildings where running water and electricity were luxuries.

Now he sat alone on one of the train's wooden bench seats meant for three. Handsome and confident, he looked much younger than his thirty years with only a touch of weariness about his eyes. A press of people stood holding straps as the train car swayed and jostled, but no one asked to sit beside him. That was just fine. Sergei enjoyed his space.

He was a striking figure in the dirt brown tunic, polished boots and gold epaulets of a Red Army major. He wore his round officer's cap at a jaunty angle. A sword and shield insignia on the blue headband of the hat announced that he was NKGB, the dreaded Soviet secret service.

He could have taken a much finer passenger train into the Hauptbahnhof, the main city train station but that was in the city center, the Innere Stadt, an international zone jointly controlled by the Americans, British and French as well as Russians. There, his arrival would have been recorded by the other Allied powers. Instead, he chose to ride in an austere passenger car on a cargo train headed for the rail yard in the Russian sector. Here he would be just another anonymous passenger. So be it.

Sergei thought of his promotion and assignment to Austria as rewards well earned during the long war. He had suffered much. Moreover, he had caused others to suffer even more. Now, that was over. Life in Vienna was going to be much better. He couldn't wait. No more freezing bunkers. No more stench of blood and sulpher. Soon, he and his family would dine in world class restaurants, attend great opera and stroll tree lined boulevards of one of Europe's grand old cities. An involuntary smile crept over his lips.

The train's other passengers watched the KGB officer and clutched their coats tight. He could see from their eyes they were wondering what could make this monster smile. It must be something truly terrible. His smile broke into an open grin as he flicked an invisible piece of lint from his knee and sat back with a deep and satisfied sigh. *"Privet Vene,* Hello, Vienna."

1400 Hours

Billy, the driver, whistled through his teeth and he bent low in the window to look up at the passing buildings. "Can you believe this? This whole block is untouched by bombing but everything around is completely destroyed, leveled. Look at these old townhouses, fancy stonework and iron decoration, wide sidewalks with trees, all perfect, undisturbed. The angels must have been looking out for this place. Okay Sir, here's the address, 37 Richertsgasse, but it's just a house, not an office."

Major Cole surveyed the fine stone buildings with their leaded glass windows and decorative cornices. There were no parked cars and no people on the street. At number 37, marble steps led to an oversize oak door with a brass plaque that read "Dr. Hans Hinkle, Praxis Psychotherapie." He had to smile. Whoever selected this location did well.

"Wait for me. I won't be very long." Cole walked through lingering drizzle to climb well-worn steps and twist an ancient doorbell. He was startled when the door cracked open immediately and a tall, stern-faced woman with steel hair and a lace collar stared out at him. He removed his cap and began in German, "Good day, madam. I am Major Cole..."

The door swung open and the woman answered in crisp British-accented English. "Yes, and you're right on time. Come in, everyone is waiting. I am Mrs. Parks and I will be your assistant." Cole gave her a warm smile which she ignored. He stepped inside to a dark Victorian sitting room with overstuffed velvet furniture, lace curtains and Persian rugs. It smelled of cigars and perfumed potpourri. Mrs. Parks took a leather valise from a walnut secretary and presented it to her new major.

"Here is everything you'll need to run your Counter Intelligence Detachment, names, dossiers, confidential assessments on your people. It contains proposed assignments and details for each. You might want to review before meeting your subordinates."

He raised eyebrows. "I'm impressed. Who provided this information?"

She paused before answering. "You may call him Trasker, although he changes his name often. He wants to meet with you at three this afternoon. He will explain everything."

"Very well, it sounds as though you have this place well in hand. Let's not keep everyone waiting."

"You don't even want to look over the paperwork? That seems a bit overconfident, don't you think?"

He forced a schoolboy grin and bent close to whisper. "I don't do well in front of crowds. Let's get this over with."

Mrs. Parks' posture made it clear she did not approve but, with a slight sniff, she turned and led him through a doorway and down a long, bare hallway that opened to an oversized room of desks and haphazardly strung electrical cables. There were teletype machines, a few antique phones and too much furniture. Maps hung everywhere.

Eight men and two women stood waiting with blank expressions. Cole strode in, cap under one arm and Mrs. Parks' valise in the other hand. He gave a cursory nod to the group.

Then, facing the array of expectant faces, his composure seemed to wither and he became a stammering Jimmy Stewart.

"Good day, I am Major Cole, the new commander of Detachment Eight. We have a"... he seemed to search for the words... "very important mission. The freedom of our country and the future of... our...ah, world... or country, maybe everything, depends on you and your...um...hard work. Well, yes. I'll get to meet each of you individually, but first, I have assignments. Please take out a piece of paper and something to write with. Ah, where is my desk?"

A movie star handsome captain with a leather-bound pipe extended a hand toward the new commander's glassed in office and wide desk. Cole took a moment to fumble with his valise, dropping a few papers. He recovered with an awkward laugh and smoothed the papers on his desk. His team seemed to share the discomfort of the moment. He began, "Johnson and-er- Mac-ma-hanan..." He looked up and two men raised their hands with some hesitation. One replied, "It's McMahan, Sir."

Cole focused on his paperwork avoiding eye contact. "Yes, thank you. I'll work on that. Anyway, you two are to work on interviewing the population and building files on possible Nazi sympathizers. Your main goal is the identification of members of the Nazi 'Werewolf' underground resistance. You will submit weekly reports to me."

Johnson spoke up, "Two people to interview the entire city of Vienna? That seems optimistic if not downright impossible." Cole shot back an irritated glance. "No, no, it's just the American Sector."

Mrs. Parks stepped forward and folded her hands before her. "Perhaps Major, it would be wise to allow Herr Honig to provide a quick overview of the Occupation Operational Rules before proceeding."

Cole nodded enthusiastically. "Yes, very good. Who is Mr. Honig, please?"

A stiff, gray haired man wearing a tie beneath his cardigan sweater stepped forward. "I am Honig. I coordinate activities with the Austrian officials." His German accent was abrupt and confident.

Cole looked concerned. "Does he have a security clearance?" he asked of no one in particular. Mrs. Parks responded, "Herr Honig has a temporary Secret Clearance granted by the Military Occupation Government. He has access to documents and activities relating to the city of Vienna and its citizens."

Cole made a face but said nothing. Herr Honig folded his hands behind his back and began a well-rehearsed presentation. "My country is divided into four sectors. The French occupy western Tirol including Innsbruck. The British have the south that borders Italy. You Americans have the north-central areas that contain the cities of Salzburg and Linz. The Russians have the east, Burgenland and Niederosterreich. Members of the Allied Occupation Forces may travel in any part of Austria as long as they are in uniform and carry travel orders with a four-power authorization stamp."

Cole interrupted, "I need a map. Does anyone have a map of this country?" The handsome captain cleared his throat and raised a bent index finger to motion as though tapping on an invisible glass. Major Cole realized the man was pointing. He turned to face a map of Austria that covered the entire wall behind his desk.

The crowd looked away and, though smirking, tried not to laugh. Cole's face reddened and Herr Honig continued in his monotone. "Deep within the Russian Sector, the city of Vienna is similarly divided among the four occupying powers with the exception of city center. The ancient city, centered on St. Stephan's Cathedral and bounded by the Danube Canal and the Ringstrasse roads, is an international joint occupation zone. Each month, the forces occupying this 'Innere Stadt' of Vienna rotate. This month, the British have responsibility. Military police duties are, however, always joint. Every patrol jeep contains four, a British, a Frenchman, an American and a Russian. No arrest can be made unless all four agree. They seldom agree and there are few arrests."

Mrs. Parks stood and thanked Herr Honig. Without comment, Cole returned to his list. "Belcher, Ryan and Roland," he looked up. Two men and a youngish woman raised their hands. "You will be hunting for the people who are assisting Nazis to escape occupied areas. You are seeking information on 'Odessa.' That is not a city in the Ukraine. It is the *Organizsation der Ehemaligen SS-Angehoren,* the Organization of Former SS Members. I'll have a list of contacts to get you started. Now, who is left?" Cole's German accent was convincing.

The handsome captain and a tall, attractive woman were the only two remaining. "You would be Woods and White, correct?" The captain stepped up and extended his hand. He flashed a grin with the self-assured bearing of a high school jock.

"Charley Woods, Sir. I'm pleased to be working for you. We've all heard stories about what you did in the war." Cole shook hands, aware that his seemed lost in the other man's grip. He averted eye contact and answered, "Stories are just stories."

The woman came forward hesitantly, probably feeling she had to follow Captain Woods' example and introduce herself.

"I'm Sherry White, a civilian contractor, Russian linguist and former translator for the Occupation Negotiations Team." Cole was happy to release the captain's grasp and take hers.

"You two will be working directly for me on special projects. I assume you both have clearances?" They nodded. "Good, we are going to become very familiar with the Russians in our area. You can begin by preparing an organization chart and background information on all Soviet officers assigned inside Vienna."

He turned to the assembled group and spoke loudly but in a cracking voice, "Thank you all. I'll be back tomorrow morning to check on your progress. Carry on." Then, to their amazement, he turned and left with Mrs. Parks scurrying after.

As he left, the agents looked at each other. "What the hell, this is the war hero we're going to be working for? The man looks like an ostrich in a uniform and acts like an idiot."

Cole heard Captain Woods trying to smooth things. "Hey, we've only seen the guy for a few minutes. Give him a chance, all right?" There were grumbles and headshakes as they wandered back to their desks.

In the hallway, he stopped and turned to Mrs. Parks. He took several deep breaths and then exhaled slowly. Rather than the fumbling, inarticulate performance she had seen a moment ago, he seemed confident and well-spoken, except for a few drops of perspiration on his forehead. "I hope I didn't embarrass you in there but I believe in…" He searched for words. "…in creating an image right away. Later, I'll build on that character. At this moment, they are confused and feeling childlike emotions. They don't know what to expect and that is a foundation we can build upon."

"We Sir?" She sounded skeptical.

He gave her a warm smile. "Yes Mrs. Parks. I will put on a show for the staff but I will always be straight with you. I need your eyes and ears. The moment we met, I knew you could be trusted. I think we're going to work very well together." She folded her hands and said nothing.

1500 Hours

Coffee shops were the very heart of Viennese life. The Occupation planners knew this and, despite shortages of food, medicine and other necessities, coffee beans were still in good supply.

The *Klatche* was a very old and cozy meeting place. Hand blown panes of amber window glass cast caramel colored light through layered cigarette smoke. Polished stone and walnut walls reflected images of men in suits arguing loudly about politics and philosophy. Crowded, noisy and rich with the smells of tobaccos and dark brew, it had probably not changed in a hundred years.

The laughter and finger pointing stopped when Cole entered. In an instant, the place froze into tense silence leaving no sound but the tinkle of spoons. He removed his cap, smiled weakly and spoke in German, "Please, I am only here for coffee." Wary conversations resumed in more hushed tones. All eyes remained on the American.

Cole surveyed the room until he found a small, puffy man in a tweed coat holding a cigarette and smirking at him from a corner. It took considerable effort to wind through the clustered small tables to reach the tweed man.

"Mr. Trasker, I assume." Tweed man nodded, motioned to an empty seat at his tiny round table and waved to the waiter as he spoke. "Major James Cole in full Class A uniform, well, you've certainly blown this as a meeting place. Pity, the coffee here is exceptional and the tortes are quite good as well."

Cole searched for a response but Trasker took the initiative. "No matter, I was ready for a change anyway. I'm even thinking of a new name... perhaps *James Mason*. Are you an aficionado of moving pictures?"

"Movies, yes I love the movies."

Trasker seemed relieved to have lightened the mood. "James Mason, the British actor, is so handsome and composed. Yes, I think I'll be Mason from now on." Then, in a casual tone, "Was everything copacetic with your arrival?"

"Yes, I think so. I have a thousand questions. May we speak freely here?"

Trasker, or now Mason, ignored the question, puffed on his cigarette and began, "You've met Mrs. Parks. She will be a great help to you. She sounds English but she's actually Czech. She's been in the business forever. No one ever suspects her. The others on your team are a mixed bag. The woman who now goes by Shelly White is not a professional intelligence asset. She's been sheep dipped, brought on as a non-volunteer, hell of a good translator though, great with Russian dialects and nuances."

Cole moved his shoulder out of the way as the waiter clattered a tiny silver tray and coffee service onto the table. Mason motioned to try the oily black coffee. "Now there's your Herr Honig, he's a real operator. The US Army pays him roughly two dollars a day. The Viennese government pays him another dollar and the Russians pay him more. Notice that Honig is the only one who drives his own car. He's making a fortune as an informant, he can afford it. Every word you say to him will reach his sponsors within hours." Trasker/Mason shrugged. "So use him freely for disinformation."

Cole was impatient. "Thanks, but first, I must ask; who the hell are you? Who *exactly* am I working for?"

"Ah yes, there's the question. You know, of course, that Wild Bill Donovan ran the OSS, the Organization of Strategic Services."

"Yes, sure, I've worked for the OSS indirectly for years."

Mason continued casually. "Ah, but Donovan was a friend of our dead President Roosevelt. J. Edgar Hoover hated Donovan and convinced Truman to dissolve the OSS at war's end, possibly because Donavan once called Hoover a fairy. Anyway, as it stands, the United States currently has *no* central intelligence authority. There's no one in charge, no one at all. Apparently, we feel invulnerable hiding behind our atom bomb. All the others, France, Britain and most of all, Russia are terrified of us and our bomb. They're in a blood frenzy of spying on America but our government is asleep to their threat. Worse, Truman has even directed that we *not* conduct espionage against our allies, specifically the Russians."

Tweed man leaned forward with a grin, "But fear not, Major James Cole, besides the OSS, there has been another intelligence agency conducting parallel operations for years. Some called it the Grombach Group after a naval officer once associated with its operational side. We haven't gone away. We're still fighting the good fight. Using liberated Nazi money, we hunt the remnants of Nazi terror and we are preparing to confront the looming threat of Communism. Western civilization, after all, hangs in the balance." He paused and drew on his cigarette for a long dramatic moment. "You control significant military assets. You'll be invaluable."

Cole fairly squirmed. "I know, or suspected, most of that but specifically, who are you? How do I know I'm not working for traitors or double agents? How can I trust? And what about my boss, Colonel Mather? Why can't I brief him on my actions?"

Tweed, or Trasker or Mason, whatever he wanted to be called, sat back and exhaled smoke. "Those are very fair questions and I don't know just how to answer. We're acting without official state sanction, spies without portfolio, and if found out we might all hang. You must not involve Mather for his own protection. For security, none of us know more than three other people in the Web. That's what we call ourselves, the Web."

After a long silence, Tweed bit his lower lip, shifted in his seat and spoke again. "Okay, here's the best I can do. You're an experienced agent. You'll know what must be done. I'll give you support. I'll give you information and suggestions but you act on your own. I will ask nothing from you except that you do what you know must be done. Sound fair?"

They drank coffee and stared for an eternity. Cole seemed to chew on something. Finally, he broke the silence. "Okay, how do I contact you?"

"We've booked a hotel room for you, number 608 in the Hotel Astoria. It's quite nice. If you need me, ask Lidia, the girl at the front desk, for the key to room '*708*'. The key is on a heavy metal fob. If she hands you the fob with the key dangling, the message will be passed. If she hands you the fob with the key pointing up, I'm not available. If she says, 'Don't you mean room 608?' there is a security problem, watch out.

Only ask Lidia. The concierge and other men who work there know nothing."

"That sounds reasonable. But what if Lidia is not on duty?"

"I'll also give you a key to room 708. The phone in that room is monitored 24-hours a day. Just pick up the receiver and talk. This is not the preferred method. There's always some risk that someone can monitor even the most secure phone."

"How will you contact me?"

"I will leave a message at the desk that your laundry is ready for pick-up."

"Where will we meet?"

"The elevator in your hotel has a board where businesses can post cards or ads. The card in the upper left corner will be the location of our next meeting. I have to go now. I brought a satchel with me. I'll leave first. You pay for the coffee and then leave with the satchel. You'll find it useful."

He paused and wet his lips. Then without eye contact he said, "Good to have you aboard, Cole. Just remember, this is Vienna. There are more spies in this city than any place else on earth. Trust no one... and always carry a gun, two would be better."

2100 Hours

A lone Jeep's headlights bounced through the darkness of an industrial ghost town. Stray dogs prowled what had been a brewery complex before it was ransacked and looted by invading Soviet troops. Now, after the occupation zones were negotiated, it fell under American jurisdiction.

Few street lights remained to illuminate a desolate road puddled and littered with garbage. Finally, the Jeep came to a stop before the one still intact warehouse. Barbed wire and sentry posts were the only hint that there might be something special about this dark building.

A uniformed man with a flashlight dismounted the Jeep to stumble and sweep his beam searching for an entrance. He was taken by surprise as a bank of blinding floodlights flashed on. Slowly he lowered the arm he used to shield his eyes as the silhouette of a guard approached and motioned toward a door. There, the visitor presented his identification papers and allowed himself to be frisked before the guard led him inside.

Blacked out windows had effectively concealed the building's brightly lit interior. Endless rows of storage racks were filled with wooden crates of varying sizes. Lost among the endless rows of boxes, Major Horatio Aalpeter occupied a tiny corner office. Officially, his title was Monument Group Comptroller, a vague and fairly unimpressive description. It was a cover. In fact, most of the financial management was actually done by the Group's aging manager, a former curator of the Leopold Museum. Horatio Aalpeter's minimal responsibilities as Comptroller allowed him access to the Group's considerable stockpile of cash. He sat comfortably obscure in his fortress of wealth.

The guard knocked on Aalpeter's door and announced, "Sir, there is a French officer to see you."

Aalpeter came out of the office smoking a pipe and holding a stack of papers. The Frenchman snapped to attention, "Captain Devereaux, at your service." A bright and cheerful sort with a ridiculous handlebar moustache, he wore the blue and gray raincoat of the French Military Police and spoke English with a decidedly British accent.

"May I say, Major, how nice it is to finally meet you."

Aalpeter returned a salute cautiously and questioned, "Finally?"

"Yes, yes. Would you like to give me a small tour of your domain? I would so enjoy it."

Aalpeter's suspicion showed in his eyes. "I'm sorry, we don't give tours."

The French policeman kept his grin and leaned a little closer. "Yes, of course, but I would like to speak away from other ears. With so many people here it is a, how do you say, like a … spider's *web*. You understand I'm sure, Mr. Trasker."

Their eyes locked in a long, cold stare. Aalpeter exhaled, his cover blown. This fellow, a complete stranger, knew about the Web and knew his code name, but why was he here? Aalpeter forced a phony smile.

"I may have been a bit hasty. I think I might be able to work in a short tour. I will, naturally, have to see your papers." Frenchy was already pulling them from his coat. He presented a passport style ID and a set of orders with the colorful Four Power seal. As Aalpeter scanned them, the Frenchman whistled, rocked on his heels and finally said, "Don't trouble yourself too much. All the approvals are real and so is the photograph."

Aalpeter didn't look up. "The photo is real? What about the rest?"

An even bigger smile came with a whisper. "Well, you know… you're in the business."

Major Horatio Aalpeter hated being at a disadvantage. He was always the one who knew secrets. Now he was completely at a loss. "Follow me," he commanded and they walked down the nearest aisle. He began like a real tour guide.

"On your right we have three full rows of the works stolen from the Baron Von Rothschild collection. These were all recovered from Neuschwanstein, the 'Cinderella' castle in Bavaria. You may have seen it on postcards."

Once they were at the back of the warehouse where the racks were empty, they had a clear view in all directions. When Aalpeter was sure no one could overhear, he stopped to confront his companion. "All right, who are you and what do you want?"

Ignoring the first question, Frenchy began his pitch. "Well, you see, I was working on Operation Sybille with some of your countrymen when a lady from Innsbrucke contacted one of my people with an urgent request. Her family, it seems, had immigrated to Austria back during the Russian Revolution. She has a sister still living in what is now the Russian Zone of Vienna. When the Soviets invaded, they killed the sister's husband, raped her and her two daughters and pressed them into service as translators since they spoke both German and Russian."

"Yes, such stories are common. What do they have to do with me?"

The Frenchman craned to look in both directions. Seeing no one, he became more serious. "She wants her sister and her, how do you say, nieces I think, extracted and protected. Now before you make some empty statement about not having any jurisdiction, hear me out, *nez pas*?"

Aalpeter said nothing. The Frenchman stepped uncomfortably close. "One daughter is working as a clerk and translator in Colonel Lushka's office. They treat her like a slave and she is sure they will eventually kill her. Since her family of White Russians fled the Bolsheviks, they consider her a traitor. Do you know this man, Lushka?"

Aalpeter was noncommittal. "The Butcher of the Balkans?"

"It's well deserved. He was responsible for the cold-blooded execution of more than ten thousand Croats who opposed the Communist invasion of Yugoslavia. Now, Lushka is KGB Colonel for Vienna." Frenchy sounded sincere. "These women could provide a wealth of information. They handle his orders and communications."

The Frenchman shrugged one shoulder and sounded a bit sarcastic. "We offered to get the sister and her daughters to a safe place in France. She won't accept. She's afraid to stay in Europe. No, she wants to live in *New York*." He pronounced "New York" with clear disdain.

"I can't do that, the Soviets are officially still our allies," said Aalpeter with no conviction. His mind was already racing.

What could these women know? Three women from right under Colonel Lushka's nose, how could they be extracted? It seemed impossible. He could feel his heartbeat quicken.

Aalpeter said, "So what you're proposing is, you pull her out and then we ship them off to the U.S.?"

"No need to complicate things. If you take the job, you do it all. We'll back out." With that the Frenchman pulled an envelope from his coat and presented it.

The chubby American major took the packet, grinned like a schoolboy and shook the Frenchman's hand. Another Op was on.

September 11, 0900

Cole was preparing notes for his initial staff interviews when his door flew open.

"I won't have sex with anyone. I want you to understand that right off."

He sat back in his chair looking perplexed. Sherry White folded her hands tightly in her lap, sat down and breathed through her nose. Her voice remained sharp. "I mean it. I will not sleep with anyone."

Cole leaned toward her and tried to sound as sincere as actor Fred MacMurray. "Miss White, no one has ever suggested you do anything of the kind. What on earth gave you the idea that we wanted to prostitute you?"

She couldn't make eye contact, preferring to scan a bare wall. "I'm sorry, I just don't know about all this spy stuff. In the movies the female spy always seduces some guy and gets him to spill his secrets."

"Ah," said Cole, "but this isn't the movies is it? We need your skills as a linguist, not a hooker." He continued in his most paternal voice. "Now, we will ask much of you. In addition to translating and eavesdropping, you may even be asked to accompany me or another agent and play a role that requires your Russian language skills. It might be dangerous. We'll try to protect you but I won't sugarcoat the facts. I am asking for your courageous help, but not the exploitation of your body."

She crossed her arms tight and didn't acknowledge. Cole needed to lighten the tone. He spoke in Russian, "So, just how did you become such an accomplished linguist?" He didn't actually care. She answered in Russian but much too fast for him to keep up.

"I am from Chicago and grew up in a blue collar neighborhood with many Russian immigrants. I played with the kids and learned a little. In college I studied Russian language and history. I was in my fourth year when the war started. I volunteered for the Foreign Service and received a posting to London. Just days after I arrived, a handsome man approached me. His name was Vander and he knew everything about me. He spoke beautiful cultured Russian, but not like a native."

Cole watched her shoulders relax slightly. "We met on a miserable day, a London day after all, and he invited me to a tiny pub. The British have such awful food. Thank God, they have great beer to wash it down."

Now she sat back and actually allowed a smile. Cole matched her relaxed posture and smile. Things were going better. He offered a cigarette from an American style crush pack. She hesitated before taking one. He lit it from his Zippo.

She blew a long stream of smoke and sighed. "An American cigarette, of all the things I miss over here, these I miss the most." He let her enjoy the smoke and waited patiently. Finally she picked up her story.

"Well, anyway, he offered me a contract job for almost five times my salary as a government employee. He talked of adventure and exotic places and changing the world. Well, here I am." She sat back and shrugged with her hands as if to say, "What's a girl to do?"

Cole looked keen to know, "So who pays you?"

Now she grinned broadly. "Do you mean, do I really work for you? Yes, I have a contract that says I report to the US

Army but I am paid from a Swiss law firm. It's really a sweet deal. Most of my money goes into a tax-free savings account and I receive a small monthly stipend to cover expenses. I live in one of the row houses on this block. It's a ten meter walk to the office. As to exactly who pays me, I can't say I really worry about it."

She seemed completely over her anxiety and looked him in the eye as she took a quick drag. "What about you? What's your story?"

He thought it pretty gutsy to demand answers from her new commander. He liked her but still, he considered carefully before answering. "I was a graduate student at NYU when I was drafted. I wound up in Intelligence when they found out I spoke German. That's about it."

Sherry White wasn't buying it. "What about the war? You went in a private and came out a major, at least that's what I've heard."

He didn't tell her that he had actually studied drama at the New York University theater center. He didn't tell her he worked with the French underground. He didn't tell her he had posed as an SS officer to infiltrate Nazi units and he didn't tell her how many men he had killed.

Instead, he politely whispered. "You know, in Intelligence, we don't tell war stories."

1000 Hours

Sergei Zelenkov tucked his cap under his arm, straightened his shoulders and prepared to meet a legend. There was no one in the outer office, so Sergei marched right to the colonel's door and knocked. There was an immediate answer in the form of an animal bellow. "Come in, come in." Stiff as a new cadet, Sergei entered Colonel Lushka's office.

The giant man sat behind a plain desk and puffed on a cigar. His eyebrows, moustache and lips formed three parallel scowling arches. His voice sounded like a cross between a bear's growl and a gravel mixer. With recognition, the expression softened. "Comrade Zelenkov, welcome."

Lushka rose to tower a full two meters, more than six feet six inches. He had to weigh almost 120 kilos, nearly three hundred pounds. His right arm was missing below the elbow where his shirt was folded and pinned. Sergei noted that his face was scarred with old wounds.

Lushka came out from behind the desk to envelop the major in a crushing hug that made him feel puny, childlike. The big man rocked back and forth as though this were a reunion embrace of long lost friends. Finally, the colonel released him and kissed Sergei on both cheeks.

"You must call me Lushka," he boomed. "Ranks are not for us. We are all Communists, all equal. We all serve the people for the glory of Mother Russia. So come, Comrade Zelenkov and tell me of yourself."

Lushka still had his great arm wrapped around the smaller man and led him back toward the desk. "There is little to tell, Comrade Lushka. I was at Stalingrad, but only from April to the victory, nothing like your service."

Lushka released his captive in order to use his good hand to hold his cigar. "Ah, we are soldiers. We are supposed to suffer. Now, I will tell you my story. I was born in the mountains of Moldova. My birth name was Dmitri Anatoli Lushkavetovitch. That is much too long a name for people to remember. The really important people in the Party have short names: Stalin, Lenin, Zhukov. Now, I am just Lushka, no middle name, no first name. Now people remember me. Sit, sit and tell me why you are here."

Sergei was taken aback. He assumed Colonel Lushka knew about his assignment. He remained standing at attention. "I am here to supervise the construction of a fence across Austria to protect our land and keep the European occupation troops out."

Lushka grinned and waved his one hand dismissively. "No, you won't be doing that. Our diplomats have negotiated a stupid agreement with Renner's provisional Austrian government to allow them to run their country as one nation. There will be no fence here." He winked at Sergei. "The fence will be at the Austrian border with Hungary. Someday, we will pull out of Austria, but Hungary and Slovakia are ours forever. That will be a better border, easier to defend."

"What then will be my job, Comrade Lushka?"

Lushka laughed and slapped his hand on his desk hard enough to make his pen holder bounce. "Ah, you, my friend, will be in charge of finding German scientists hiding like rats here in Vienna. You will be in charge of our part of *Operation Alsos*. We know they are here. They want to escape to Italy and maybe South America. None of my people can find them. We want Doctors Klein and Finklestein and even more, we want one man, Doctor Werner Heisenberg. Comrade Stalin himself wants this man captured. These are the brains we need for our future weapons programs."

Lushka's head bobbed and his eyes went unfocused as though he was having some kind of internal conversation. After a full minute of silence he resumed, "You will have available all the resources I possess. This is top priority, top priority. Stalin wants this. We must not let these Nazi bastards escape."

Sergei had questions but before he could ask, the door slammed open and an Amazon of a woman burst into the room. Lushka beamed as he shouted, "Svetlana, my flower, come meet our new Comrade Zelenkov."

She wore a plain Red Army uniform with no rank, ribbons or unit patch. Large breasted and strongly built, she carried herself like a man. Braided straw hair fell to plain black shoulderboards on broad athletic shoulders. Polished knee-high boots had small straps at the top. It was the uniform of a political commissar, an all-powerful commissar. Even Lushka would defer to a commissar if politics or patriotism were involved.

"Lushka, my hero, what have you brought me? This one is pretty, no? Is he a present for me?" With that, she reached over to Sergei and grabbed a big, meaty handful of his butt. Startled, Sergei jumped and almost let out a yelp. He didn't believe this was happening. A KGB major did not get fondled, even by a commissar.

Lushka broke out laughing. Svetlana laughed. Sergei looked stricken. She still had hold of his ass.

"So, pretty man, what do you want here?"

Sergei tried to keep his composure. "I am KGB. Colonel Lushka was just giving me an assignment." She still had hold of his ass.

"Lushka," she demanded, "Give him to me so I can indoctrinate him."

Lushka belly laughed. "Svetlana, am I not man enough for you?"

"Of course, my hero, you are better than a horse but you know I love the pretty ones. I will return him to you still intact, just a little tired." She kneaded the butt cheek as though it were fresh dough.

Lushka was still laughing. "No, my little flower, you are frightening him. He fought at Stalingrad and does not frighten easily but you are too much woman, even for a Hero of the Soviet Union. Maybe, if you are a good girl I will detail him to you someday, but not now. Come and give me a kiss."

She gave Sergei one last squeeze, hard enough to leave bruises, and then went to attack her colonel. Throwing both arms around his neck, she wrenched his head to hers and planted a kiss that must have sucked every bit of air from his lungs. After writhing against the big man she pulled back, wiped her mouth and gave Sergei a long, lecherous stare.

He still stood at attention but a slight tic developed in one eye. *What have I fallen into? These people are crazy. These people I work for are crazy. My wife and son are coming here.*

This was going to be our wonderful adventure. I was not supposed to be working for crazy people.

Svetlana went back to hugging Lushka, who smiled with his lips but the other two arches, his eyebrows and moustache, retained their scowl and it was a cold, heartless scowl.

1400 Hours

Cole was growing weary of the interviews. More than anything, he was tired of trying to overcome the first impression he made. Perhaps, if he seemed more authoritarian, these interviews would give him a better feel for his subordinates.

Johnson and McMahan had been easy. Both had administrative backgrounds. Competent but unimaginative agents, neither impressed Cole as having the talent or the balls for covert work. He would leave them to their task of interviewing a couple hundred thousand Austrians. Maybe they would find something of value, who knows.

Belcher and Roland were different. Both were aggressive with a disdain for authority that bordered on insolence. Captain Belcher was older, maybe 35 or 36. He had a thick, muscled body and receding hairline. and could easily blend into a crowd of Austrians. Lieutenant Roland was younger and taller with a shock of blond hair that smacked of former Hitler Youth. He would be okay.

Lieutenant Cynthia Ryan was a petit black haired woman who could pass for Italian despite her Irish name. She wore her hair pulled back and piled on top in the 'Victory Roll' style to honor working women like Rosie the Riveter. She had bright inquisitive eyes that didn't miss details. Her tomboy attitude held promise of success as a field agent. She wore slacks and crossed her legs like a man.

Now, he had only to interview Captain Charley Woods. When they met, he had an instant dislike for Woods and his frat boy arrogance. Cole had always been intimidated by such men;

too cool, too confident. Even Woods' stiff-armed handshake offended Cole.

"My first name's Charley but in school they called me 'Ruly' because my teachers always said I was un-ruly."

Cole ignored the light hearted comment. "Thank you for the organization chart of Russian Occupation Forces, Captain Woods. I know it came right out of their phone book. Now, to more important things, how's your German?"

"It's passable but not good enough to be taken as a native speaker. I've never really had a knack for languages. I'm more of a relationship man. You know, I get to know people and build trust, get them to confide in me."

"Do you think you will get to know many German people if you can't speak their language?"

"Well, yeah, that's going to be a challenge but I'm really good with people, especially women."

"So you want to be a Romeo spy?"

Woods sat back, crossed his legs and grinned. "Hey, I'm here to serve my country, whatever it takes. Know what I mean, Sir?"

"Do you have any combat experience? Your record doesn't show it."

"Not real shoot 'em up experience. I was stationed in the Canal Zone during hostilities. We tracked down some German and Italian agents but I've never shot anybody."

"Has anybody ever shot at you?"

Woods grinned wide. "Just a couple of jealous husbands."

Cole feigned a smile. "Okay then, I have a surveillance mission for you. I want you to follow this man and report his activities." He slid a manila envelope to the captain who picked it up, tapped it on the desk and then rose with a nod and a grin.

Cole tried to overcome his dislike but couldn't.

September 13, 0830 Hours

McMahan knocked on the major's door. He seemed excited. "Sir, I think we're onto something. Could you come have a look?" Johnson was waiting before the big city map with a wooden pointer. "We started our interviews here by the train station. Surprisingly, most people were happy to talk to us. It was almost as though they were glad that someone was interested in them. Most of them felt they couldn't speak freely about anything since the Anschluss, when Germany annexed Austria. They wanted to tell us all the terrible things the Nazis did and how glad they are to be in *liberated Austria*."

Cole showed impatience. Johnson continued, "But here's the thing, we heard a story over and over about a group of Nazi academics hiding in the Soviet-controlled Donau area. They may number as many as 80 or 90, just hiding until the 'Odessa' group can get them smuggled out of country."

Cole looked dubious. "Odessa, the association of former SS officers, operated primarily in Western Austria with strings of safe houses along routes they call 'Ratlines.' They normally pass from Salzburg to the Brenner Pass and then on to Genoa, Italy where they sail to some other country. There have been few reports of Odessa operating in Vienna."

McMahan answered. "I can only tell you what we heard. These scientists are kept in groups of four and moved often to avoid discovery by the Soviets. We know of three possible houses used by these rotating occupants. There are probably many more. The men in these groups are all over the age of 40, speak High German dialect and seem to have no money."

Cole crossed his arms and looked at the push pins in the map. "These are the safe houses?"

Johnson nodded. "We went into the Soviet Zone and made walk-by inspections of these three houses. Hopefully, we aroused no Russian interest."

"I also hope that's true. Do you know any more about the Germans? What kind of academics are they?" Cole was frowning deeply. "Do you think the reports are credible?"

Johnson shrugged, "We just don't know. Without being able to conduct thorough interviews with the people inside the Russian Zone, I don't know how we'll find out—and those interviews would be a clear violation of the Occupation rules."

September 20, 0830 Hours

Major Cole was almost in his seat when the auditorium was called to attention. Colonel Mather strode to the podium and slapped down a thick folder. He faced the crowd with anger in his eyes.

"It has come to my attention that some in my command have overstepped their authority in regard to our Russian allies and I stress the word 'allies.' There are serious allegations that some, and, lucky for you I do not have specific names, have made offensive remarks to Russian soldiers and officers and treated them almost as enemies. This is unacceptable and will not be tolerated."

He paced with hands on his hips looking like a headmaster about to dole out punishment. Then he turned to the crowd. "I am instituting a new policy with full support of General Mark Clark and the Occupation General Staff. We will immediately begin to participate in social events and public ceremonies with *all four* allied powers. To that end, Vienna is no longer designated an unaccompanied tour. All field grade officers with a rank of major and above will be authorized individual housing on the economy. Spouses will be allowed, and *strongly* encouraged, to come here. Moreover, I have set a goal of having all families reunited by the first of December."

There were murmurs throughout the crowd. Mather raised his hands for quiet. "The war is over. We are in transition to peace. Remember that. The peace will be won only through cooperation and respect. We are here to rebuild the world not to renew old animosities. Are there any questions?"

Hands went up all over the auditorium. Colonel Mather didn't seem pleased. He pointed to a man in the front row. The man stood and asked, "Yes Sir, what about children?"

Mather frowned and answered, "Children of pre-school age will be permitted. Those between grades one and twelve will be sent to boarding schools in Switzerland until we can set up English language schools within our zone. Any other questions?" It sounded like a threat to prevent further challenge.

The standing man continued, "Do you mean we have to send six-year-old kids to a boarding school in a strange country?" Mather brushed over the question, "It's just temporary."

Another stood without being recognized. "How do we opt out of this policy? I don't want my kids separated from their mother."

Mather was getting really irritated and his voice became shrill. "Individual requests for exemption will be considered only for demonstrated hardship such as unique medical needs documented by a physician. That's enough questions. A directive memo will circulate this morning. Paperwork must be submitted by Monday. We have already begun appropriating adequate housing in the local community. That is all." Mather walked off the stage to a chorus of chatter. No one even called the room to attention.

Cole was elated. Not only would he get to be with his wife but social events offer a bonanza of access to the other powers, particularly the Russians. This was an invaluable gift to the spy community. He rushed back to tell his detachment.

0900 Hours

Horatio Aalpeter did not attend the briefing but word travelled quickly. He thought of all the possibilities as he turned to a large map of Vienna. Where did the American and Soviet Zones touch? Perhaps he could find a house that would serve

31

his needs. He picked up his field phone, spun the crank and told the operator, "Major Aalpeter of Monuments calling, G-4 housing officer, please."

1000 Hours

Over the centuries, countless soldiers had marched across the Danube River. Mongols, Turks, Vikings and Cossacks had invaded and been repulsed. Christian Knights and Crusaders sallied forth to battle and claim lands, leaving footprints in history and monuments in stone.

Today, it was Captain Charley Woods who strode with purpose over the Donau Canal Bridge into the Soviet Zone. He looked sharp, very military, as he flashed his orders at the Russian control point guard, a bored young conscript who showed no interest in the pompous American.

Woods wore an American Army uniform but carried a trench coat slung over his arm. He tried to be inconspicuous but that was impossible. His look and bearing were uniquely American. He smiled. He walked tall. He greeted strangers with a cheery nod, looking them directly in the eye. No one in Occupied Austria behaved with such arrogant self-confidence.

Once across the bridge, Charley tucked his service cap in his belt and donned a wide-brimmed felt hat from under his coat. Then he put on the raincoat and a pair of sunglasses. With his collar pulled up, the disguise was complete. It worked well. No longer recognizable as a soldier, he looked instead like a comic book version of an American spy.

Carrying a tourist map, he pretended to take in the ornate buildings and winding cobblestone alleys. Actually, he was searching for the KGB headquarters. Once he found the huge pink limestone building, he began circling, watching which doors were most used and where officers usually came and went.

Completely by chance, he saw a Russian officer coming down wide marble stairs flanked by stone lions. This could be his target. Charley checked the photo he carried and compared it to the man. No question, this could be his man. The target set a quick pace forcing Charley to bump and shove pedestrians as he hurried to catch up. The streets seemed suddenly very crowded. Luckily, he was tall enough to see over heads if he bobbed and stretched.

After several blocks, the target entered another building and Charley had a chance to catch his breath. He took in his environment, just as all good agents were supposed to do, and saw two men staring at him. Both were beefy specimens wearing identical ankle length black coats and matching hats despite the mild September weather. They made no effort to hide their interest.

Charley felt suddenly vulnerable. He wasn't really doing anything wrong. He was allowed to enter the Soviet Zone. He had orders. He was in uniform—sort of. The men started toward him.

He began to walk, hesitantly at first, glancing over his shoulder. The men split up. One crossed to the other side of the street. Both increased their pace. No question, they were after him. Charley broke into a slight jog, cutting through the crowd, pushing when he had to.

He came into a shopping area with stalls set up in front of stores. Some of the shoppers took offense at the American's rudeness and shoved back. The black coats shouted in Russian. Charley broke into a full run. Black coats ran as best they could in their confining outfits and shouted even louder. The crowd drew back before the chase and watched with a mix of curiosity and suspicion.

Charley cut and wove like a linebacker, easily besting the black coats but he wasn't sure of the direction any more. At a major intersection, he panicked. Which way was the bridge? Shadows had been to his left as he crossed. He had to put the shadows on his right. He ran but the roads weren't straight. In a few blocks he was again turned around. Bystanders eyed him with apprehension, this comic book spy on the run.

A boy, no more than seven, grabbed at his coat and held up a begging palm. Charley brushed him aside but the boy persisted. The kid was dirty and thin with fingernails dark from dried blood. He must have been working in the rubble piles. "Please," he pleaded, in whining German, "for my mother. She will die without food." Charley pawed in his pocket and produced a coin. He didn't notice its denomination. The boy grabbed it. His eyes widened and he ran off shouting.

Charley resumed his effort to get oriented but was interrupted as a dozen or more kids raced at him from the alleys. They were all clones, urchins with ragged clothes and dirty hands but sharp, dark eyes. They mobbed him, jumping, grabbing and shouting. He tried to push them away but they were like ants on sugar. In desperation, he plunged his hand deep in a pocket and slung a handful of coins onto the cobblestones. The street sharks in short pants abandoned him to swarm after the precious copper coins. Charley took off at a dead run.

He was panting now. Sweat ran from his hatband down his forehead into his eyes. Where to go? He heard a Russian shout from somewhere and launched into another dash without direction but he was getting winded. He had to calm down and make a plan. Then he saw the giant Ferris wheel, the Prater amusement park on the west bank of the canal. Head that way.

In minutes, he emerged from the labyrinth of medieval alleys onto the bank of the canal. Just ahead lay the bridge, but there, on that bridge, milled a half dozen Soviet troops. Unlike the conscript who had been there earlier, these soldiers with AK-47s stopped every pedestrian to inspect papers.

"Oh shit," he said aloud. What could he do? There was no other way across the canal. He could try to swim but they might shoot him in the water. He could hide and wait for them to go away. They probably had more patience than he. There seemed only one choice. He stripped off his raincoat and hat, tossing both away. With his service cap back on, he straightened and tried to look confident and military if somewhat sweaty.

With grinning bravado, he walked up the bridge toward the guards. They shouted and motioned at him. He presented his orders. They shouted louder. He shrugged to show he didn't understand. They poked him with their rifle barrels. He pretended to become irate and shouted back.

An Austrian city policeman stood back and watched the whole affair. The local police had been reconstituted for only a few weeks and no one understood just what authority they had, least of all the police themselves.

Just as it seemed things were getting out of hand, a Jeep pulled halfway up onto the bridge. It was a "Four-in-a-Jeep" patrol. The policemen got out. The Frenchman and the Brit stood back out of the way. The Russian began screaming at the bridge guards. The American came to Charley and whispered, "What the hell are you doing, Captain? The Soviets reported you were out of uniform following one of their officers. Are you trying to get yourself killed?"

Charley mumbled something about sightseeing. No one was going to buy that. They herded him into the Jeep while the Russian policeman and the bridge guards continued their screaming match. Finally the Russian disengaged with a disgusted wave and crammed himself into the now severely overcrowded Jeep. Then they were off, now "Five in a Jeep."

1530 Hours

Major Cole drummed his fingers on the desk. He put on a stern Orson Wells Citizen Cane scowl as Captain Charley Woods entered and saluted.

"What in God's name were you thinking?"

Woods shifted from foot to foot. "Well, I was just following orders, Sir. You told me to follow this Russian guy and find out about him. So I went over to KGB Headquarters and started looking around, that's all."

Cole leaned forward, puckering until he had no lips. When he spoke, his voice quivered. "You did no research. You had no plan and no backup. You didn't even tell anyone where you were going or what you were going to do." Now he turned sarcastic. "And then... and then, you screwed it up. You know we are prohibited from surveilling the Russians. What that actually means is we are prohibited from *getting caught* surveilling our good buddies. You broke the cardinal rule. You got caught."

Cole spun his chair around to face the wall map. He secretly smirked as he let Captain Woods stew for 30, maybe 45, seconds. *There, that's about long enough.* He spun back to see Woods' head drooping.

"You do realize that you weren't even following the right man? In the long run, *that* might be a good thing. At least you didn't alert them to our interest."

Woods started to speak but Cole cut him off. "Effective immediately, you are restricted to the office. You will review and analyze all reports before they get to me. Hopefully, we can minimize the damage from your little escapade. That is all. You're dismissed."

Woods stood and saluted before leaving. For the first time Cole could remember, the captain had no smart retort. James Cole watched the handsome man retreat, head bowed and moping.

As the door closed Cole whispered to himself, "Well, that felt good."

September 21, 0745 Hours

Mrs. Parks knocked and then maneuvered her way carefully into Major Cole's office carrying a silver tray and tea service. "Good morning, Sir. I thought you might care for a cup of tea to start your day."

James Cole was surprised. "Well, thank you." He half rose and pointed to a clear space on his desk for the tray. She poured and he sipped for a second before speaking.

"Well, now that you have been here a week, how do you feel about your band of misfits?"

Cole smiled, "I was hoping you might share some of your insights Mrs. Parks. You seem an astute judge and you've spent more time with them than I. For instance, I appear to have misjudged Johnson and McMahan. They have done a remarkable job of coaxing information from the Austrian population and then carefully coordinating their data. In just days, they have focused hundreds of leads on fugitive German scientists down to some solid information. We're almost ready to move."

She sipped and settled as she balanced her saucer. "Yes, I too have been surprised. Johnson, on his own initiative got Belcher and Ryan to follow a handful of suspects. It all seems to be coming together quickly." She seemed properly impressed.

Cole set his tea aside and folded his hands on the desk. "The Ryan woman, I notice her manner is rather masculine. Do you think she's a little... funny? I mean, does she like men?"

Mrs. Parks put on an amused smile as she shrugged. "All I can say is that every time Captain Woods enters the room, Lieutenant Ryan finds some excuse to face away from him and bend over. I suspect she thinks her best asset is where her ass sets."

Cole laughed, surprised that his little lady caretaker had made a slightly off color comment. She smirked from behind her tea cup. "Which brings us to your problem child, what are you going to do about our Captain Woods? He seems an utter incompetent. Surely you aren't going to keep him on after his amateur stunt in the Soviet Zone?"

"Actually, I am. An incompetent can be valuable in some circumstances. In Woods' case, he is an incompetent who makes the ladies knees go wobbly. Who knows how that ability might be employed?"

She didn't like that answer. Mrs. Parks pursed her lips uncomfortably and asked, "Please forgive me, Sir, but I feel compelled to probe a bit. When you arrived, you played a bit of a fool. Then you explained that you wanted your people to depend on themselves not you. After watching you work, that really doesn't ring true. Am I missing something?"

Cole winced and spoke in his carefully measured voice. "You seldom miss anything, dear Lady. I told you I would always be straight with you and I will." For a full half minute, he said nothing. "I am an actor, a highly trained actor. I have been told I have a unique ability. I also have debilitating stage fright, a rather unfortunate limitation for an actor. I can perform with passion before a group of five. Six people begin to make me nervous. Seven rattle me to the point I forget lines and eight or more leave me nearly catatonic with anxiety."

Her brow wrinkled as she tried to understand. He went on, "What can you do as an actor if you can't perform before more than an elevator load of people? Well, I chose intelligence. I play out roles before small groups, rather effectively I think. I'm using my skills doing something that matters. This is my lot."

Mrs. Parks thought deeply. "Well, thank goodness. That explains everything. I was quite afraid that your chameleon behavior changes might indicate emotional instability. Now, it all makes perfect sense. We must make sure that all future meetings are conducted in smaller groups."

Her relief was obvious as she sat back in her chair and took a long sip. Neither spoke for a moment until she asked, "Do you care for my tea? I find it relaxing to add a shot of brandy."

James Cole leaned forward, stared deep into her eyes and smiled a boyish grin. "Not even a little." She laughed and he copied her laughter. They sounded like a couple of girls around a Canasta table.

CHAPTER TWO-OCTOBER

October 1, 1700 Hours

"Your laundry is ready for pickup, Sir."

"Yes, thank you so much, Lidia." James Cole smiled pleasantly to the clerk behind the hotel counter. She was a hard looking woman of undetermined age, somewhere between eighteen and thirty. However many, they must have been very hard years.

James went to the metal cage elevator and scanned the cork message board. It was filled with business cards, most old and dog eared. But in the upper left, a crisp new card read *Bistro Cheval Blanc*. Cole noted the address and went to change clothes. He looked forward to a French meal in the "White Horse Bistro." Even though he had worked with the French resistance fighters, translating the restaurant name was just about the limit of his French.

He arrived promptly, this time in civilian clothes that did not create a stir. The restaurant was a closet, crammed between storefronts. In better weather, diners would take outdoor tables on the wide Viennese street. That was out of the question in rainy early October.

James Mason, as he was now to be called, sat waiting. They shook hands and Mason made an elaborate show of pouring and complimenting his own selection of wine. They sat and chatted and watched the other patrons. None seemed to be paying attention. The waiter, who hadn't bathed since summer, appeared in a worn tuxedo with an apron that dragged the floor. Cole thought he looked silly and smelled like vinegar.

Once they had ordered, Mason began, "Your people have done excellent work documenting stories of the German scientists in Vienna. I have to say, though, there's something odd going on. We have assumed these Nazi professors were simply hiding while the Odessa organization made arrangements for them to escape down into Italy. That normally takes just days but these eggheads, who are reported to number almost a hundred, have been waiting more than a month. That just doesn't make any sense."

Cole was amused that along with the name of an English actor Mason seemed to have acquired an English accent to match. "So, what do think the problem might be?"

Mason shrugged. "I wish I knew. I'm thinking it may be time for you to raid one of their safe houses and bring a few of them back for interrogation. My only fear is that might scare the rest right into the Russian's hands. It's a tough call."

Cole nodded, "More than that, I'm not sure we have the resources to handle the extraction of more than one or two targets, particularly if they aren't cooperative."

"Yes, I agree. I have something in the works that will eventually make that much easier. I'm getting you a house with an excellent view. I think you'll find it quite acceptable," Mason said.

"Well, thank you. I'm not sure how that will help but I appreciate it, nonetheless. On a less pleasant note, I'm sure you've heard about my idiot Captain Woods' adventure in the Soviet Zone. I've put him on administrative duty."

Mason grinned as he drank. "No real harm done, it might actually make him more careful. He's still your best Romeo. You can't afford to waste him. Such men can be incredibly useful. I may have some ideas for him but that's for another time. Right now, I have a more urgent problem for you."

Cole looked for butter but found only schmaltz, rendered pig fat. Their soup arrived in delicate, hand painted Limoges china cups. He wasn't sure why he knew such a small detail.

Mason blew on his spoon and whispered, "There is a girl, a White Russian, who works for the KGB Colonel Lushka. She's desperate to get out of his control and might give us a load of information. Her background data and a recent picture are in the envelope under your napkin. Every night at 1800 hours exactly, she goes to the news stand in Kaiser Wilhelm Platz to buy a newspaper. That's your best opportunity for contact. She uses the name Anna Kerkova to protect her family. Her real name is Anna Petrov. You might use that to get her attention."

"Sounds interesting," said Cole. "What can we offer?"

"Ah, there's the problem. You see, she wants her whole family pulled out of Soviet control and shipped to America. That's going to be dicey. Here's my proposition. Tell her it will take a while to set things up but, in the meantime, she needs to provide us information. That way, no matter what happens, we get something. She's a secretary for the crazy Russian and probably has access to most of his records. It could be very productive."

October 2, 1750 Hours

The next evening, Cole wandered about Kaiser Wilhelm Platz carefully checking his watch and inventorying the crowd. Everyone seemed to be appropriately engaged. There were no men pretending to read newspapers. There were no random wanderers. It seemed safe to make a contact.

At one minute before six, or 1800 hours military time, he walked to the newsstand as though in a hurry. He wore older woolen clothes with very European touches like animal bone buttons and leather-trimmed cuffs. His hair was slicked back and he had a knit scarf around his neck. Even his size-twelve shoes were hand stitched and badly worn. No one took note of him.

A small line formed as the evening newspapers were set out. Cole searched faces but did not see his target. He bought a paper paying with an old Reichsmark coin. Then he saw her. He stopped, stared and broke into a wide smile.

He spoke in cheerful Russian, "I know you. Anna Petrov, don't you remember me?"

She was instantly frightened and turned her face away. He grabbed her arm gently and spoke in a calm deliberate voice. "Anna, do not be upset. I am a friend. I can help you. I can help you and your family. You can trust me." She wasn't convinced. Her face paled and her eyes searched for an escape route. Austrians waiting in line seemed interested in the exchange.

"Anna, come sit with me and let me explain. You have nothing to fear, I swear it." He led her by the arm and she came haltingly. At a park bench, they sat and he offered her a chocolate bar, a rarity in the Soviet Zone. Cole was patient and non-threatening. She took the chocolate and broke off a small piece, carefully folding the wrapper to save the rest.

"I am an American and I know of your family's situation. I think I might be able to get you over to the American Zone and then out of Austria. All I ask in return is information on the Russian, Lushka."

She took a hurried bite from her piece of chocolate. "You want my family dead? Lushka is a monster. I have seen him strangle a man right in his office. He thinks nothing of murder, cares nothing for humanity."

"Then we must get you out of there. Where are your mother and sister? Are they close?"

"I live with my sister but I have little contact with my mother after she was sent to Leopoldsdorf. I only see her sometimes on Sundays. I never know when she can come. I cannot leave her. I cannot. They would kill her for vengeance if I left."

Cole shook his head slowly. "This is a major problem. We can get you and your sister across the border any time but your mother may be a challenge. Is there some way you can set up a meeting in advance?"

A tear tried to escape her eye and her voice became shaky. "I don't know. I will talk to her the next time she comes to visit."

Cole turned to the practical. "I will need a picture of you, your sister and mother for passports. There is a camera in my bag. Use it to take the pictures. I have also given you cigarettes and some fruit. I know these are hard to find here."

She reached down and picked up his cloth bag. "Is there any more chocolate?"

He smiled. "No, I'll bring more next time."

Her breathing relaxed. "How will we meet next?"

"Here at the same time. After all, you must have your daily newspaper. Now tell me of Lushka."

She began hesitantly but quickly turned animated as stories tumbled out of her. The whole time, James Cole scanned the crowd to be sure they weren't being watched.

"He is the worst. When the Anschluss turned Austria over to Germany, we were frightened. When we heard the Soviets were invading Austria, we were truly terrified. But, the first Soviet troops that came were kind to us. They were the real fighters, the men who took Vienna. They shared their food and sent their doctors to help our people. They acted like liberators and we were proud to be Russian."

She hunched her shoulders and looked at hands folded in her lap. "But the fighters left after just a few days and were replaced by others. Those men were brutes, thugs. They raped my mother in front of us, not once but over and over. And then they turned to my sister and me. I wanted to die. I expected to die. It lasted for days. Finally, a woman commissar came and took us away. We thought she was our savior. We were wrong."

Cole tried to calm Anna. He didn't want a scene in a public place.

She shook herself and wiped her eyes. "They made us translators. They made us servants. We still get beaten for any minor thing and sometimes for nothing at all. Lushka likes to hurt people. They will kill us. I must get my mother out." She turned to him with eyes that did their own pleading.

"I will help you, Anna. I will."

October 3, 0800 Hours

Billy Connors looked unusually cheerful as he held the car door for Major Cole. "Morning Sir, happy to be at your service." Cole climbed in and settled without comment. Once behind the wheel Connors said, "Where to this fine morning?"

"Just drive around the city. We need to talk."

Connors smiled wide at the prospect of more black market business.

Cole looked out the window made his pitch. "I need vehicles, two medium sized trucks and three cars and I need them day after tomorrow."

Connors bit his lower lip. "That's a tall order. It can be done but it will cost big time. How much are you willing to go?"

"One thousand US dollars. You negotiate and keep the difference between what you pay and the thousand. I don't care about condition except they must be running. I just want them to be inconspicuous."

Connors hesitated before he asked, "When do I get the money?" His question was answered by a package tossed into the front seat. He pulled it close to his leg and reached in to touch the money. It felt right. It felt sweet. This major was going to make him rich. His moment was interrupted.

"Billy, I want to talk to your documents forger directly. I need to verify the quality of his work to make sure my requirements are met exactly."

"Well, okay, but you have to pay through me."

Cole leaned forward so Billy could feel breath on his neck. "Son, you'll do what I tell you. I'll make sure you get your cut but you don't make the rules." There was a moment of silence before Cole continued. "The Danube River is no stranger to bodies. Almost every day another is fished out."

Billy Connors tried to sound nonchalant as he said, "Major, are you threatening me?"

Cole lit a cigar and blew a stream of smoke before he answered in a Humphrey Bogart voice, "Yes."

October 9, 1600 Hours

The meeting in Major Cole's office included five people, his maximum comfort level: Johnson, McMahan, Belcher, Roland and Ryan.

He assumed the posture of a tough wartime leader, a regular Douglas McArthur. Clearing his throat, he began, "You have all done well at your assigned tasks but now, I must ask more of you." He paused for a bit of drama. "I am about to ask you to take on a terrible risk, both for your personal safety and for your future. Moreover, I am asking this in direct violation of our international occupation agreements."

He had them, every eye focused, every hair on end and he savored the moment. "We are going on a raid to kidnap Germans from the Russian sector. Make no mistake, this is a criminal endeavor and it is *not* voluntary. You *will* go. I take full responsibility but that will be little comfort if you are captured or killed. Your family will know only that you were on an unauthorized mission. Therefore, I encourage you *not* to get captured or killed."

A moment of weak laughter died quickly. "Today is Tuesday. We go on Thursday night. Spend tomorrow assembling an outfit, a working class Austrian outfit, and getting your affairs in order. Our briefing will be Thursday here in the office at 1600 hours. Eat a big meal. It will have to last all night. Tell no one. Act as though there is nothing unusual going on. Any questions?"

They had thousands of questions but it took a moment for anyone to speak. Cynthia Ryan was first. "What about me? Isn't there a restriction about women being used in combat?"

Cole was dumbstruck and momentarily lost his McArthur persona. "Are you serious? I just ordered you to conduct an unauthorized mission into Soviet controlled territory to kidnap civilians, possibly including the use of deadly force and your big concern is the limitation on women in combat?"

She was quick to respond. "Now don't get me wrong, I want to go. I just wanted to be sure I was included."

Belcher growled. "You'll be great. We'll use you to draw fire. The Ruskies love to shoot at women."

She stood up quietly, squared her shoulders and walked over to Belcher. Blinking twice, she smiled and then smacked him hard on top of his balding head. After a moment of indecision, the other men broke into laughter. Even Belcher joined in.

Cole continued, "You can bring your own weapons or select from those I have assembled in the closet. Make sure you're comfortable with your outfit and your weapons. Sanitize everything, no identification or personal effects. If captured, your cover story is that you accidentally wandered into the Soviet sector. It's weak, particularly dressed as you will be, but stick to it."

The questions went on into the evening. No one asked to be released from the mission. No one even hinted of qualms. This was real live spy stuff, real combat. It made blood flow and spines stiffen. This was what it was all about.

October 10, 0730 Hours

Wednesday morning, before the coffee perked, Sherry White banged on Cole's office door. He looked up at a red cheeked woman with murder in her eyes as she slammed the door behind her. "Why have I been excluded? There's something big happening. It's in the air like day-old fish. I am a part of this organization and I demand…"

Cole leaned back in his chair and tossed a pencil onto the desk just as he had seen Gary Cooper do. "You demand nothing. You are entitled to no answers. You are a valued member of this detachment but you are a civilian translator and analyst. You have no training in other aspects of our duties."

He stared her down for a long, uncomfortable moment. Then with a conciliatory arch of his eyebrows, he added, "You're the brains, not the brawn, of this unit. As our most believable member, it will be your responsibility to present an activity signature so no one suspects the six of us are out playing cowboy." As an afterthought, "And while you're at it, let slip to Herr Honig that we are doing a dress rehearsal for a possible probe into Besamberg. That'll keep our little double agent hopping."

Sherry calmed but her cheeks still glowed. "Honig is a spy?"

Cole nodded. "And you are our utterly trustworthy civilian stalwart. I need your unquestioning support." He leaned forward with his most sincere look. "If you let us down, some may die. I'm really counting on you."

She didn't know what to do. Cole watched her eyes for hints of tears. There were none. *She's tough*, he thought. *Too bad she's not military.*

1130 Hours

Sergei Zelenkov reviewed his morning messages. One about the American Intelligence detachment suggested a "probe" of some sort into Besamberg. He looked at the map. What could be the American's interest? Nothing of importance was happening there; at least, nothing he knew of. There were no corroborating sources. Still, something must be afoot. The Russian major sat back and pondered his options. Finally, he slapped his hand on the desk and called his adjutant. He needed spotters at all the bridges. He would find out what the Amerikanskis had in mind. Perhaps he could even catch them in the act.

October 11, 1500 Hours

Early October had been unusually mild and pleasant in Vienna but it was about to get stormy and not just from the weather. Thursday rolled in under the shadow of dark thunderheads.

Lieutenant Cynthia Ryan was itching to go when Belcher finally announced it was time to get dressed and assemble in the parking lot. Two battered trucks waited behind the Richertsgasse office. From a small window, Herr Honig pulled aside a curtain and peered intently.

The five, now clad in their pseudo-Austrian outfits, gathered and checked their gear. There was good natured banter until Major Cole appeared, looking confident and self-assured. Lieutenant Ryan thought his voice even sounded a little different.

"All right, here we are. Two trucks, we'll go three in each. Belcher drives the first, McMahan the second. We take different routes to arrive at this building discovered by our team."

He unrolled a blueprint style street map very obviously shielding it from Honig's window view and pointed to a location on the map now becoming dappled with raindrops. Cynthia stretched to see over the men's shoulders. "We'll cross the canal here on the southernmost bridge. It will almost certainly be unmanned at night in this weather. We then park behind the building in this alley. After that, we'll have to play it by ear."

McMahan apologized, "I'm sorry we didn't get better information. We did a couple of walk-by's but could never get inside to scope the building. All we know for sure is that it's a four story monstrosity. The back alley side has been heavily damaged by bombs and the ground floor is vacant. We saw a single set of stairs around an internal courtyard. It seems reasonable that the German scientists will be housed on the top floor if they are actually there."

Cole continued, "We'll just have to feel our way. At least the weather will be on our side. Rain is forecast all night. That will keep most people indoors. The big unknown is how well armed these guys are and how willing to fight. Regardless, we stay tight. We provide mutual protection. We grab our Nazis and we get out. Everybody gets out. Wounded or whatever, we leave no one."

Cynthia turned to load up and Cole added one more thing. "Oh yes, I have a three battery flashlight and a camera flash for each of you." He handed out small silver dishes with battery packs. "You have four flash bulbs. In the darkness, these can blind and incapacitate an opponent. Just be sure to close your eyes tight when you fire it."

With that, they boarded trucks and lumbered off into the storm. There was little talk as they bumped along. Cynthia was the only one who even tried to keep a conversation going. Cole and Belcher ignored her banter.

The rain swept bridge was, as Cole had told them to expect, unguarded. They drove across into the Soviet Zone and immediately entered a world of dark, winding cobblestone alleys. After ten minutes they were very close. Cynthia realized she was breathing hard. She tried to be calm as she muttered, "It's pitch black. There's no electricity in this part of town. Christ, we'll be fumbling around in a blackout."

She turned to Belcher and grabbed his arm. "Don't let me get lost, okay?" Her voice became a whisper. "I've always been afraid of the dark. Stay close, please stay close." Belcher, sensing her anxiety, put aside his normally combative attitude. She thought she could actually see a faint glint of a smile. "Don't worry. We'll all watch out for you... and you watch out for us too, okay?"

They parked behind the huge building and waited. There was no response. No one came out shooting. No one seemed to notice. After an eternity that was probably no more than a few minutes, Cole stepped out of his truck, raised his collar against the weather and motioned for the others. They shuffled quietly though pouring rain to stand, almost in awe before a dark square structure that filled a city block. A pile of collapsed rubble angled toward them like a giant brick landslide.

Beyond the debris, the building's interior was exposed but it was too dark to see anything inside. This was going to be like blindfold mountain climbing in a monsoon. Cole led into the soggy darkness and they followed, mostly by sound. There was huffing, groaning, squishing and an occasional curse when someone stumbled.

Cynthia was amazed that her eyes were slowly adjusting to the oily blackness. She began to see vague shapes, but only if she looked slightly off center. She was concentrating hard to stay oriented. Suddenly, she was grabbed by the shoulders.

Almost by reflex, she fought to twist free of strong hands but then she smelled something familiar. Cigarette and mint, it was Belcher. He gripped her tight but slowly, even in her dark visual fugue state, she realized that just inches above her head, an outcropping of splintered and broken wood threatened to impale her. Belcher had, as he promised, looked out for her.

She put her hand on her scalp and whispered, "That would have hurt." Without answering, Belcher helped her up and onto the dark landing of an interior balcony. She caught her breath and tried to decipher the shapes around her.

It seemed to be a long straight passageway with a metal hand rail on one side and doors on the other. Cautiously, she stood and began walking. To where, she had no idea. A flight of stairs led up to the third floor; still no sign of life. She climbed unsteadily, one foot at a time, forcing herself to breathe in the darkness.

The third floor was equally lifeless but above them she heard the faint sound of a violin. Finding another stairway, they inched upward toward a dim glow of yellow light. She could see Major Cole ahead, bent and cautious as he crept forward. None of them realized he was in the process of assuming a new role.

Footsteps, she heard heavy footsteps approaching and saw Cole flatten against the stair wall, pistol ready. Ryan watched, more fascinated than frightened as she slipped her own handgun from its holster and clicked off the safety. She had done well in marksmanship training and felt pretty comfortable with guns.

In the dull light she could barely make out an elongated shadow moving across the wall. It was the shadow of a man, large and bony. She could tell no more. Then his upper body came into the light. Shaved head grown to stubble, bony face of a well pounded boxer; it was a frightening face. He wore a filthy undershirt and suspenders for military pants, German military pants.

Cole suddenly broke from the stairway and, to everyone's surprise, tackled the big German who grunted in surprise. Cole was taller, faster and more athletic. The German was stronger. They tangled and twisted. Then Cole got clear and delivered a clean kick to his opponent's knee. The German went down with a scream. Cole punched him square on the forehead. That rocked the man back on his knees. Cole took a breath, cocked back his arm and delivered a fearsome knuckle punch to the Adam's apple.

The fight was over. The German rolled on the floor clawing at his throat and making terrible gurgling noises. The raiding party gathered around like traffic accident bystanders to watch the man's agony.

Cole was breathing hard but still spoke in a controlled voice. "This guy doesn't look like any scientist I've ever seen. He's just a guard." Then he pulled out a silenced .22 pistol, calmly aimed at the German's temple and fired a single shot, little more than a poof.

There was a quiet chorus of gasps as the group stepped back in unison. Cole turned and marched off. One by one, the others followed. Cynthia's eyes lingered on the lifeless quivering body before joining the others.

They were all intent, sneaking along the wall toward the light source. Music grew louder. An open door allowed them to glimpse into a large room of ragged furniture. They could see three painfully thin older men listening to a fourth who played a violin by the light of a kerosene lantern. Cynthia Ryan saw Major Cole wet his lips.

They waited for what seemed a long time. There was no reaction. Then, Cole lowered his gun and stepped boldly into the room. The old men gasped and clung to each other in obvious fear. One of them, a balding gnome, spoke in German. "Are you Russian or German?"

Cole replied in his best German, "Neither, we are Americans."

The men collapsed into tears. "Oh God, thank God, it is the Americans. Have you any food? We cannot remember the last time we've eaten."

Cole ignored the request. "How many other guards and what armament do they have?"

"There is just Heindrick in the hall and Fritz up on the roof. Fritz is lazy. He is probably asleep. Please get us out of here and get us some food, please."

The men still clustered together until the gnome stepped apart and forced his quivering lips into a smile. He stood as tall as he could. "I am Doctor Herman Vogleman of the University of Leipzig. We were made prisoners by the SS during the last days of the war. They wanted to take us all to Italy and then somewhere in the desert of Arabia. We were supposed to create new weapons for the Reich. Hitler was very interested in jet engines. He wanted a fleet of super jets."

"There will be time to talk of that later. Now, we must get you to safety and get you fed. Do you know a quick way out of the building?"

Almost as an afterthought, Cole directed, "Belcher and Ryan go up to the roof and try to capture this Fritz. Don't take any chances. If he doesn't come easily, kill him."

Without comment, the pair trotted to the last stairway and climbed into another black void. Cynthia followed, mostly by sound. Belcher paused and raised an arm as a halt signal. She didn't see it and bumped into his back. Then both froze. He leaned over and said softly, "Listen, the old Professor was right." She cocked her ear and heard the soft purr and snort of a man sleeping soundly. They continued forward on tip toe.

Cynthia took out her flash, nudged Belcher and he nodded. She pointed it toward the snore and whispered, "Close your eyes in one, two, three, now." She squeezed her own eyes closed, yelled "Achtung!" and pressed the button. Even through her tightly pressed eyelids, the flash was bright.

Eyes open, she flicked on her flashlight and took a moment to focus the beam. In that same moment, Belcher lunged forward at the big, thick bull of a dazed German. Unfazed by the American's sudden attack, Fritz tossed him off like a bedcover before lumbering to his feet. Belcher bounced away into darkness as his flashlight rolled away and went out.

Cynthia shined her beam directly into Fritz's face as he fumbled for a machine pistol strapped to his side. Belcher, lost in the dark, seemed in no position to help. She had to do something. Shifting her pistol to her left hand, she stepped forward, raised her flashlight and, with all her might, slashed downward making a great arc of light across the roof. The big flashlight thudded against rock-hard skull and the lens shattered. Pieces clattered on the floor. There was a long moment of silence and total blackness. Cynthia crouched with her pistol clamped in both hands trying hard to keep her balance in the darkness. Her heart pounded and her breath came in quick gasps. She heard Fritz stagger and then drop like a head-shot buffalo.

When Belcher's flashlight finally came back on, she sagged with relief and almost cried.

1813 Hours

The trucks sat waiting as Cynthia hurried down a dark stairway, motioning for Belcher to hurry as he dragged Fritz's huge body. It took four people to push the comatose German into Cole's truck.

Headlights appeared down the alley and Cole immediately ordered everyone into the truck. The moment he was in, they took off. A lightening flash illuminated the way to the bridge back to safety in the Innere Stadt.

At the bridge, a Russian soldier hunkered against the downpour and desperately tried to write something on a paper pad that was much too wet. He turned to a portable phone and cranked furiously but, in the rain, it didn't work either. He swore as the trucks rolled past him into the American Zone.

Finally calm, Cynthia sat back and thought, "*We left the dead German's body. We weren't supposed to leave anyone behind.*" But she said nothing.

2030 Hours

Once settled before a great fireplace in the cottage safe house, everyone relaxed. The scientists introduced themselves between brief bouts of tears. They had been captives of the renegade SS troops for six long months. Vogleman continued as spokesman. "We were rounded up in March and kept in a small castle outside Berlin. There were 106 of us all together, representing all areas of engineering and physics."

He sighed, "Then the Allies came closer. In April, our guards were ordered to take us to Salzburg and then on to Genoa. We were told that we would have a world class research campus somewhere in the desert where we would build war machines."

Cole interrupted, "How did you wind up in Vienna?"

"Good question. We were in buses headed south when the guards told us Munich was under attack by the Allies and we would take a detour through Linz. Something went wrong and the guards became upset. They argued and the officers punished several of them. We kept driving and driving. We complained that we were tired and hungry but the guards no longer listened. When we finally arrived in Vienna we were kept in a hotel for two weeks."

Cole asked, "That would have been April, correct? That would be the fall of Berlin."

"Ah," said Vogleman. "Yes, that makes sense. The officers set up an elaborate scheme to rotate us from place to place. We were always in small groups, usually four men. We moved every week, always in the dark of night. We think that as soon as the Russians overran Vienna, the officers all ran away leaving the guards without guidance or resources. Without someone to give orders, they were helpless. Worse, they lived in fear of discovery by the Russians. We never went out. Over time, we ran out of everything. We truly expected to starve."

Cole put on his good will ambassador face. "That will not happen, sir. We will feed you and get you clothes. You will be transported to America and given houses and jobs with good pay. You will be able to study without fear."

He hesitated and looked perplexed as he asked, "How is it, sir, that you were not discovered by the Russians? They had thousands of NKVD soldiers out scrutinizing the population to find Nazis."

Vogleman shook his head. "We don't really know. Perhaps it was because we were only housed in ruined buildings after the Soviet occupation. Before that, we could actually go out to stores and go on walks. Afterwards, we were true prisoners held in the most deplorable conditions."

Vogleman grew sad and looked away. "What about my Marta? If we go to America, how can we ever find our families?"

"We have a repatriation system, sir. All displaced persons must register. After we locate your family members, they will join you."

The others had gathered close and listened intently. Just then, Cynthia Ryan brought in a tray of soup and bread with cheese. The Germans attacked the food. Vogleman interrupted his chewing. "You must find Finklestein. He is the most important theoretical physicist we have. He was an embarrassment to the Nazis because he was a Jew. If they had given him the tools he needed, Germany would have had an A-bomb before America. You must find him before the Russians."

October 12, 0545 Hours

Sergei Zelenkov looked dapper in a pressed uniform with a bearskin overcoat draped over his shoulders. He slapped gloves against his free hand and surveyed the damaged building, squinting as he looked upward. With a resolute posture, he climbed a set of stairs as a Russian soldier stood at attention and held the door open. Inside, Russian guards surrounded a sobbing woman as she knelt in the center of a ruined room. Sergei circled her, watching intently. She followed him with tear-reddened eyes.

He gave an order in Russian and soldiers grabbed the woman by her arms and forced her to the floor. She cried out but they pressed her down hard with her face flat on the cold stone. Major Zelenkov stood close. He knew she could see the reflection of her face in his polished boot. Carefully he raised one foot and placed it on her neck, easing on more and more pressure as he bent low.

In a soft, almost compassionate voice, he whispered in German, "Mother, do not force me to harm you. A man has been killed in your building. Others have been kidnapped. Great crimes have taken place under your roof. We must assume you are involved, maybe responsible."

"No, no," she cried, voice muffled against the stone. "I just rent the rooms. These men came to me months ago and offered to rent a whole floor. No one else will live here. One whole side of my building is destroyed. I have no electricity or water. I need the money. Please believe me. I never asked questions. I know nothing of what went on. I needed the money to live."

Sergei released a little of the pressure. "Who were these men? How did they pay you?"

She struggled to straighten her neck a bit. Her jaw was still jammed against the floor. "They were German, not from here but somewhere around Berlin. I could tell by their accents. They were unpleasant men. I was afraid to talk to them, but they paid in cash." She strained under his boot. "Every month they paid, always on the first day. October is the first month they were late but I was afraid to go and ask. I never went up to the top floor. I'm glad they're gone."

Sergei stepped away, releasing the woman. "I believe you, mother. Tell me everything you can about these men."

She sat up rubbing her neck but her eyes were still wide with fear. "There were always six men but they changed every week. They paid 100 Reichsmarks a week. No one paid that much for a damaged building. I didn't really care who they were. They didn't hurt anything. I don't know how they managed up there without water or power. They had to carry water up four flights just to flush toilets. There was no heat and no electric light. I will never be able to rent again without utilities. Can you help me get the utilities back?"

Sergei only smiled. "No, nothing will change. If anyone contacts you or if more men show up, you must call me. I will pay you for the information. Do you understand? Yes, that's good. Now, can you tell me how many different groups of six men have stayed here?"

The landlady shrugged and swayed from her position on her knees. "I don't know. Perhaps seven or eight groups, I can't be sure. I never went up there."

"Thank you for your help, madam." Sergei was calculating how many men may have passed through.

0600 Hours

James Cole sat alone in his office. It had been a long night. The raid had gone well. All four scientists were safe in the cottage. The man he knew as James Mason should soon arrange transportation for them. Fritz, the German guard, was locked up downstairs waiting interrogation. Cole could relax. He poured bourbon into a water glass and chuckled at the slight tremor in his hand. It didn't matter. There was no one to see.

His solitude was short lived. Lieutenant Cynthia Ryan entered the office area looking freshly scrubbed and bubbling with enthusiasm. She flicked on a light switch and saw him. "Good morning, Major."

He mumbled, "You sound like a damned cheerleader. What time is it anyway, six or six thirty?"

"Pretty great night wasn't it, Sir? It was a real adventure. I've never seen anyone killed before. In fact, I've never seen a dead person except in a coffin wearing lots of makeup. How did it make you feel? It had to be awful, just shooting the German like that."

Cole deadpanned. "It was the expedient thing to do."

Cynthia rattled on. "I was so excited I couldn't sleep a minute. Thank you for including me. I'll never forget you for it." She paused, looked at her shoes and approached his desk. He thought he saw her bite her lower lip before speaking. "And Sir, you were so great. I've never seen anyone so brave and so calm." She looked up at him with big soft eyes.

"Jesus Lieutenant, are you flirting with me?"

She flustered, "Oh, no Sir. I mean not if you didn't want—I mean, no, not at all."

He scowled and downed his bourbon in a single gulp. "We have a lot of work to do. There will be a meeting tonight at 1600 hours. Now get out and quit being so damned cheerful."

She stumbled backward, started to salute, seemed unsure and then turned to run out the door. Cole laughed deep in his throat and poured another glass. *"She flirted with me. She actually flirted with a skinny misfit like me. That might be the high point of my week."*

1600 Hours

Four o'clock came quickly. The detachment mood was upbeat after a successful operation and everyone expected this to be a congratulatory meeting. It wasn't. Major Cole came in feeling haggard.

"We have reports of Russian troops all over the site of last night's adventure. All the bridges into the Soviet Zone suddenly have three guards and they are checking identification on every vehicle. I have to believe we've been compromised. If so, that means the Russians may be aware of the other scientists. Roland, how is the interrogation of the German guard proceeding?"

Captain Roland stood. His blonde hair seemed unnaturally light, almost albino. As the most proficient German speaker, he was chosen for the interrogation. "The man is Fritz Gaerbor, a former SS sergeant who saw action primarily on the Eastern Front. He has been wounded three times, once in the spine. He blames his injuries for his capture by a woman and a fat man."

Belcher fumed, "Fat man?"

There was a round of laughter. "Sergeant Gaerbor has been on guard duty with the scientists since early April. He was one of the junior men and had little information on what was planned, except that he expected to eventually reach a safe base, possibly in Syria. In Vienna, that plan fell apart. They have waited for months for Odessa to move them on. Their officers abandoned them with little money and less guidance. But they are SS, loyal to the death. They were going to guard their prisoners until the last man dropped."

Roland made direct eye contact with Major Cole. "He knows of seven different holding locations and he has personally guarded nine groups of four prisoners. They rotate the guards to prevent them from becoming sympathetic to their scientist prisoners. I have a list of names and some approximate addresses. I doubt the sergeant is outright lying. He just isn't smart enough to keep his stories straight, but I would rate his accuracy with names and places as quite low."

Cole stood before the assembled detachment and picked up the lists. "Woods, plot these locations on a city map. Mrs. Parks will begin an interagency search to find who these men are and what value they have to the United States." For the moment, James Cole seemed to have overcome his anxiety in groups larger than five but he was starting to sweat.

"We have to consider that the Russian reaction may just have been spurred by the discovery of the German guard's body. But I think the stakes have just gone up and we must be very, very careful what we do next. We know there are at least thirty two more high value resources out there. We must find a way to get them out."

Johnson raised a hand like a schoolboy. "Sir, I've spent the day with the four professors. When they were in the Berlin castle they were free to mingle with each other. I too have a list, but mine has 106 names, each identified according to his specialty. Most of these scientific areas mean nothing to me but, at least six of the men are involved with nuclear weapons, A-bombs."

1800 Hours

That evening James Cole made his normal rendezvous with Anna Petrov at the newspaper stand. It was unseasonably warm and pleasant and everyone in Kaiser Wilhelm Platz seemed relaxed wearing shirts and light clothing. They sat and talked more than usual.

James had worked out a routine where both carried identical satchels. Normally Anna would set hers down as she opened her change purse to pay for her paper. James would drop a coin and make the switch to his identical satchel as he bent to pick it up. His bag was always filled with food, scarves, money and, of course, chocolate. Hers held photocopies and carbons from Lushka's office.

This night's paperwork contained a bombshell. Back in his office, Cole rifled through the documents until he came to teletype printout that read, *"Confidential informant reports that a covert American operation conducted last night resulted in one Nazi soldier killed and five others kidnapped from a building at 67 Krather Strasse. This information confirmed by Major Zelenkov who followed an Austrian registered truck with license AU67:78 which crossed the Taborstrasse bridge and continued through the city to 37Richertsgasse in the American Zone."*

"Shit," Cole shouted as he stood and paced frantically. "How could they know? It had to be Honig, but how did he know? Okay, maybe he knew the truck's registration but how could he know the address." It occurred to James Cole that he did not even know the street address of the raided building. He simply worked off the map which had no numbers. "And, if the Russians were actually watching, why didn't they act? They would have been on sound legal footing if they killed us all. Something is terribly wrong."

October 13, 1730 Hours

James Cole asked Lidia for the key to room 708 at the Astoria Hotel. She responded with the key dangling. The message would be passed. James went to his room to wait. He hadn't slept for two days and fatigue suddenly hit him with such oppressive weight he collapsed backward into his bed.

From deep in his near-coma, he heard knocking but it seemed distant, unimportant. It came again and again. Very slowly, Cole emerged from the liquid, floating sleep. Though his eyes could not yet focus, he managed to sit and then fumble his way to the door. A well-oiled bellman waited with a hotel envelope which he presented and then stood patiently waiting for a tip. Cole closed the door in his face.

The envelope held a simple note. Shaking his head, the printing on the note began to focus. It said only, *"American Bar, 2000."* Cole slapped and then shook his face. He needed to think. What the hell did American Bar mean? What time was it? The note said 2000, eight o'clock. Where was his clock?

In just ten minutes, he washed his face, dressed in civilian clothes and made it downstairs. It was five minutes past eight. A quick stop by the front desk and Lidia gave him directions. Luckily, it was a short walk.

The *American Bar* turned out to be the name of a swank little establishment with a huge reproduction of the Stars and Stripes over the door. Inside, it was completely dark. Black light made silhouetted figures invisible except for their glowing shirt collars and cuffs. Glass topped tables were lit from beneath. White drink tumblers, illuminated by the black light, seemed to float, glowing in space. It was a bizarre, otherworldly effect.

The music was jazz and the talk muted. Tuxedo clad waiters wove invisibly through the darkness. A huge Onyx and brass bar stood illuminated only from behind.

"F. Scott Fitzgerald would have loved this place," said Cole aloud. James Mason sat alone at the bar drinking from a tall glowing glass. James seated himself and ordered a beer. Mason smacked his lips and whispered, "What's up?"

James Cole looked around. The bar was almost empty at that early hour. "I think we've been compromised. The girl from Lushka's office passed a dispatch that accurately identified details of the mission. I am concerned that our organization's penetration is deeper than Honig's casual observation."

Mason sipped without reaction. "I have no information about that. Test your people. Throw out several pieces of bait and see which one gets a nibble. That will narrow your search."

Cole, now becoming more alert and coherent said, "That makes sense. I have an uncomfortable foreboding that we are running out of time. I have a list for you. It's an unsubstantiated batch of names and specialties for the scientists in Vienna."

Mason dropped his napkin and stepped off the barstool to retrieve it. Cole passed the paper as he bent over. Work done, Cole and James Mason spent the remainder of the evening drinking. It was a good natured, relaxed time, just two spies passing the hours. Much later, and after many drinks, Mason toasted with a shot glass of Jaegermeister. "Here is to my favorite spy, to you Hernando."

A drunken Austrian at the bar next to them spoke gravely English. "So you are Americans, yes? You are now our masters."

Cole waved a limp hand. "No, no, we are your protectors."

The Austrian belched loudly. "So, who do you protect us from?"

Mason leaned forward and grinned, "From other Americans." They all laughed.

Cole turned back to Mason and weaved just a bit as he raised his glass. "Okay, but who is this Hernando fellow?"

Mason put on an exaggerated frown as though pondering a great question. Then he raised a finger to make his point. "Why, you are my friend. That is your code name. I thought you knew."

Cole took a great long breath followed by a watery belch. "Hernando, why on earth am I Hernando? Don't I get to pick my own name? I'm not Spanish or anything."

Mason shrugged. "Better that way. Our most important agent is man code named Phyllis. Hernando's not so bad."

Drinking done, they paid and stumbled limp and loose into the chill of night. Cole saw their reflection in a store window and broke out laughing. There he was in his own skin, not playing some role. He draped a limber arm over the much shorter Mason and pointed woozily. "Look at us, Mutt and Jeff, one too tall and one too short, both ridiculous." His laughter faded into a deep sigh and he sounded almost sober as he said, "Who could imagine the things we have done?"

Mason, now seriously drunk, hung on Cole's shoulder and made his boozy point with a wandering raised finger. "Not to mention the things we have yet to do. The most dangerous man is always the least likely. Beware the harmless, beware of... us."

They both broke into childish laughter bordering on giggles.

October 14, 1600 Hours

Cole sat alone in his office staring at the map behind him. In late afternoon, he began calling people in, one at a time. To each, he gave a firm thank you and a bit of information about upcoming raids, along with a stern warning not to discuss anything about their conversation. Last to be briefed was Sherry White.

She sat down with a 'what's up' look. She was a good sized woman, tall, confident and imposing. James could easily imagine her playing high school field hockey and giving the other girls grunting body blocks.

"First, let me thank you for your help in keeping our operation secret." She shrugged, "How could I not keep it secret? You told me almost nothing."

"Yes, that's true. That's why I'm telling you now. We're going back in for more of the scientists." He spun to the map. "We're headed for the church on Rotenster Ring right off the Prater. It should be an easy pick up. Again, we'll be depending on you to keep up appearances just as you did before. I can't tell you how much I appreciate your dedication."

She looked at him with knit brows but said nothing. He stood and shook her hand and that was that. The bait was all set. He had given everyone a different story and sworn each to secrecy.

October 15, 1200 Hours

The day blew in on gusty winds that spit grit in your eyes. Three trucks with new license plates pulled out of the detachment parking lot and headed in different directions. Belcher and Ryan went north. Johnson and McMahan went east. Woods and Roland went south. None knew the others' destination.

Crossing the bridges into the Soviet Zone, each team had been instructed to open a letter. Woods was the passenger in Roland's truck. He fumbled and tore at the envelope letter and read loudly. "You are to do a dry run only. Drive by and inspect your assigned building. Pay particular attention to activity and defenses. Then return and report."

Woods tossed the letter. "That's just great. He still doesn't trust me. I get sent on a mission all right, but mine is just a dry run. I can't believe it. I'm sorry you have to suffer because of me."

Roland didn't seem concerned. "Hey, you don't know this has anything to do with you. We'll just do the drive by and report as ordered. No cause for concern. We'll be at our target building in about two minutes."

Woods continued to sulk as they slowed to creep past their target, an aging apartment building. The street was absolutely empty; no pedestrians, no traffic, no life... until they passed beyond the building. There, two Russian tanks and a score of soldiers hunkered behind a wall. Roland slowed almost to a stop but one of the soldiers made a sweeping motion with his gun to move on. Woods sat very straight. Here he was *again*, out of uniform in the Soviet Zone.

Roland accelerated and they made an uneventful return to the detachment. There, Cole took reports from each team. They were all frustrated by the cancellation but only the Woods/Roland mission had encountered Russian troops.

1830 Hours

Cole called Mrs. Parks in and explained his quandary. He looked depressed, almost panicky. "I gave each team different destinations to see which, if any, were leaked. Of the three teams, one drove right into what looked like an ambush. This can't have been Honig. I leaked a completely bogus address for him. No, I must conclude that either Woods or Roland passed information to the Russians. There seems no other logical explanation. What do you know of these two men?"

She sat, prim and serious, "After our good Captain Woods' adventure I took some pains to investigate his background. I have discovered that he overstated his academic credentials and had two arrests for public drunkenness as a college student, but no convictions. He comes from a wealthy family who apparently covered his misadventures with political influence. He might not be a saint but I see nothing that might suggest treason."

Cole continued to look pained. "To tell you the truth, that's pretty much as I expected. Woods might be an arrogant buffoon but he doesn't strike me as a traitor. What about Roland?"

"In all honesty, I haven't looked at him very carefully. He's quiet, capable, doesn't create a stir ever."

Cole shook his head. "The man you never notice. The man you never suspect. Beware the harmless man. See what you can dig up."

October 16, 1800 Hours

Cole arrived early for his evening exchange with Anna. She was right on time but seemed nervous. Brushing by him, she did an expert exchange of satchels, so good it caught him by surprise. She coughed into her hand and said, "I'm being followed. Check the back of the news stand." He let her pass without recognition and walked in the direction she had come. Several people passed him. One held a newspaper. Why would a man already holding a newspaper go to the newsstand? James Cole walked by and sat down on a bench to watch. The man did, indeed, seem to be following Anna.

After they were gone, Cole walked behind the stand. Sure enough, there was a scrap of paper stuck on a nail. He scanned the area and saw no one watching. Then, pretending to have a coughing fit, he leaned against the wall and arched his back as if retching. His fist closed over the note and he drew his hand to wipe his mouth. He read a printed address, 322 Kohl Strasse. How would he find it? Did he even dare risk searching about with a satchel full of stolen documents?

James Cole walked the plaza looking for street signs, no Kohl. From the thinning crowd, he selected a bent old lady pulling a wheeled shopping basket and addressed her using his best German, "Excuse me, Madam, where is Kohl Strasse?"

Without looking up, she pointed a crooked finger. James thanked her and set off. Two blocks and he found the cross street. Number 322 was just two houses in. Now what? He watched and waited but he didn't have to wait long. Anna appeared, looked in both directions and motioned him to come in.

Once inside, she began rattling like a scared child. "Major Zelenkov has set up an operation to catch Americans trying to kidnap people in our area. I am frightened that they may be looking for me. They may have traced some of the information I gave you."

"There, there. Nothing can be tracked back to you. I promise. Just keep your normal schedule. If you are worried about being caught, don't copy anything for a few days. Wait and see what is going on."

She began crying softly. "My mother came yesterday and I took pictures of her. They are in your case. She cannot come again until November 11, the day of the Fasching Parade."

Cole tried to sound comforting. "That will be perfect. The parade will fill the streets and give us opportunities to move the three of you. Be ready."

October 19

"The tunnel is nearly done. We have enough information to act." James Cole shared his tea and his excitement with Mrs. Parks. She didn't seem completely convinced.

"You still have no confirmation of these locations or people. You don't really know what the Russians are doing. If we have been compromised there may be no scientists left to extract. You could be chasing ghosts or worse, walking into a trap."

Cole sat back and sipped. He thought for a time before answering. "That's all true but if we don't act soon, these scientists may starve or their guards might just kill them and make a run for the border."

Mrs. Parks reached for the brandy. "If you choose to go, I would be quite sure of my backup plan and my escape strategy. To me, this is unacceptably high risk. You don't even know if Professor Vogleman and the others' memories are accurate."

"All true, all true, and yet, I feel I must act. We have reliable information that the Russians are about to tighten travel restrictions into their sector. And there is some Russian major trying to sabotage our operation. It will be much more difficult to get our German geniuses out if we delay."

She toasted him with her tea cup and forced a smile. "All my best wishes go with you."

October 22, 0930 Hours

The operation was a complete surprise to everyone at Detachment Eight. It was not only the short notice, but the totally new strategy that caught Woods and the others unprepared. This time, the trucks were loaded with food and the teams were to be dressed in Austrian workers' blue coveralls. Major Cole's briefing brought open mouthed amazement. This was going to be more audacious than anything they had imagined and it was going to happen right now.

Roland, still under suspicion, had been sent to Salzburg to a meeting. Honig, the resident informant, was sent to the Vienna city hall to research records. Sherry White and Mrs. Parks were left to run the detachment and make everything appear normal.

The others were again set up as three teams of two each. At noon, they rolled. Five locations with three trucks in just a couple of hours; it was a lot to ask.

Cole rode with Charley Woods who spoke little as they drove, thinking he was still on probation in Cole's eyes. They approached their target, an abandoned hotel, and parked in back. Each of them lugged a box of bread and sausages and marched through the back door as though they owned the place. Climbing the main stairway, Cole shouted in harsh German, "SS men, come out and get food. It is time to go."

No one appeared. They continued to climb and Cole's shouts became more insulting. "Dumb bastards, we've come to take you south. Get out here and help us carry this damned food or we'll throw it away." The major's accent sounded native German. Everything about him; his bearing, his tone even his posture, made him completely believable as an SS officer.

On the third floor, a man in tattered clothes jumped from the shadows and poked a rifle at them. Cole never missed a step. "Put that damn thing down and give me a hand. We have very little time. We need to make connection with your transportation in just half an hour. Get everyone together."

Woods said nothing. His own accent could expose him. The group of Nazi guards and scientists gathered quickly drawn by the smell of meat and bread. That was enough to overcome any fears or doubts. Cole kept checking his watch. "Achtung, attention, we must go. Bring only what you can carry. Hurry."

Like children, they scurried to obey. Once in the back of the truck, the Germans found beer and candy. Overwhelmed by the food, there were no questions and no arguments. No one really paid much attention to the two phony Odessa agents in the front seats and the drive was uneventful.

They pulled to a loading dock at the rear of an abandoned U-Bahn subway station where Cole pulled back the truck's canvas flaps. He wore an apprehensive look and put a finger to his lips to signal everyone to stay quiet. Looking furtively left and right, he motioned them to follow him. The Germans, now suitably submissive, crept behind the truck, each carrying an armload of food. Inside the dock, they hurried down a dark, cobwebbed stairway.

The deeper they went, the darker it got. At the bottom of the long staircase, Cole opened a large double door and shone a flashlight inside. The six men entered and turned back to see him hold up two fingers and whisper, "Two hours." He slammed and locked the door.

Climbing back up, he exhaled deeply and laid a hand on Woods' back. "That was a lot easier than the first time." Woods didn't seem to understand. "But what are we going to do with them now? We're still in the Soviet Zone." Cole just smiled his goofy smile.

1100 Hours

Johnson and McMahan arrived with another load of six Germans. Again, this group marched dutifully down the steps as Cole directed only to be locked up with the others. Once free of his passengers, Johnson almost collapsed against the wall. He blurted loud and in English, "I can't believe we pulled it off," only to be hushed by the other Americans. Cole grabbed him by the lapels and yanked him up the stairs.

As they stumbled and climbed, Cole hissed, "They follow orders. They are used to following orders. When we acted authoritative, we gave them an excuse to fall back on old habit patterns and follow orders. I thought it would work. I prayed it would work. They wanted to be bossed and were willing to overcome doubts about us and become submissive. Now, *you* be quiet and don't screw this up."

Johnson nodded compulsively. "I still can't believe it worked." He was covered with sweat even on this chill October day. Cole slapped him hard on the back and said, "You did a good job, now go get another bunch."

Belcher and Ryan arrived even before Johnson's truck left. Cole again acted as tough drill sergeant rushing the German men downstairs. "This is just too easy," he said to himself. Two more loads and Cole's team had exhausted the list of Vogleman's addresses. He then dispatched all three empty trucks back over the Russian bridges with one driver each. They had dummy papers in case they were stopped, gambling that none of the Russian guards could read non-Cyrillic writing.

Now to take care of the SS guards, Cole took a deep breath and unlocked the double doors. It was pitch black inside and a roar of complaints greeted him. "Attention," he barked. "All SS men come with me. You will be given worker's coveralls and taken by truck to Switzerland. Come to shower and change clothes. All others wait."

Ten filthy, grumbling soldiers followed Cole. They were unhappy about being confined in the darkness but still so glad to be fed and moving again it didn't matter all that much. They marched smartly across the subway station to a tiled bathroom where Cole stopped them with a command. "Halt. Here you must disrobe before cleaning yourselves. Inside the bathrooms, there is no light and no hot water. You are SS warriors, you can handle the discomfort. When you are finished, come back here and get clean clothes. You and you, here are flashlights to help the others. Be thorough. You have ten minutes, no more. Go."

71

When they had all disrobed and crowded their way into the bathrooms, Belcher and Woods came quietly out of the darkness with chains and locks. Cole moved quickly to pull accordion style folding gates across the entrance. Chains rattled and locks snapped but there was no need to worry about the noise. The Germans were laughing and singing as they showered. Cole, Belcher and Woods gathered up the Germans' weapons and started down the subway tunnel to join the herd of scientists being assembled.

Woods looked back and said. "How long do you think those barriers will hold them?" Cole shrugged. "Long enough for you to go back and toss these into the crowd." He opened a small bag containing three hand grenades. Woods stopped, feeling instantly horrified, "You want me to just kill these men?"

"They wouldn't hesitate to kill you if given the chance."

"But... but, I was never trained to use hand grenades. I don't know..."

"Captain Woods, these men will destroy us all if given a chance. This is combat and they are the enemy. You know how to use a grenade. You pull the pin, count to three and throw it. I suggest you take cover right after that. Belcher, McMahan and I will march the others through the abandoned subway tunnel to the American Zone and meet up with our trucks. When you have taken care of the SS, follow us. I'll meet you at a small tunnel about half a mile down on the left. I'll be waiting. Don't screw this up."

Cole left to join the shuffling crowd of German scientists. Most of them were still desperately cramming food. They didn't know where they were headed and probably feared they might not eat again for a long time.

1140 Hours

Woods paced the shadowy subway platform like an abandoned puppy. Suddenly aware he had to piss, he stood on the subway platform and faced the recessed tracks. He was trying to be calm but his hand shook, painting urine all over. He wasn't sure he could do the grenades but he had to try. There was no choice. Introspection ended with shouts from the bathroom behind him.

Turning, he faced a crowd of angry, naked men pressing against the metal spider web gates. Muscular arms groped through the gates reaching out for Woods. All singing done, there was now only hostility in the SS men's voices. Charley Woods could only imagine what they would do if they got loose. Against the press of their weight, the gates bowed out and looked flimsy.

He reached into the bag, took out the first grenade and held it close to his face. There was so little light he wanted to be sure he could see to pull the pin. The grenade consisted of a grooved ball, a pin and a lever; nothing else. Should it be so simple to kill? Then the Germans charged the gate in a coordinated wave slamming against the metal. They backed off for another attempt. It wouldn't hold for long. He put his finger through the ring of the pin.

With a suppressed whimper, he yanked much harder than needed. The grenade went flying from his hand and bounced along the floor until it hit a metal cross bar. It rolled back lazily in the darkness. Charley could hear the grenade's grooved edges making tiny clicking noises against the tile.

A live grenade—he started forward to pick it up. No, that was stupid. What to do? He leaped from the station platform to land on the recessed tracks three feet below just as an explosion cracked above him. The concussion echoed repeatedly growing softer each time. For a long moment he stayed on his hands and knees breathing hard, smelling his own urine and trying to collect.

As ringing in his ears cleared he heard voices, Germans screaming with rage. Soon the crowd of muscular murderers would swarm him. But then there were other voices, brisk military voices shouting in Russian. Woods rose just enough to peek over the tiled platform edge. Russian soldiers poured down the stairs with rifles leveled at the gaggle of naked SS men.

Woods crouched low and began to shuffle down the tracks. No one noticed him. He broke into a run, bent and breathless in the dark. It took a long time for the voices to fade behind. Finally, he dared to stand up in the darkness and breathe. The two grenades left in his bag banged his knee and he discarded them. Afraid to use his flashlight, he stumbled along dragging one foot on the train rails as his only guide.

After an eternity, he saw a faint light ahead. Drawing nearer, he could make out Major Cole standing beside a ladder that lay against the broken rubble completely filling the tunnel. Cole started climbing and motioned for Charley to follow. Instead, Charley Woods leaned his head against the ladder and paused long enough to get control of his breathing.

He was alive... but he had screwed up again. Steeling himself against the criticism he knew was coming, he looked up and then climbed. At the top of the 20-foot long wooden ladder, he pushed aside a burlap flap and was amazed to find himself in a fancy wine cellar. Major Cole waited with a look of anticipation. Together they pulled up the ladder and Woods leaned back against a stone wall, exhausted.

"It was a disaster." Cole said nothing. "Just as I was about to toss the grenade, Russian troops stormed down the stairs screaming and shooting. I got one grenade off but I don't think it took out many of the Nazis."

When he said it like that, it didn't sound so bad. Maybe he would still come out of this okay.

October 23

The next morning all Cole's scientists were moved to one of Detachment Eight's row houses. It was a grand reunion for them. They could talk freely. They were being well fed and clothed. They were clean and safe. For that, they rejoiced, full of hope after so many months of desperation.

James Cole sat in his office reading through the message traffic provided by his informant Anna. It was apparent from those messages that Colonel Lushka was furious and the target of his wrath was a Major Zelenkov. Somehow the Russian major had known details of Cole's raid and had intended to capture the Americans. But Cole and his people moved too fast. Zelenkov's men followed the American's trucks but were too cautious and did not assemble their troops fast enough to catch the Americans who suddenly and mysteriously disappeared.

Despite his anger at Zelenkov, the communiqué Lushka sent to Moscow was upbeat. It described the capture of several Nazi SS guards who, under torture, revealed the location of an additional 70 German scientists. All those scientists had been captured within hours. Two scientists suffered gunshot wounds. All German SS guards were subsequently liquidated.

Cole felt the air go out of his lungs. Seventy scientists now in Russian hands; he had failed to protect them. Worse, he led the Russians to them. Damn, he thought he was so careful. How did the Russians know about his raid? He had been cautious to the point of paranoia. How did they know? Honig didn't know. Roland was out of town. Where was the leak? The only person who knew the complete truth was... Mrs. Parks.

CHAPTER THREE-NOVEMBER

November 1, 1545 Hours

Her mother had insisted on calling her Deborah. Her high school friends called her Debbie. She had always wanted to be called Deb but now, it didn't matter anymore. The soldiers bringing in boxes of her household goods called her Mrs. Cole and in the most respectful tones. She liked that.

She liked everything about her new position as Mrs. *Major* Cole. Who could have imagined that James Cole, awkward scarecrow of a man, could have made her life so wonderful? He must never, ever find out she only married him out of fear that she might be pregnant—and not by him.

For young James—no one ever thought of calling him Jim or Jimmy—the timing had been perfect. He had come back to her small upstate New York town trying to find his parents before shipping out with the Army but he came home too late. His mother was dead and his father long gone. But she was there.

They met in a soda shop. That was just a week after Deb's thoroughly unsatisfactory transaction in Bobby T. Gerrity's Ford roadster with the gear shift gouging her ribs and her head banging the glove box. She didn't know much about sex but she knew pregnancy was a very real possibility. She needed a husband in a hurry and Bobby T. lost interest as soon as their two minute wrestling match was over. James appeared as if on cue. He was a real gentleman, though certainly no heartthrob.

She went after him shamelessly and they were married after a one week courtship which included no real intimacy. Quickie marriages were common with the war raging. Who would have dreamed her fallback husband would become an Army officer, a major yet? Who would have dreamed he would bring her to Vienna and this fairy tale setting? Who would have dreamed she would live in such a house? Actually, it wasn't just a house; it was a mansion, almost a palace. Old and ornate, it was huge beyond all reason.

She stood in the ballroom and let her eyes flow over the marvelous spectacle. A glistening black grand piano sat on elaborate inlaid flooring. The walls were covered with fringed velvet drapes and paintings of ostentatiously dressed men she did not know. Even the massive gilt picture frames spoke of sumptuous elegance. Polished brass bannisters on two curving stairways led to a balcony crowned by a pair of crystal chandeliers that sparkled in the filtered light of stained glass skylights. This would be such a perfect setting for a cotillion. Did foreigners have cotillions?

"Mrs. Cole?" Her reverie was broken by the maid. She still couldn't believe it, a maid?

"Yes, Hurta."

The maid's name was some unpronounceable foreign thing but Deb called her Hurta and she always answered. The thick, ruddy woman wore a scarf on her head and a sour look on her face. "Ma'am, the men wish to speak with you."

Deb Cole rose to her full five feet two, smoothed her dress and tried to look imperial. "Yes, Hurta, bring them in."

Two Army soldiers in work uniforms removed their hats as they entered. "Mrs. Cole, we're done for the day. We have most of the wiring in the tunnel complete but there are still a couple of hot wires loose. It is important that no one goes down there until we're finished. I'd hate to see anyone hurt."

She smiled sweetly. "Thank you Sergeant, I'll see that no one goes near the tunnel." She had no idea whether he was a sergeant. All this military stuff was still alien to her. On top of that, she had no idea there was a tunnel or why she should care.

Including their wedding, two furloughs and the three days after she arrived in Austria, Deb and James Cole had spent a grand total of 28 days of married life together. For the rest of their two and a half year marriage, he had been away at war. She knew next to nothing about him or his job. But, in truth, she didn't much care.

She hugged herself tight and almost cooed as her eyes ran up the decorative columns to skylights that bathed her in heavenly light. It was like a cathedral, a magical setting fit for a princess. God, she loved this place.

November 2, 1630 Hours

Sherry White had been summoned to the Cole residence to check out a fancy new telephone switchboard. The signal intelligence team worked secretly for over a week with men of the engineer corps and now they felt ready.

As her car approached, she was amazed at the size and grandeur of the place. It must have forty rooms. Statues flanked the entrance to a landscaped garden with a fountain. As they pulled up to the house, a red cheeked woman with the downtrodden bearing of a peasant met her at the door. Sherry assumed the woman was Austrian and greeted her in broken German.

The peasant woman returned the pleasantry but Sherry stopped short. There was something in the woman's voice. Sherry spoke again, this time in Russian. Again, the woman responded, now in fluent Russian. They talked for a while and the woman became more social.

"What is your name, Madam?" asked Sherry.

"Charlotte Huntsov," the woman responded. "But Mrs. Cole calls me Hurta. I think she misunderstood when I introduced myself. I don't care what she calls me."

"You sound educated and you have a slight accent, Ukrainian perhaps."

Charlotte Huntsov smiled. "You have a good ear. Yes, I was born in the Ukraine but that was long, long ago."

Sherry was interested now. "So, why is a woman who is obviously educated, refined and well-spoken working as a housekeeper?"

Charlotte made a half laugh. "For food, of course, my husband was a Cossack. His people made the very bad decision to fight with the Germans *against* the Russian Army. When the Germans surrendered, he and his soldiers turned themselves over to the British thinking they would be safe. They were wrong. The British shipped tens of thousands of Cossacks back to the Russians who killed them all. Now, I must do what I can to feed myself and my daughter and avoid the damned Russians. They will kill us as quickly as they killed my husband."

They walked in silence for a time. Sherry pondered the story. Something didn't sit well. The more she thought, the more she doubted. Finally, she stopped and confronted the housekeeper in a soft, even voice.

"Charlotte Huntsov, I don't believe you. You would have to have been carefully checked out to get a job working for a senior American Intelligence officer. No wife of a man who fought for the Nazis could get such a job. So, someone must have paid a fortune to bribe people and forge documents to get your appointment. Tell me the truth. Who are you really working for?"

For a long terse moment Charlotte Huntsov's face churned as her lips tried to find words. Sherry became impatient. "It will do you no good to lie. I will know. I am a trained agent." That was, of course, untrue, but it sounded good.

Charlotte wrung her hands and her voice cracked. "What will you do to me?"

"Tell me the truth and I will protect you."

"The truth," Charlotte laughed without mirth. "Who knows what is true. All I know is that my husband may not yet be dead. He is in a concentration camp. They will keep him alive as long as I report what goes on in this house. If I fail, he will surely die a horrible death."

"So, you are working for the Russians?" Charlotte nodded, looking at her feet. "Good, I will talk to my boss. I think we can work something out. We will pay you to provide false information to your Russian handlers."

Charlotte looked suspicious. Sherry tried to be reassuring even though she was making promises well beyond her authority. "We might even be able to get your husband freed. I can't promise that but I'll try. No matter what, we will be able to get you and your daughter safely out of Vienna at some point… if you help us."

Charlotte looked up and her eyes clouded. "This is possible? I will do anything to get my daughter away from here. My husband, I fear, is lost. He fought the Russians. They hate him. The Allies think he is a Nazi. There is no place left for him. He is a lost man.

Sherry shrugged slightly. "No one is lost until the final gunshot. We can try."

Their conversation was interrupted by Deb Cole who swirled into the room in her crisp powder blue shirtwaist dress. She sounded prissy. "Hurta, who is this woman? I demand that you ask me before you allow anyone into my house. Do you understand?"

Sherry tried to be cordial. "Ma'am, I am Miss White. I work for your husband, Major Cole. I will be doing work in your cellar on a regular basis. I do not wish to trouble you with my comings and goings since I will be operating at all hours of the day and night. I have my own key and I will make every effort not to disturb you."

Deb looked as though she was just about to explode. She inhaled deeply and her nose rose as high as her eyes. "I didn't know there was a woman in my husband's detachment, let alone a woman with a key to my house. I forbid you to enter without my permission. This is my house and I..."

Sherry cut her off. "Ma'am, this house belongs to the US Army. It is my workplace. I will make every effort not to inconvenience you but I do not need your permission to enter and do my job. Do you understand?"

Deb was shaking as she spun and stomped away to telephone James Cole. Sherry looked at the housekeeper and shrugged. "Write down all the information you can about your husband. What is his name? Where is he being held? How do you communicate with him? What specifically, have the Russians told you and what have they demanded of you?"

Charlotte padded off to start writing. She could hear Deb Cole in the next room screaming into a telephone and that made her smile.

1700 Hours

Sherry opened a heavy oak door that led down into a dank wine cellar. Army engineers had just installed a light switch that revealed a basement made of fitted stone with a low ceiling and great support beams grown black with age. Empty alcoves that once held casks and bottles now gathered dust.

She walked to the far wall, hesitating at the sound of a small, scurrying creature. Ahead, a new door opened to reveal a freshly dug tunnel and steps that now replaced a rickety ladder. She was about to begin her climb when a voice below called, "Who's there?"

"Sherry White, I'm coming down." A man appeared at the foot of the stair only to immediately step back out of view. She thought that was a consideration to her modesty as she descended wearing a skirt. At its base, the tunnel opened into an endless void dimly lit with red lights.

The man reappeared. "I'm Sergeant Richardson of G-2 Signals Intelligence, attached to Detachment Eight."

"I'm Sherry White." She extended a hand and he returned a tentative shake.

"Ma'am, I didn't know I'd be working with a woman. Can I ask your rank?"

She grinned. "I'm a civilian so you don't have to worry about the 'sir' stuff and don't worry Sergeant Richardson, I won't bite. I'm a Russian linguist. Could you show me the equipment?" Her voice echoed off tiled walls beyond the rubble. He pointed the way with his flashlight and she followed.

"Ma'am, this is a portion of the Vienna U-Bahn subway that's been cut off as a result of Allied bombing. We dug the tunnel and made this big fake rock to hide the entrance when we're not working here. It is important that you always replace the rock when you come down." With that, he activated a switch and an electric motor slowly drew the rock back until it looked like part of the collapsed concrete and stone pile.

"The Austrians are very efficient people. They were considerate enough to run their electrical, water and telephone lines through these subway tunnels for easy access and repair. That's great for us, easy access to the telephone cables. I've built a switchboard that will allow you to plug into any phone line and listen in." He smiled proudly. "Watch your step Ma'am. These old rails can be dangerous in the dark."

Richardson was right. Walking on gravel and crossties between the subway rails required care. She resolved never to try it in heels. She also decided to wear a heavy sweater next time. It was downright cold inside the tunnel.

"Do you see the paint stripe across the tracks? Once you step over that, you're in the Soviet Zone. Well, actually, you're under the Soviet Zone. We're coming up on an abandoned subway station. The Russians have sealed it off at street level.

Down here, it's completely intact and the electricity still works. Your work station is set up in the old station master's office. There are big glass windows so you have a great view. You can see everything around you even though it's pretty dark. A bunch of doors in the office give you lots of options for escape routes."

"Escape routes?"

"Well, yes Ma'am. We are in the Soviet Zone and just a stairway away from the street."

She made a face and climbed metal stairs into an expansive office. There, Sherry faced a standard 1940's telephone switchboard; over 100 receptacles on a four foot square board. Above each, a tiny light indicated it was in use. Unfortunately, she could only listen to one line at a time.

She plopped into a swivel chair, put on the headset and began plugging into one after another. Satisfied, she turned to Richardson. "So, how's this going to work? I spend my shift listening. What do you do?"

He was taken by surprise. "Well, I guess I'm here in case anything goes wrong. I can repair the board or troubleshoot connections or whatever. I will also act as lookout and provide protection."

Sherry nodded and smirked. "Can you make coffee?"

November 7, 2300 Hours

It had been almost a week and Sherry was slowly adapting to her four to midnight shift in the tunnel. Sergeant Richardson turned out to be a pleasant enough but incredibly dull companion. He spoke little, read his Bible in the dim red light of the Station Master's office and sometimes mumbled to himself while staring into space.

Sherry had become a real voyeur listening to one conversation after another. If it was German, she unplugged and moved on chasing the tiny lights that indicated open lines. When she heard Russian, she lingered to get the gist. Tonight, she heard a unique voice speaking French. She didn't know ten words in French but this was unusual. They were far from the French Zone. Even more unusual, the voice on the other end spoke Russian.

She barked, "Richardson, turn on the recorder." He stumbled into the back as she turned back and pressed the headset to her ears to listen open mouthed.

It was almost eleven when Sherry White stormed up the stairs to Major James Cole's bedroom and pounded on the door. "Are you awake? I need to tell you something."

Deb Cole flung open the door. She looked small and mousey as she wrapped herself in a flannel robe. Her voice was shrill as a bird's. "What in hell do you think you are doing invading my boudoir?" Behind her, Cole was fumbling for his pants. "It's all right, Deb. Just relax."

"It is not all right. This woman has no right, no right at all…"

"It's all right, Deb. I'll just be a minute." He pushed by his wife as he zipped his fly and pulled suspenders over a sleeveless tee shirt. Deb stamped her foot and slammed the door behind him. He motioned down the stairs.

"Okay Sherry, what is so important that you got me out of bed and brought the wrath of my darling wife down on my ears. I won't hear the end of this for a long time."

Sherry was excited. "I've intercepted a Frenchman who spoke terrible Russian talking to a Russian who spoke terrible French and they were talking about us, *Detachment Eight*. They were talking about *us* and specifically about the scientists we've captured. They intend to conduct a raid into our territory and capture the thirty or so men we control. There is one, in particular, they want. His name is Klein."

"Do you know when this will happen?"

"Soon, but I didn't get enough context. I need someone who speaks French to review the tapes. I was only getting part of the conversation. I did get this, however. The Russian's name is Zelenkov and the Frenchman is Devereaux."

They reached the kitchen and Cole poured two glasses of Bourbon. He ran his hands over his face and sighed. "This whole thing is like a Kaleidoscope. At every twist, the whole picture changes completely. Now, we have the French helping Russians. My maid is a Ukrainian Cossack spying for the Russians. Honig spies for everyone. Our office is compromised. I need a drink."

November 8, 1500 Hours

Cole crammed into the hotel's metal cage elevator along with a mob of pushing, grumbling Austrians. He craned to read the bulletin board over the mob's heads. There, in the upper left corner was a torn brochure for Stephansdom, the Cathedral of St. Stephan's. This would be the location for the urgent meeting he had just requested with Mason.

Cole knew the church was bomb damaged and certainly unheated in an early November suddenly turned unseasonably bitter but there wasn't time to change into warmer clothes. It was a short but frosty walk into the shadow of the battered but still imposing building. Before the bombings, the enormous roof had been embellished with a hundreds of thousands of colored tiles depicting a double-headed Austrian eagle. Now it was gone. Still, what remained was a grand monument of soaring buttresses and statued vaults. He walked around the perimeter enduring cold that made his nose run and his breath cloud.

He was beginning his second circle when he saw Mason in a black coat and fur cap talking to a Priest outside one of the massive doors.

Mason waved to Cole and spoke to the priest in German, "Ah Father, here is my good friend. Please tell him the story of the inscription." Cole blew into his hands and nodded a greeting to the priest who nodded back while keeping his own hands deep inside his robe.

"Guten tag," replied the priest. "I was just explaining that the initials 'O5' carved in the stone here are to honor the Austrian resistance fighters. Many died fighting Hitler's troops. Sadly, most Austrians were not so brave. The majority accepted the Anschluss passively when the Nazis annexed our country. To our North, the German priesthood largely capitulated to the Nazis without complaint. We Austrian priests however, refused to cooperate. Many went to concentration camps and few of them ever returned."

The priest inclined his head toward James Mason. "I was just telling this gentleman that we also resisted the efforts of the Organization of former SS to help Nazis escape our country. The Odessa people threatened us and even killed one priest, but we never hid a one of them or vouched to get passports. That is something the Italian priesthood cannot say."

Mason held out a gloved hand and said, "Thank you Father, you must be cold. We will take no more of your time." The priest ignored Mason's offered hand, smiled and made a slight bow as he left. Mason shrugged and clapped his hands against the biting cold.

Cole hunched and recapped the last day's events. Mason registered no surprise, as though he already knew all of it. Cole was shivering and wanted the meeting to end quickly or, at least, move inside.

Mason appeared in no hurry. He leaned back to see the O5 in the wall. "I brought you here for this. Mrs. Parks already told me about Honig. She's been researching him a bit. It seems his birth certificate is fake, a very good fake. It shows him being born in 1905 here in Vienna. All the signatures and stamps look real. Even the paper is properly aged. The only problem is the watermark. It bears an emblem of the Austrian Republic which had not yet been created." Mason pointed up. "This is what we know of Honig. He was O5, a resistance fighter."

Cole's teeth chattered as he clenched his arms tightly across his chest. "So, he was a hero? Why is he spying on us now? He should be helping us create a democracy for his country. And, why in God's name would he pass information to the French? This makes no sense."

"Actually, it does. The O5 was much more than a bunch of freedom fighters. They were mostly communists. Before the war, this town was called *Rot Wein*, Red Vienna. The communists were a major force then. There is still strong support for the cause and, despite the atrocities of its army, for the Russian state."

Cole could take no more and, with an apology, began walking up the steps to the church door. He grabbed a huge iron ring and struggled to swing open a massive door. Mason followed. Once inside, it was only slightly warmer but, without the wind, it seemed bearable.

Mason continued with his story. "Honig isn't Austrian and he isn't German. He's French, from the Alsace border area. His real name, we believe, is Henri Meil. He grew up in a German speaking area but hated the Germans he had to deal with daily."

"But why is he here? Why didn't he fight Germans in France rather than Austria?"

Mason gave a little eyebrow gesture. "He did. He was captured and sent to a concentration camp outside Munich. On the way, his prisoner train was attacked and wrecked by Allied aircraft. He escaped to find his way south. Here, he joined the Austrian fighters."

"Where did his attraction to communism come in?"

"When France fell to the Nazis, it was assumed they were just overwhelmed by the Blitzkrieg. In fact, the French had not had a functioning government for many months. They were locked in a self-destructive battle between conservatives and liberals. Many conservatives so hated their liberal opponents, they saw the Nazis as a better alternative. Those hard core conservatives became Milice, collaborators. Many liberal hard liners were, or became, communists and later resistance fighters. Honig was one of them. For him, a German-speaking Frenchman stranded in Southern Germany, the O5 was a natural move."

Cole's shivering lessened. "So he spies for the French who support the Russians? Could this get any more complicated?"

Mason shook his head. "Well, yes actually. Honig officially works directly for the Austrian National government. Their de facto leader, Chancellor Renner, operates from the Soviet Zone. We consider him a Soviet puppet. Still, Honig is a diplomatic pawn. We can't *arrest* him. We must rely on other measures."

Cole hugged himself tighter to calm his shaking. "Other measures?" He tucked his chin thoughtfully. "All right, I'll take care of it. I'll be glad to get rid of him. We've just found a microphone under my desk. I suspected Mrs. Parks but I think my 'leak' is simply Honig and his bug."

He became more earnest. "What I need from you now is a safe place for my scientists. I must move them out tomorrow with little commotion. Mrs. Parks translated a taped conversation that indicated the Russians intend to raid my building tomorrow at 1500 hours. Can you help me?"

Mason pursed his lips and stood lost in thought for a moment. Then, he nodded to himself and said, "Yes, I know where to hide them. Load them up as inconspicuously as you can and deliver them to the bombed out parking lot of the old University Technik in the city's American Zone. We have thrown together a temporary Displaced Persons camp there. It's filled with refugees waiting to have their credentials verified before we move them west to more permanent camps near Salzburg. We will hide your scientists in plain sight, mixed with a few hundred other refugees."

The meeting done, Mason looked pleased with himself. Cole just wanted to get somewhere warm.

November 9, 1445 Hours

Friday afternoon was no warmer. Snow peppered the gray skyline and a harsh wind chased it along the streets. The detachment's buildings were now empty. Mrs. Parks took an unsuspecting Honig out to a late lunch. Everyone else moved to a nearby building with a clear view of the entrance to the detachment's parking lot with its imposing ten-foot brick columns with a massive stone lintel spanning the gap. From that vantage point, they watched the building where, until yesterday, the scientists had been held. They watched and waited.

Three o'clock sharp; two Russian trucks careened into the parking area with wheels spitting snow and gravel. Shouting troops streamed out of the trucks at a dead run. Finding a locked door, they kicked it in without hesitation. A dozen soldiers in belted long coats and egg shell helmets charged into the building fanning machine guns before them. Others spread out in a defensive arc around the trucks.

Cole, watching from the nearby window, leaned out and gave a signal. Just down the alley a truck started its engine and began to lumber slowly. As it moved, a long chain behind the truck stretched taut. The truck struggled, spinning tires as it pulled against one of the brick parking lot pillars.

Russian soldiers watched helpless as the huge brick and stone column cracked, tilted and came crashing down in a cloud of dust. Rubble now blocked the parking lot entrance trapping the trucks. There was intense shouting. Soldiers from inside the building came out shrugging apologetically to a team leader now screaming spittle. Soldiers milled in confusion. No one seemed to know what to do.

Cole stayed concealed as he shouted in Russian, "Hands up. You are under arrest." He ducked back inside to watch and laugh along with the rest of the detachment. The Russian team leader looked around in desperate confusion. He pointed his pistol up in the air searching for the source of the invisible voice but could find no target. In a rage, he grabbed the hat off his head and slapped it against his knee.

Lieutenant Cynthia Ryan hung up her phone and announced, "I have just notified the Four-power security force of an armed attack on an American office building." Cole grinned and returned to his window.

It was quite a show as the Russians tried to ram their trucks through the rubble pile. The first truck only managed to bash its front end into a mangle of bent metal spewing a geyser of radiator steam. The second truck did better, climbing and bouncing to the top of the pile, but there, it bottomed out to teeter helplessly rocking back and forth.

Russian soldiers mobbed the truck shouting and shoving and finally pushed it over the top. Once free, the truck slid down the loose brick mound to slam hard onto a cobblestone road and raise a cloud of dust and snow. Two trucks worth of troops climbed frantically over the brick pile and leaped into and onto their last vehicle. They hung from running boards, canopy posts and open doors as the bent and sagging truck lumbered out of sight in light falling snow.

James Cole opened a bottle of Austrian Wine and poured for a toast. "Here's to the Russian bear who has never looked so foolish." There was a chorus of "here, here." Cole let out a deep breath; now to deal with Honig.

1600 Hours

Mrs. Parks walked into the detachment laughing as she pulled off her shawl. Herr Honig must have just told her a joke. The entire staff stood waiting. Cole stepped forward. "Herr Honig, as you are well aware, the Russians just attempted an unsuccessful attempt to kidnap our guests."

Honig did a commendable impression of an astonished man. "I knew nothing…"

"Not quite true. You provided the information necessary for them to dare such an action. Let's step out onto the balcony. I could use a cigarette and, I suspect, so could you." With that, Cole was off. Honig looked from face to face in a desperate search for support from anyone in the crowd. He found none.

The normally haughty Honig came out to the balcony that overlooked the parking lot. Cole offered an American cigarette but didn't light it for him. The major turned and leaned on his elbows to survey the scene below. One wrecked Russian truck still lay against the pile of bricks that had once been a stately column.

"So, no one was killed in today's adventure. We knew the Russians were coming and we made fools of them. I'm afraid your Soviet employers now know you are compromised. You will no longer be of use to them. Worse, you have committed an act of aggression against the American Occupation Force."

Cole drew on his cigarette and exhaled a long stream of smoke into gentle snowflakes. "So, what do you think will happen now?"

Honig was quiet for a full minute, probably thrashing for a story to tell. Finding none, he cupped his hands and lit his own cigarette. "I suppose you mean, who will kill me. What do you propose?"

"Ah, there's the question. I have a choice for you to consider." Cole held the cigarette in his lips, pulled out his pistol and cocked the slide. A single ejected shell tinkled like a sleigh bell as it bounced on the deck. He set the gun on a ledge and took the cigarette in his fingers.

"Here's how I see it. The Russians are a lost cause but you may still have credibility with the French. You could tell me everything there is to know about Devereaux and his people and then feed them false information as I direct."

Honig's head fell. His voice was soft, defeated. "No, never. I am a patriot. I want to see a world where all men are equal. The communists will be the salvation of our race. I will not betray my cause. I will not."

Cole picked up the gun and inspected it. "As I see it, you now have two choices. You can become a double agent or a double amputee." He aimed the gun at Honig's knee. "If I were you, I would consider postponing my crusade to save the world. You will not be much of a revolutionary in a wheel chair."

Honig fumed and cursed under his breath. He knotted fists and clenched his teeth so hard he bit his cigarette in two. He said nothing and focused a bitter stare at the horizon. The silence went on for an eternity. Finally, Cole grew exasperated. "All right, then, pick a leg, right or left, your choice."

Honig hissed. "I know that voice. I often go to American movies to learn accents. You sound like the actor Jimmie Cagney."

Cole ignored the comment. "Okay, I'll pick for you. We'll start with the left. Please lift your leg so I may have a clean shot." Honig turned and flashed a look of pure hate. Cole steadied the pistol in both hands, cigarette still dangling from his lips, aimed and pulled the trigger.

The hammer clicked and Honig flinched dramatically, but there was no explosion. Cole grinned. "I must be out of ammunition. Give me a second to reload."

The breath went out of Honig's lungs and he sagged with one hand on his chest. "All right, I will tell you about the French but I will do nothing to harm the people of this or any other nation. Communism is the future. It is the hope of millions."

Cole was still grinning. "The hope of millions? Well Monsieur, do you think it will help people survive the brutality of the Soviet dictatorship? I doubt it. You are an unwitting tool of the bloodiest tyrant left in the world. Now you will help us. You will do what you are told or we will hand you over to the communists you so love and they will turn you into dog food. Do you understand?"

The muscles in Honig's temples pulsed and his jaw ground. Lieutenant Ryan interrupted, "Sir, there's a call for you. It's urgent."

1615 Hours

Mason stood and paced at the extent of the telephone's cord. His face was tight. The Russians had just kidnapped Christian Weiss, code named 'Phyllis'. The Swiss diplomat was not a real intelligence operative. He would never hold up to torture. Mason didn't know exactly how deep Phyllis' knowledge went ,but it was extensive. All the Web organization's secrets were threatened. Everything was at risk. He waited for Cole of Detachment Eight to answer. "Come on," He pleaded into the air. "There's no time. They have three stolen staff American staff cars that were used in the kidnapping—answer, damn it."

1618 Hours

James Cole made a panicky call to Colonel Mather. He shouted into the phone. "Sir, I have just been informed that there are Russian agents driving American staff cars to your parking lot. They are setting you up to take the blame for a kidnapping. You must apprehend them. This is extremely urgent. You must stop these men and arrest them."

Mather shot back. "Have you lost your mind, Major? The Russians would never do such a thing. There must be a rational explanation for their use of our staff cars, if it's even true. Now calm down and get a grip on yourself."

"Colonel, my detachment has just been attacked by Russians. If you don't stop these men you will be committing an act of treason and I will personally file charges against you."Mather screamed, "Don't you dare threaten…" but the line was dead.

1619 Hours

Cole, Belcher, Roland and McMahan screamed out of the parking lot in a battered Mercedes and sped toward the U.S. Army headquarters. Inside the car, the stern faced men, still in their Army uniforms, were checking weapons and loading clips. There was going to be a fight and they had little time to prepare. The fake staff cars would soon have to cross the Ringstrasse, a beltway that surrounded the inner city. There, they would meet the men of Detachment Eight.

Roland saw them first and shouted over road noise. Belcher rolled down his window and poked out a carbine. Cole hit the throttle and accelerated wildly past the first two olive drab cars. In each, Russians in military uniforms stared back at the Americans with a mix of amazement and concern. Coming alongside the lead car Cole shouted, "Shoot the driver."

Belcher fired a series of quick shots that shattered the car's windows. The Russian swerved frantically, smacking the American's car broadside. As they bounced together, rubbing doors, Belcher flailed trying to get a clear shot at the Russian driver. The Russian in the passenger seat blasted away with his pistol. In wildly careening cars, neither could keep his aim steady. One of the Russian's shots hit his own driver in the head. Blood splattered the window as the driver slumped and his car veered off to strike a curb. It bounced, rolled onto its side and skidded in a spray of sparks.

Cole's rear window exploded in a shower of glass. He slammed the brakes hard and caught the second Russian car by surprise. The Russian driver hesitated just a moment before panic braking. That moment was all it took. He smacked into the rear of Cole's skidding Mercedes, bounced and rebounded from the impact.

As the American's crumpled Mercedes skidded to a stop, Roland flew out the back door with his .45 pistol blazing into the windshield of the third car. It was coming fast and he barely dove out of the way as that vehicle slammed into the other wrecked cars. Four cars now formed a pile of bent and shattered metal. A suspended wheel continued to spin making a week, week, week sound.

Cole, with pistol drawn, shouted in Russian, "Everybody out with hands up." He was answered only by groans from inside the three stolen staff cars. A quick scan showed all the Americans standing and unhurt. Well, McMahan had a bloody forehead gash. No one else seemed injured. A distant siren wailed and Cole ordered them to run. The four men in US Army uniforms took off down a small alley and were immediately confronted by an Austrian City Policeman who blew a whistle and commanded them to halt.

Two rifles and two pistols were his only response. The unarmed policeman dropped his whistle, raised both hands and stepped politely out of the way. As Cole and his companions sprinted their way through the labyrinth of back streets the number of sirens increased, but they were becoming more distant. Behind a row of small shops, the quartet of runners finally paused. Coughing and breathless, they bent, hands on knees and tried to collect.

Cole, looking as gangly as a stick figure, spoke between wheezes, "I don't know what will come next but I'm proud of you all. We may have prevented a major blow to the reputation of the United States. We may go to jail, but we go as heroes."

There were a few coughing nods but no one doubted that there would be serious consequences for killing Russian allies in an apparently unprovoked attack. Still, there were no regrets. Belcher even forced a smile as he wheezed, "Hell of a good fight, boys."

1800 Hours

Mather, hearing of the shootings on Ringstrasse, was on the phone to his commanding general demanding a manhunt be launched for the attackers. He just knew it had to be the renegade Major Cole and the out-of-control gang of hoodlums. After all, Cole had called to warn him the Russians were coming. The conversation was interrupted by a captain with a pained look. Mather yelled, "Not now, I'm on the phone with General Brandt. "

The captain persisted, "Sir, you need to hear this." Mather covered the mouthpiece and glared. "Sir, those staff cars were stolen. They were being driven by Russian soldiers in NKVD uniforms. It also appears that they match the description of cars used in the abduction of a Swiss diplomat less than an hour ago."

Colonel Mather sat frozen but fuming. Finally, he controlled his voice and spoke into the phone, "Sir, I have just been given new information. I'll have to call you back." He hung up but his face was still as tight as a clenched fist.

1900 Hours

Across the canal, a Major Barkov stood uneasily before Colonel Lushka and gave a stammering report on the partial failure of his mission. "We have the Swiss man but our drivers who were to plant stolen cars by the American headquarters were all shot. Police of all occupying powers are swarming the crash scene."

Lushka snickered, then chuckled and finally rolled with laughter. He slammed his hand repeatedly against the desk. Tears welled in his eyes as he pointed at Barkov. "So you came here to do Moscow's plan and it was a disaster. Now somebody has to take the blame. I was not involved. So, Comrade Barkov, who do you think it will be?"

Then Lushka extended a thumb and forefinger in the international imitation of a pistol. He closed his thumb and went "bousch," the sound of a gunshot. Barkov found no satisfaction in Lushka's humor.

November 10, 0800 Hours

Sergei sat stiffly dreading his meeting with Lushka. He expected that the colonel was angry and there was much to explain. He reviewed his failures. To begin, he had not been successful in finding the German scientists. Instead, he had to wait until the Americans showed him the way. Then he had been too cautious in his effort to catch the American raiders. True, his own soldiers had later captured more scientists than the Americans but his failure to find Doctor Klein remained a humiliation. And now, the embarrassment of the failed attack on Detachment Eight's compound must be explained.

Anna, the timid secretary, clutched a clipboard to her chest as she came out to the waiting area. She avoided eye contact and whispered, "Colonel Lushka is ready to see you." With a deep breath, Sergei straightened and marched into the office.

Lushka boomed, "Welcome my friend, Comrade Zelenkov. Come in, come in." He motioned to a seat and Sergei sat, grateful to avoid a bear hug or worse, Commissar Svetlana's advances.

Lushka plopped into his great chair and began with a voice that seemed weary. "We have just captured Christian Weiss, who has been spying for the Americans. While you were busy distracting the Americans, Barkov's group grabbed the phony Swiss diplomat who infiltrated the Austrian government."

Sergei came out of his chair. "My colonel, you have another group do my work? Have I failed you so badly that you must have others replace me?" He realized that his voice was just short of soprano and his face felt flushed. Lushka held out his hand, palm down and motioned to slow down.

"Hush now. That was not my decision. Many decisions are now being made by Moscow directly. I am no longer in complete control. But that is not important." The big man seemed to shrink a little right before Sergei's eyes. "My friend, when you came here, you said you wanted to build a fence. Now, you get your chance."

He tossed a map at Sergei. "Most of the border between our Zone and the Americans' is defined by the Donau canal but there is one stretch of twelve kilometers where anyone can walk across. You will build a fence along this area. I will give you 300 soldiers to do it. But it must be built it in one day so no one will have time to complain. Can you do this thing?"

Sergei was taken aback. "Yes, of course I can do it, but why? You said we would be leaving this country soon. Have things changed?"

Lushka stood and stretched his huge arms wide. His right sleeve flapped limp and lifeless where the arm and hand had once been. He sighed deep. "So much has changed. So much is changing. The war is over. Now we are waging *politics*." He shook his head and his normally bombastic voice grew dejected and hollow. "Our time is drawing to an end, Sergei. You and I are old warriors. Now, our once fierce Army is becoming a nest of snakes. No one can be trusted. Build your fence, Sergei. Build your fence and be happy in your work."

The giant turned toward a window and stared in silence. After a minute, Sergei gathered his things and left quietly trying not to disturb the big man. Once outside, he paused to consider. Building a fence was a trivial job. But he knew he could do it well.

His mind was already hard at work planning. Despite the routine nature of the task, it was honorable work. Better, it was a concrete accomplishment. Everyone could see and touch his fence.

He knew the western allies, the Americans, French and British, had an Armistice Day holiday next Sunday, November 11. That was the same day as the local Fasching Parade. Everyone in Vienna will be distracted with their holiday plans. He would begin his fence work on Friday night. All government offices would be empty for the weekend so it would be done before any formal complaint could be filed. Once built, it will be impossible to get a four-power agreement to dismantle it.

Sergei walked and plotted. Twelve kilometers, one fence post every two meters would require 2000 fence posts. Four strands of barbed wire meant almost 5000 rolls of wire. Four per post required 8000 spikes. He would use 50 men to string and nail wire. The other 250 would dig post holes and tamp in posts. It should take eight hours if everything went well but, of course, nothing ever goes well. He would plan for twelve hours.

He almost broke into a whistle but that would be inappropriate for a KGB officer. Still he could not stop smiling. He was working at something tangible. Later, he checked the weather forecast. It would be cold but clear. Sunset would be early but the moon would be a quarter full. That would be enough light.

November 10, 1800 Hours

Despite the harrowing day, Cole still managed to arrive at the newsstand promptly at six. With his mind still frazzled by the Russian raid, the diplomat's kidnapping and the shootout with Russian drivers, he just wanted this to be an ordinary drop, quick and easy. That was not to be. Anna came, stepping fast and she wasn't alone. Two women followed, each of them lugging a large suitcase. They shared an intense, almost frantic look.

Anna spoke in Russian, "Please sir, you must help us. Everything is crashing down. We must get out tonight. Here is also my mother and my sister. It is no longer safe for any of us here."

Cole looked around the square but saw nothing suspicious. He became an understanding uncle and tried to calm her. "I'm sorry Anna, we're just not ready. I don't have things set up. You must wait until tomorrow, Sunday."

Her voice became increasingly shrill. "No, that will be too late. The Red Army is in chaos. Many will soon die. I am sure of it. Just get us to some place where we can hide. I beg of you, help us."

Cole grimaced and tried to come up with a plan. "All right, come with me. We will work something out. It will be a very long walk. Can you all make it?" He looked at the mother.

Anna was the spokesman. "We will do whatever we must. My mother is strong. She will not slow us down. You should know I have brought many important messages for you. You will see how terrible things are."

Cole led the way and they marched smartly for seven blocks trying not to be noticed as they carried luggage. He scanned constantly but saw no one following or even paying attention to the tall man and his three women companions. Anna was, however, wrong about her mother. The old woman had bad ankles and made constant whimpering noises as she struggled to keep up. Cole took her suitcase but she still stumbled and flailed as though every step brought pain.

Arriving at the closed U-Bahn station, Cole made them wait in the shadows as he went to scout. All front doors were locked. He had neither keys nor tools. He did have a gun but dared not shoot off a lock. Instead, he walked back to explore the loading dock where his team had so recently smuggled scientists. It was a shambles. Russian troops had smashed windows and doors. Glass littered the ground and trash piled everywhere.

Summoning the women, Cole lifted each over a concrete barrier so they could crawl through a broken window. Once all three were safely inside, he contorted his own awkward frame through the small opening using care not to disturb protruding glass shards. That might alert watchmen or guards.

Inside, it was too dark to walk safely. He took out his Zippo lighter but it was out of fluid. Sighing, he put it away and pressed on. "You must follow me. I will hold Anna's hand. Each of you two join hands and hold onto the straps of her luggage. We have a very long walk ahead. Once we go down the stairs it will be completely black and we must walk over loose stone and iron rails. You must be very careful. There is no need to hurry but you must not allow yourself to get injured. If you fall, it will be difficult to help you in the dark. Do you understand?"

He could barely see them nodding like bobble heads. After another deep breath, he took Anna's hand and they began a terrifying journey down into a world so dark it was like wearing a black velvet hood. There was no up or down, no left or right, only forward. The mother whimpered and the sister breathed like a struggling pack horse. Anna was silent except for an occasional word of encouragement to the others.

Ordinarily, Sherry White would have been working the communications console inside the subway but tonight she was busy coordinating passports for the German scientists. That was going to be a big problem, a problem he dared not share with the three women. Without Sherry, there was no one to turn on the red guide lights that led to the end of the tunnel. Without those lights, he had no idea how he would find the switch to operate the fake stone door. That stone was their only way out of the subway tunnel.

He found the hand rail and followed it down stairs onto the tracks. They walked and stumbled, for what seemed like hours, before he tripped, falling to his hands and knees into a rubble pile. "Halt," he commanded. "We are at the end of the tunnel. You must stand here while I search for the escape door."

"No," Anna screamed in the darkness. "Do not leave me. Do not let go. Please don't."

He pried loose from her clutch and whispered, "I must." As he pulled away, she began sobbing. Bending low, he ran his fingers over dirt, broken brick and torn metal. His hand snagged repeatedly. Warm blood ran down a finger.

He just couldn't remember where the switch was hidden. Worse, he couldn't be sure just where he was in relation to the fake rock. The tunnel was almost 20 meters wide. He could be anywhere along the collapsed rock pile. Finally, he bumped against solid concrete, a subway wall. He had gone too far. Damn, he should have paid more attention when he was last here.

Cole could feel chill sweat running down his backbone. He was becoming more and more disoriented in the inky void. The sound of women crying gave him his only slight spatial anchor. He turned in that direction and asked in frustration, "Don't any of you smoke?"

Anna was quick to answer. "Yes, we all smoke."

"Well, do you have matches?" There was a sound of snaps and leather straps being loosened and then a blinding burst of light. It was just a wooden match but with their dark-adapted eyes, it seemed blinding. Cole tried to take in as much as he could before the match burned out. The rubble stretched out before him in a mural of confusing shapes and textures.

Six feet away and knee high, was a recess in a brick pile. That struck a memory chord. He started toward it just as the match flickered and disappeared. Still, a tiny glow from the spent match helped him keep his bearing. He felt around until his hand slid into the gap among crumbled pieces of wall. There, there was a toggle switch. He pressed and an electric motor began to hum. Immediately a sliver of pale light appeared and grew until the large rock moved enough to reveal a rough wood staircase dimly lit from above.

The women came, weeping, stumbling and desperately clutching their suitcases. As they climbed up into the wine cellar, all three began to sob in earnest, but now it was a gasping chorus of joy. Cole followed and activated the switch to close the concealing rock below.

"Ladies," he said with a relieved smile, "welcome to my home."

They were still in the process of calming and trying to breathe normally when Deb stormed down the stone stairs. She folded her arms and demanded. "What are these women doing in my house? Your dinner is waiting upstairs and here you are with a bunch of women in the cellar. This has got to stop."

James Cole clenched his teeth and played the peacemaker. "*These women* have just escaped from the Soviet Zone. They will be spending the night with us. Please be a good hostess and have Frau Huntsov prepare a meal for them."

Deb turned with her arms still crossed and left as though swept away by a sudden gust of wind.

1900 Hours

Lushka had ordered the fence built immediately. For some reason, it could not wait one more day. Sergei had his men measure and plant a small red flag with a hammer and sickle where each fence post was to go. Along the projected fence line, some dirt mounds had to be leveled and a few structures demolished. Owners protested but the appearance of a Soviet KGB major quieted them immediately. Only one old woman had the courage to challenge him to his face. Sergei found her amusing and directed that the fence be routed around her little garden. She folded her arms defiantly and stood her ground to make sure the soldiers obeyed.

By afternoon, they were ready. Just as he hoped, no government official had complained or even noticed the activity. That gave Sergei confidence to start digging. At seven that night, more than 200 soldiers with posthole diggers and spades attacked the line of small flags. By daybreak, the Soviet Zone was guarded by a new four-strand barbed wire fence.

Locals saw it as a curiosity. The old lady found her garden was now fully under Soviet control. Movement to the American Zone was no longer painless.

Major Sergei Zelenkov gathered his work force and presented them with cases of vodka. He toasted their hard work and they broke into spontaneous song. It was a job well done.

November 11, 0600 Hours

Cole rose before dawn and tried to anticipate the day's coming events. He had on his uniform pants and shirt but he still wore slippers and the tossled hair of a rough night. The coffee was just beginning to percolate when he heard a rap at the door. Shuffling and grousing, he opened to the door to confront a sunny Lieutenant Cynthia Ryan.

"Morning Sir, hope I'm not too early." He only grunted. "Well Sir, yesterday, when you and the boys grabbed guns and ran out the door, you left us without any guidance. We didn't know what to do with Honig, so we let him go. I followed him. I'm actually getting pretty good at this surveillance stuff. I used all the techniques we learned in school, concealment, random street crossing, passing and back tracking. I even took different hats to do simple disguise changes."

Cole held up his hand. "That's wonderful Lieutenant, but where did he go?"

She beamed, "He went into the French Zone. There is a little Bed and Breakfast there. All the cars in front had French Occupation license plates. I went in and ordered a beer. While I was sitting in a back booth and—get this—I saw Devereaux. There were five or six men huddled and shouting at Honig. Believe me, they weren't happy."

Her report was interrupted by another knock, this one more forceful. Cole opened the door and confronted two serious looking American military policemen. "Major James Cole?"

"Yes, I'm Cole."

"Sir, we have orders to take you into custody. Please come with us. And, is there a Mrs. Huntsov here?"

Cole made an ugly face. "Yes, she is my housekeeper. What do you want of her?"

"Sir, we have orders to bring her in as well."

Deb came down the stairs in a terry robe and trilled. "Another woman... you have another woman in my house. What in the world is going on? Are we running a brothel?"

Cynthia's face turned hot and she launched toward Deb. Cole grabbed her arm. "My wife is not your biggest problem right now. You must get back to the detachment. Belcher is senior. Tell him he is in charge. Your first priority is to bring Honig and Devereaux in for questioning. Use whatever means are necessary."

Then turning to his petulant wife, he commanded, "Deb, get my shoes, NOW."

0730 Hours

James Cole, now wearing shoes but no tie, entered Col. Mather's office and stood at attention. He did not salute and he did not speak. Mather looked as though he just finished sniffing a skunk's butt. He sat back in his chair and glared. Finally, he spoke in a tremulous voice.

"I believe you said you would keep it off me when the shit hit the fan. Well, the fan is full and I feel covered. I cannot prove that you and your people attacked those Russian drivers and killed three of them right in the middle of the International Zone—in broad daylight. I cannot prove it but I have no doubt that it is true. What do you have to say for yourself?"

Cole straightened and imagined himself as Alfred Dryfuss facing an unfair tribunal. "If you can't prove it, Colonel, neither can anyone else."

Mather scowled deep, "That's your answer? No one can prove it?"

Cole responded, "A better question might be, what were Russians doing driving stolen American sedans? Where were they headed and what did they intend to do... to you, Sir?"

"To me, what on earth makes you think any of this involves me?" Mather rooted in his desk drawer and grabbed his pipe with more force than necessary.

"Sir, I'm sure you're aware those cars were used in the kidnapping of a diplomat less than an hour earlier. The Russians were going to plant them in front of your office and accuse you of the kidnapping."

"And you know this how?"

"Through careful spy craft. Think what you will, my people saved you from a political debacle. Now it is the Russians who must explain why their uniformed NKVD soldiers were found in the stolen kidnap getaway vehicles."

Mather filled and tamped his pipe. Cole noticed that his hands were shaking slightly. The colonel avoided eye contact as he bought time for an internal debate. Finally, he bit down on his pipe stem and spoke through gritted teeth.

"I don't like you, Cole. I think you look like a fool and act like a gangster. It's unbecoming. I must admit, however, that you have accomplished much. Though the weekly reports you submit to me are pure works of fiction, I have kept up with your activities. I know you have, in your own mind, served your country well even as you disobeyed my orders to respect and cooperate with the Russians."

James Cole's brow wrinkled for just a second. "How exactly, Sir, have you kept up with me?"

Mather puffed as he lit up. "Your housekeeper, Mrs. Huntzov, works for me. She's really quite capable. Not too complimentary of your wife I'm afraid."

"But I thought she worked for the Russians. I've fed her nothing but misinformation."

"Yes, you thought you were quite clever but she saw through it all. As I said, she's quite capable. You don't think I would really allow the wife of a Cossack Nazi to get close to my intelligence chief. No, she worked for the OSS in the Balkans for years."

Mather continued, "I know you have some sort of tunnel in that mansion of a house where you live. I know that you have caught some German scientists and that Herr Honig bugged your office. By the way, Mrs. Huntsov won't be coming back to work. I have reluctantly come to the conclusion that constant surveillance is pointless."

There was a long awkward silence before Cole spoke. "If you do trust me, I need some help. I can't get my scientists out of Vienna. I need orders for the 'Mozart Express' troop train."

Mather puffed. "You need more help than I can give you. President Truman has issued a directive that no German with Nazi ties can be given asylum or employed by the US. An Army group in Munich has had some luck in forging background material to give some of their captured rocket scientists a sanitized history."

Mather was calmer now. After a moment of thought, he added, "You may not have heard but your 'Pond' group is in chaos." Cole gave no indication that he didn't understand. Mather continued, "With the dissolution of the OSS, terrible infighting has erupted for control of American intelligence. Hoover has demanded the FBI have overall authority but Truman distrusts him. The military services are like hens in a pen, squawking and fluttering. Your group is disintegrating. It was composed mostly of Army and some civilian operatives. Now they're refusing to cooperate or share information. I would be very careful whom I trusted. Well, I must draft a formal complaint against the Russians. That will be all, Major."

Cole saluted smartly and left. Once outside he pondered two statements. "When did I become his 'intelligence chief' and what the hell was the Pond?"

0800 Hours

James Cole decided a walk from the Army Headquarters to his detachment's building might clear his head. It was a crisp November day and the sun felt good on his face. That warmth matched the overwhelming relief he felt knowing he would face no criminal charges over the shooting of Russian drivers. Thank goodness he and his men used the untraceable old Mercedes supplied by Billie Connors. Now he could forget that worry and get back to finding a way to smuggle his scientists and Anna's family out of country.

The moment he opened the detachment's office door, he felt a buzz, a nervous energy left over from yesterday's events. A bandaged and bruised Roland met him, excited and stammering, "What do you know about the fence?"

Cole shook off his coat and frowned. "What fence?"

"The fence that appeared magically last night along the American-Russian boundary, has something changed? Are we not permitted into the Soviet Zone anymore?"

"I don't know? I'll find out."

Cynthia Ryan was next, "I got the three women settled into your house. Your wife is not thrilled. When's your housekeeper coming back?"

"She's not. Have Sherry White go over."

McMahan elbowed his way forward. "I've talked to French intelligence. They have no one named Devereaux on their staff and they deny knowledge of any involvement with the Soviets."

"Check the Occupation Authority Registry. If he's allowed in Vienna, he'll be listed.

Sherry White shouted over the crowd, "The passports are ready for pickup."

"Good, pick them up and then go to my house."

Mrs. Parks waited her turn, "Mason is waiting at the Central Café. You should hurry." Cole nodded, blew a puff of air and said nothing. He simply picked his coat up and left.

"Wait," shouted Woods. "I have information on Zelenkov."

"So do I," said Cole and he was gone leaving the whole crowd staring after him. After a second, they seemed to come out of their trances and launched back into their various duties.

0855 Hours

The Central Café was an ageless slice of Vienna. High ceilings, stone columns and subdued conversations among elegantly dressed high society made it clear that this was not the place for tourists or common folk. Mason was, as usual, seated at a small rear table. Cole was still in military uniform, still without a tie. He sat, enduring Mason's look of disapproval.

"In a rush this morning?"

"Arrested, no time to dress properly."

Mason sipped his espresso. "Arrested by?"

"Mather, but he mellowed after we had a talk. He says we should be worried. The Pond is drying up. What, if you please, is the Pond?"

Mason scanned the room. Seeing no threat, he said, "We call ourselves the 'Web.' That includes many small intelligence cells here in Europe. The larger organization at the Pentagon is the 'Pond.' Mather is right, everything is coming unglued. Old allegiances are being broken. Trust is evaporating. There is no intelligence chain of command, not at any level."

Cole accepted a coffee and pastry, an artful trifle with a swirl of strawberry jam and something that looked like whipped cream. He knew from previous experience that sugar was a rare commodity in post-war Austria and the pastry would be bland.

"That sounds grim but I feel confident that we can still operate. We know the goals. We'll just have to be independent."

Mason raised an eyebrow. "I'm glad you feel that way. It's not going to be easy, so much is happening all around us. Truman has offered up all A-bomb secrets to the British and Canadians. The French are furious that they were excluded. They have directed their agents to make the 'Bomb' their top priority. Much worse is a report from a source deep in the Kremlin that Stalin has almost everything he needs to have an operational bomb within two to three years. Don't plan a vacation, Hernando. You're going to be busy."

Cole sat back and studied his cup. "You know the difficulty we've had getting transport for our scientists, Mather says the boys in Munich have dummied up resumes for some rocket scientists to meet Truman's 'no-Nazi' policy. I might give that a try."

"Of course, but that will only be needed later once we try to get them out of Austria. Our immediate problem is getting them through the surrounding Soviet Sector to Salzburg in the American Zone. The Russians and their Austrian stooges have orders to check every passenger trying to board the Mozart Express."

Cole looked thoughtful. "I just learned that their fake passports are ready. Perhaps I can send them one or two at a time hoping to get past the emigration desk. But I think all persons in civilian clothes have to be checked against a permit log to verify travel." Mason leaned forward conspiratorially. "I have another plan… as long as they aren't claustrophobic."

1030 Hours

Woods drove while Cole surveyed the fence. "Amazing they could build this in one night without raising alarms. It seems well done. It won't stop a man with a wire cutter but it will certainly deter normal traffic. More important, I think, it sends a message. The brief era of Soviet cooperation and trust is over."

"It may be electrified," said Woods.

Cole thought for a second and then said, "Stop the car, we'll check. He found a pair of jumper cables in the trunk and hooked one red clamp to the top strand of nearby fence. Then he successively tapped the black clamp to each of the other three strands. There were no sparks. He touched the back of his hand to the fence, nothing. As he turned back to the car, he saw a small soviet flag marker mashed into the dirt. He picked it up and shook it clean, a souvenir.

Back at the car he paused, "You said earlier that you had information about Zelenkov."

"Yes, I met a lovely lady in the central Registry. She has no record of anyone by that name but she has contacts in the Russian bureaucracy who sometimes tell her of undocumented officers. They confirmed that he exists. They are willing to sell a copy of his personnel record for $50 American. She also says the other girls in the Russian classified records section of the GRU work for starvation wages and will do anything for a little money."

Cole grinned like a schoolboy. "I have just lost my informant over there. Buy the record. Cultivate the girl and try to set up contacts. The GRU is a competitor of the KGB. They keep files on each other. This could be a gold mine."

Woods's shoulders straightened as though he had finally done something right. He seemed relaxed enough to ask, "What did you find out about Zelenkov?"

"He's KGB, assigned to watch us and recover our remaining scientists. He had a trap set for us on our last raid but he failed to move fast enough. That's why he pulled the stunt in the detachment parking lot. He was trying to recover. But when that face-saving effort also failed, his reputation has sunk very low. He's desperate to succeed against us. The diplomat's kidnapping, however, was not his doing."

Woods cocked his head. "What kidnapping?"

1850 Hours

James Cole came home, to what he knew, was going to be an unpleasant evening. Sure enough, Deb was waiting with both barrels loaded. He didn't have his coat off before she began.

"No housekeeper? No cook? Just who do you expect to take care of this museum? I want you to know this and know it well, I am not a servant. Do you understand me?"

Cole looked exhausted. "Where are the three Russian women?"

"That's what you care about, those threadbare foreign women. I am alone in a building the size of Grand Central Station with no help and you worry about the welfare of a bunch of foreigners. Well, they're gone. That tunnel woman who works for you had a talk with them before she went down to the cellar. What does she do down there anyway? Well, she hadn't been gone ten minutes when they used the phone to call someone and talk that crazy foreign talk. A car came and they left. At least I won't have to fix dinner for that bunch. Who knows what they eat."

James Cole looked his wife in the eyes. What had he ever seen in her? He felt sadness and a twinge of disappointment as he turned away saying, "I'll be back in a minute."

"Don't you walk away from me," she trilled. "I'm making soup for you."

He climbed down into the tunnel and followed the path of red lights until he came to the subway station. There he climbed to the booth where Sherry White sat listening through oversized headphones. Sergeant Richardson snapped to attention. Sherry was too intent to notice. He tapped on her shoulder and she jumped in surprise yanking off her headset as she did.

"Oh, my goodness. I'm sorry but you scared me, Sir."

Cole tried to be cordial. "What happened to the three women?"

"I gave them their passports and left them in your house up above. What's wrong?"

"They're gone. I was supposed to be protecting them. Did they say anything to you?"

Sherry thought. "No, just that they were grateful to be free of the Soviets and thankful to you. I had them review the details of their passports to make sure they were okay. I wasn't much help. I barely speak German and don't understand a word of French."

Cole looked confused, "French?"

"Yes, they each got both Austrian and French passports." There was an uncomfortable silence until Sherry asked, "Did I do something wrong?"

2100 Hours

Cole ignored the hour and any trace of caution as he marched down a dark cobblestone alley that smelled of cabbage and spoiled wine to bang on an unlit store's back door. After several minutes of relentless hammering a voice from inside shouted, "Go away, we are closed. It is late, go away."

Cole made sure his voice registered the fury he felt. "You betrayed me. Open the door or I'll burn the place down with you inside." He stepped back and drew his pistol. The door cracked just enough to allow a peek. Cole kicked it hard and sent the peeker sprawling. He straddled the man who now curled on the ground shielding his face with both hands.

In his harshest German, Cole said, "I won't hurt you. I want Herr Rolf. Where is he?" The squirming man flicked one arm toward the hall. Cole reached down, checked the man for weapons and finding none, stepped over him into the hall.

Rolf rose to see what caused the commotion. He wore a jeweler's lens and eye shade. Small, round shouldered and balding, he looked like an elf roused from his work table. Hardly a threatening figure, Cole still held him at gunpoint.

"What have you done? You made the Austrian passports for the three women I asked for but you also made French passports, why?" Herr Rolf was not intimidated. He removed his eyepiece and stared down the barrel of Cole's gun. He was probably used to threats given his clientele.

"Your man came to me and offered me triple the original price. He said the French passports must be ready by yesterday at noon. For that money I dropped all my other work. Are you not pleased with the quality of my work?"

"Who was this man? Do you have a name?"

"Yes, yes, of course. It was Captain Devereaux. He said he worked for you. I had no reason to distrust him. He knew their names and all the personal information you provided for the Austrian passports. What is the problem?"

Cole let the gun sag to his side. "That man is a Russian agent. I don't know why he wanted French passports but the women are gone, kidnapped."

"Oh my God," said Rolf. "I am so sorry. He paid with the same money you use, Austrian Military Schillings. It all seemed to be in order. I saw no reason to suspect."

Cole ran his free hand over his face. How much more screwed up could things get. "How are you coming with the other men's documents?"

"It's a very large order but it goes good. I think a few more days. Some of the paper must be treated to make the seals look old. Everyone is suspicious of a passport that looks new. To be believable they must look worn with all the right seals and border stamps. A few days and they will be ready."

Cole turned and left with a mumbled apology for his accusation.

Devereaux, who the hell was he and what was he up to?

2245 Hours

Back at home, Deb was already asleep. He went to his study and unlocked the briefcase containing Anna's copied documents. The stack was at least four inches thick. It was slow going. Although he spoke passable Russian, reading Cyrillic writing was a challenge. He had to sound out each letter in his head to get the meaning. He kept notes on a yellow legal pad, recording the date of each message and a short summary of its contents.

This was just too slow. He left his desk and climbed down into the tunnel again where he asked Sherry to leave her listening post and come help him. She was cheerful, probably glad to leave the tedium. Once back in Cole's study, she set to work humming and scribbling. He stood over her and noticed for the first time that she wore a subtle perfume.

"Thank you for doing this," he said in his most paternal voice. She looked up at him with a sweet smile and Cole fought the temptation to put his hand on her shoulder.

"Oh my God, she mumbled, "this is an absolute gold mine. Every page is a new revelation. After reading one teletype, she shook her head in disbelief and read it again. Turning to Cole she translated.

Now he did put his hand on her shoulder and felt the warmth of her body. "Dear God," he said aloud, "I've got to get to Mason."

November 16, 1400 Hours

Each of the four flatbed trucks carried two 10 foot square wooden crates bound by straps. American Military Police rode in Jeeps with .50 caliber machine guns. One Jeep led and the other followed the convoy. Arriving at Aalpeter's warehouse, they parked and began loading under guards' watchful eyes.

1415 Hours

Across town, a battered old bus squealed to a stop in front of the University Technic. Once a sedate campus of landscaped malls, lawns and cobblestone plazas, it was now a tenement of tents and shanties populated by a thousand ragged souls who wandered without purpose. Barbed wire ringed the school with makeshift guard towers at the corners. This was a Displaced Persons Camp, a DP center, to hold war refugees, most from Eastern Europe, as they waited and waited in desperate hope for some sort of disposition or repatriation.

Major Aalpeter, wearing his Army uniform, dismounted the bus with a clip board looking very businesslike. He approached an Austrian guard who did not salute. In formal German, he told the guard, "I am here to collect the men on this list. Please assemble them for me."

The guard took the list without interest, scanned and handed it back. "Nothing can be done without the administrator's approval. You must submit a request in writing. Aalpeter put on his angriest face. "You go and get the administrator now."

With an insolent sneer, the guard turned to his companion and whispered something. The other man left with a brisk stride. The guard lifted his chin making him a full head taller than Aalpeter and said, "Things are different now. You Americans

can no longer give orders. We work for the United Nations
Relief and Rehabilitation Directorate, not you."

The second man soon returned with a woman. Big and
boney, she had a farm worker's body crammed into an ill-
fitting, coarsely woven suit. "I am Frau Zigler. I am charge here.
What do you want?"

Major Aalpeter gave her a condescending look. "You seem
confused, Madam. This camp is located in the American
Sector of Vienna. Although we have allowed some resumption
of Austrian control in city affairs, your new United Nations
organization has no official standing and you are in charge of
nothing, at least, not yet."

She drew up huge breasts like a rooster preparing to fight.
"I am the camp administrator and I demand…"

Aalpeter leaned into her face. "You assert an authority you
do not have. I, on the other hand, can back up my demand with
many guns. Do you need a demonstration, or will you behave
sensibly and comply with my request?"

The administrator showed teeth like a menacing dog. The
guard, watching the exchange, now stepped forward and tried
to push Aalpeter away. The major, in turn, grabbed the guard's
wrist twisting it backwards and driving the man to ground.
With his free hand, the much smaller American wrestled the
guard's rifle away and slung it into the street.

He released his grip, stood and straightened his uniform
jacket. "Now, if you please, collect these men for me. They are
going home."

Frau Zigler folded her arms in an obstinate pose. "It cannot
be done. We have only today taken over the camp from your
army. We do not even have a list of names. It will take weeks
to get organized."

Aalpeter pushed by her through the gate and into a crowd
of dirty, milling DPs. In a voice that seemed impossibly loud
from such a small man, he shouted. "Attention, attention, I need

Professor Vogleman and all other university professors. Come quickly."

The crowd began to murmur and whisper among themselves. Messages were passed. Frau Zigler said, "There is paperwork that must be filled out." The guard leaned over her shoulder and reminded her that no forms had yet been created.

In less than fifteen minutes Herr Vogleman and all the others had assembled. Aalpeter checked them onto the bus giving each man an Austrian passport and an envelope with documents that described a fictional previous life devoid of Nazi affiliation.

Huge airbrakes hissed and the loaded bus rumbled back toward the Monument Group warehouse. As they rolled, Major Aalpeter squatted in the aisle beside one man with a great shock of gray hair. "Herr Doctor Klein, can you tell me please why the Russians want to capture you above all the others?"

Doctor Klein made a kindly smile. "This is so? I can only think it may be because I authored a paper once with Heisenberg, the man who suggested the 'uncertainty principle.' You know him I'm sure." Aalpeter gave no indication. "Well, anyway, I think they must believe I share some of Professor Heisenberg's genius. I'm afraid they would be very disappointed to discover my strength is in experimental design, not nuclear physics. I hope this will not disqualify me from going to America?"

"No, of course not," said Aalpeter who then stood and looked over the crowd. The other scientists jabbered like excited children talking about what they hoped lay ahead. They certainly didn't expect it to be packing crates.

Aalpeter gathered them before the flatbed trucks and made his announcement. "You will go first to Salzburg in the American Zone. To get there, you must secretly ride a train through the Soviet Zone. Here is how you will do it without detection. Each crate is filled with expensive artwork. These crates will be guarded and may not be inspected by the Soviets or anyone else. You will climb ladders into the tops of crates which will then be sealed. Be sure to use the bathroom before we leave. It will be many hours before you are again free to move about. In each crate you will share the space with a fortune in famous art. Please do not piss on these priceless treasures." He paused, expecting laughter. There was none.

"All right then. Use the bathroom and then pick up a box of food for your journey. We have thirty minutes before you leave." He smiled at them. "Before you lies a new life without war or fear. You are going to America."

He looked as sincere as he could and hoped to hell it was true. He still had no idea how he was going to get them to the States.

1800 Hours

The scientists had been elated at being free from the DP camp. It was supposed to be a safe place where refugees were researched to be sure they were not Nazis. Once cleared, the DPs would be reunited with whatever family could be found in their home country. Those without family had to find a country willing to sponsor them. In the post-war recovery, not many nations were generous about accepting immigrants. To the German scientists, the DP camp had seemed like just one more prison. Even though they were fed and given blankets, it was still a prison.

Now they were free, if you could call being nailed into a wooden box free. They settled in for a long journey of isolation and discomfort. Once inside the boxes, forklifts tossed them and banged them about until finally they felt the lurch and repetitive clatter of wheels that told them the train was moving and they were on their way.

Relieved, they opened food boxes and were delighted to find wine, sausages and vegetables. The vegetables were a particularly rare treat in war-ravaged Austria. They ate and drank, respectfully avoiding damage to the many boxed and wrapped masterpieces that were their travelling companions.

2030 Hours

In Salzburg, a youthful Captain Mercer paced as the train pulled in. The Mozart Express was an American train, a troop transport used to support the USFA, United States Forces Austria, units in Vienna. Its interior was considered sovereign American territory exempt from Soviet or any other interference, but in 200 kilometers of travel through the Soviet Zone, who knew what could happen.

To add to the captain's problems, there were no forklifts available for offloading his precious crates. He would use Army trucks that backed up to train cars to winch the crates off.

After an hour of screaming and arguing with Austrian officials, his crates were finally convoyed off to a guarded salt mine where the Monuments Group stored its treasures. Once inside the huge cave, the crates were opened and the scientists helped out.

Captain Mercer shouted for attention, "Who speaks English?" Then, with more urgency, "Anyone, I don't speak German?" After a moment, a smiling Vogleman came forward and answered.

"Good day to you, sir. Many of us speak your language. They will translate for the others. First, let me say how grateful we are for your efforts. We intend to be as helpful as possible. Can you tell me, please, what happens now?"

Relieved, the captain's shoulders settled. "We have purchased a chalet for you in the mountain country south of Salzburg. You will be billeted two to a room. There is a cook who will make your meals and a car and driver to take you shopping. I have some money for you. Each man will receive $500 US. You may exchange to any currency you wish at any bank."

Vogleman politely asked again. "Then what?"

The captain's face tightened. "I wish I knew. We have transportation to Genoa, Italy and a ship to New York all arranged. Our problem is US visas. Our State Department is being difficult. I expect to solve that problem in just a few weeks." "Weeks, it will still be weeks?"

In a diversionary move, the captain changed subjects. "I have here a list of family members who have been located. There will be a lady at your chalet who will work with you to set up travel clearances to get them here."

Vogleman pressed, "Will we be guarded?"

"No, you are free to come and go as you please. You can even arrange your own transportation if you choose."

Vogleman's look was intense. "This is true? We can do as we wish?"

The captain nodded. "You are free, sir. We will help you as we can but you are free."

The men began a slow soft clapping that grew louder until it matched the intensity of their smiles.

November 17, 1300 Hours

Cole went to Lidia at the hotel desk and asked for the key to room 708. She looked both ways and whispered the code words, "Don't you mean room 608?" There was a problem. He took the key to 708 and found the telephone he had been told of at his first meeting with Mason. Without dialing he picked it up and listened.

A cultured voice replied, "Yes."

"I need to speak with Mason."

"Not possible just now. Can I be of help?"

"This is Hernando…"

"Yes, I know. What do you need?"

"I have urgent information. I must speak to Mason immediately."

"Hm-m-m. Go downstairs and out the front door. I'll meet you there. I'll be in in a tweed overcoat and matching deer slayer cap." The line went dead.

Cole wasn't sure what to do. He didn't know to whom this voice belonged. Could the man be trusted? He was on the secret phone; he must be okay. Just play this by ear. He marched out of the hotel and into the cold. The man was waiting, hard to mistake him in his Sherlock Holmes outfit missing only the Meerschaum pipe.

Sherlock extended a hand. "How do you do? I'm Winston Etherington, late of his Majesty's Secret Service, now a freelance operative. I am well acquainted with you, Major, or Hernando if you prefer. You are, no doubt, a bit suspicious of me and that's appropriate, but rest assured I am well versed in current Web operations."

Cole began tentatively, "I have come across something critical to US intelligence. I must speak to Mason."

"Out of town for two more days, is this information specific to the Web?"

"No, but I don't know where else to go."

"I see," said Sherlock Holmes. "Well then, come and walk. We'll see if we can't find someone appropriate for such an important revelation."

They strolled, a bit too slowly for James Cole. He wanted to get the information passed. Sherlock became a tour guide. "This is the Opera District, wonderful old architecture, but then where in Vienna is there anything else? Ah, there is where the Vienna Boys Choir rehearses, wonderful sound. They castrate them, you know."

Cole inclined his head. "What? That's ridiculous. That would never be permitted even in a country dominated by the Nazis."

"Oh yes, the practice goes back centuries. Poor families would fight to get their children accepted into the program. When the monks who ran the place were sure a boy had talent, they would snip off the old boy berries. That kept their voices from changing as they matured. If you are an aficionado of classical music you will have noted some segments designated for 'castrati,' the berryless boys."

Cole didn't quibble but he didn't truly believe it either. Approaching an enormous museum, Sherlock announced, "Well, here we are. Go to the reception desk and ask to speak with Dr. Curtis Winters, American Ambassador to Austria for Cultural Affairs. They will ask if you have an appointment. Say you were to meet him at 3:17 but hope it will be convenient now."

"What happens if they say no?"

"I'll wait here for ten more minutes. If you can't get in to see the Ambassador, come back."

Cole left the bright sunlight and entered the dark, tomb-like museum. He had to pause until his eyes adjusted. At a leather-bound reception desk, a white haired man in a vest and bow tie folded his hands and seemed intently interested in the American officer. Cole approached and repeated the line Sherlock had given him verbatim. The bow tied man looked over the top of his glasses and clarified "You were to meet at 3:17?"

"Yes, I hope it is convenient." Bow tie kept his impassive stare as he peeled an admission ticket from a roll as though Cole was just another visitor and pointed up the stairs. "Third door on the left, knock twice." Cole made a slight bow with his chin and bow tie did the same. As the major left, bow tie picked up a telephone and cupped his hand over the mouthpiece.

The third door on the left was already open as he approached and a muscle bound man in a suit stood waiting with his hands clasped loosely before him. As Cole neared, the man lifted his arms level with his shoulders as a sign for Cole to do the same. Suit frisked him, removed his shoulder holstered pistol and silently motioned with a head bob to enter.

Inside was a paneled office with wall-to-wall bookcases and overstuffed leather furniture. The chair behind a large polished wood desk was empty. Cole entered and allowed his eyes to dart around the room as he stood waiting. Framed diplomas and awards, a few statues and, of course, bookcases; it was generic professor stuff. After a few minutes, a panel in the wall opened and a tall man in an afternoon coat emerged. His waistcoat, vest and tie were all matching gray. His trousers were striped and he wore spats.

"Hernando, I believe." The elegantly dressed man made no motion to shake hands or even offer a seat. "Sorry to keep you waiting. One must be careful these days. I am Ambassador Winters, senior member of the Vienna Web. I have followed your exploits closely. You have done well. So, this must be quite important to risk coming here. What do you have?"

Cole straightened to attention. "Forgive me, sir, but how can I verify your identity?"

The Ambassador raised eyebrows and then smiled as he steepled his fingers with an indulgent look. "You contact James Mason through Lidia. The last time he spoke with you, he told you that the Pond was dissolving. You volunteered to continue without much help from those of us higher in the chain. Does that satisfy your concerns?"

Cole bit his lip. "Yes, I suppose so." Then, with no more hesitation he began. "Joseph Stalin has been poisoned. As of two days ago, he was alive and expected to survive but he will be impaired for a while. The assassination attempt was the work of a group of Red Army colonels. A purge has already begun at the top and will almost certainly flow downhill. The Russians are in total confusion. No one knows who will die next."

The Ambassador tapped his long pianist's fingers over the desk. "And you know this how?"

"Until we pulled her out, we had an informant in Colonel Lushka's office. She copied his documents and messages and passed them to us."

Now acutely interested, the Ambassador sat forward. "That makes sense. It explains the fence, the kidnapping and the sudden chill in Soviet relations. We may be at a turning point in our Alliance. How reliable is your information?"

"I can tell you the informant is terrified. She even escaped from our safe house. We've lost track of her."

The Ambassador scowled. "Mason will be back in 48 hours. Be sure to brief him. He'll keep me up to speed. Thank you."

Cole started to leave but hesitated and asked, "Sir, do you know anything about a French Captain Devereaux?"

The Ambassador nodded a negative and Cole left, not quite sure if he should have saluted.

2200 Hours

Cole sat before the great stack of papers Anna had given him. Sherry White had made extensive notes but she only made it a quarter of way deep in the thick pile. Still, the information was terrific. He was learning just what the Russians knew and how they operated. Then he came to a barely readable onion skin copy on which Sherry had written, "Oh, my God."

He held the tissue thin paper up to a lamp but it was probably a third or fourth carbon, too faint for him to decipher. Sherry's note read, "Can't get it all, but this is addressed to General Colonel Shimetriev, *Secretariat of the Supreme Soviet, personal and confidential.* This has got to be really important. Tomorrow, I'll try to get the paper treated to increase definition."

Cole sat back and mumbled. "Secretariat of the Supreme Soviet, who and why would someone in Lushka's office communicate with such an important agency?" He took the shade off his lamp, smoothed wrinkles and stretched the paper close to the bulb. Straining, he could barely make out the signature, Svetlana Borsky. He didn't know the name.

He was about to set the document down when he noticed a trace of handwriting on the original top copy which could have read "with deepest love." It was hard to say. So many Cyrillic letters are similar. He was trying to remember Russian phrases used to close a letter when he heard the phone ringing. The only phone was downstairs. He raced down the winding marble stairs being careful not to slip in his stocking feet.

It was dark in the entrance hallway and he groped for the oversized receiver before answering. He spoke his name breathing hard. A small German voice answered, "This is Anna. I am sorry to leave without correctly giving thanks. I ask you please, not to look for me. My family is safe."

Cole answered in German, "Where are you Anna? Why did you leave?"

"I must leave. It is not safe with the Americans. I must now tell you the truth. I was always working for the French really. Mssr. Devereaux employed me and my sister to get information on the Soviets. He said he could not receive my information directly. He did not trust his own people, so he used you. I passed things to you and somehow he got them."

"Honig and the bugged phone," said Cole. "But why did he pass information to Zelenkov?"

"I don't know," said Anna. "Perhaps it was a trick to gain confidence. He is very interested in Zelenkov. I am sorry, I must go now. Thank you for rescuing me. Thank you for my mother and my sister and for me and thank you also for the chocolates. I will always remember you."

The line was dead. Cole shuffled to the kitchen and found no coffee. Damn, he needed a housekeeper. Deb was almost useless at all this domestic stuff.

November 18, 0925 Hours

Mrs. Parks overheard Woods bragging about his contact in the Vienna Occupation Central Registry. He waved around a manila folder with perhaps a dozen sheets of paper. That must contain the documents he bought with his fifty American dollars. She watched as he went to refill his coffee cup and then slid into the office and flipped through the folder. It was in Russian, a language she barely spoke. She gritted her teeth and retreated to call Mason.

She spoke softly so no one could overhear her conversation. "One of our agents has obtained a GRU personnel record for a Soviet Major Zelenkov. I can't read it but it is stamped with wreathed hammer and sickle seals of a classified document."

She listened for a time, nodded but took no notes. Finally she hung up without saying good bye and sat with her hands folded. Nothing on her body moved as she planned her next move. Then she put on her sweet little English lady smile and went looking for Lieutenant Cynthia Ryan.

"Ah, there you are, dear. Do I recall correctly that you were trained in signal intelligence?"

Cynthia shrugged. "Well yes, but as an analyst only."

"Nonetheless you would recognize a High Frequency transmitter if you saw it, would you not?"

Cynthia thought for a second. "Well sure, it's pretty much like a HAM radio set and I used one of those as a kid. Why do you ask?"

"I believe we have such a radio stored in the loft of the building next door. Would you consider taking a look? I think it could be a useful tool for us. Take Captain Woods with you. He's a strapping lad and I'm sure he'll have no difficulty hefting the thing. I appreciate this so much."

Cynthia looked over at Woods. He was, indeed, a strapping lad. She smiled back at Mrs. Parks. "Sure thing, I'll do it right now." After a brief conversation which involved Cynthia Ryan tilting her head and toying with a loose curl of hair, Woods locked the folder in a desk drawer and they were off to explore the dark, close quarters of the attic next door.

Mrs. Parks waited till they were out of sight and then went to Woods' desk with a stack of paper for his in-box. With one hand, she pretended to sort through the papers while the other hand expertly picked the drawer lock. It was amazingly simple. Removing the folder, she walked casually to the building's Victorian setting room, took out her cigarette pack camera and quickly photographed each page. Another trip back to Woods' desk and the folder was safely home.

It was almost two hours before Woods and Ryan returned. He lugged a huge metal box with outsized dials and meters. Cynthia trailed along almost skipping. They had obviously enjoyed their mission to the attic. Mrs. Parks shot them a stern look and pointed where she wanted the radio. Ryan tried to suppress a trace of a giggle and Woods struck an aloof chin-up pose. Mrs. Parks suppressed a smile.

By early evening, the developed film negatives were on Major Aalpeter's desk. Although he struggled with the Cyrillic, Mrs. Park's photographed copies made it clear this Zelenkov fellow was no ordinary Soviet officer. Page after page of commendations, all with those peculiar words of Communist double talk they used to say something without actually saying it. This man was valuable.

November 20, 0855 Hours

Colonel Mather brushed by Fraulein Gint and almost knocked her off her feet. Without apologizing he paced behind his desk and motioned her to take notes. He began dictating in a tight, rapid-fire voice. He waved his pipe with one hand while the other motioned wildly.

"To all section chiefs, the commanding general of Armed Forces Austria has directed that all travel to the Soviet Sector of Vienna by military personnel be limited to official business. Recent events have made it necessary to exercise increased vigilance against possible compromise of our people and our position vis-a-vie the Russians. To reiterate, no American military member may enter into the Soviet Sector without specific approval of his commanding officer and the issuance of a 'gray card' authorization."

He plopped in his chair and glared at the young woman. "Get that typed up with my signature block. I want it distributed to everyone in G-2 by this afternoon." He dismissed her with a wave of his fingers.

Once alone, the colonel began an angry speech to the walls. "This is a complete over-reaction. Colonel Bukinev has assured me—assured me—that the fence is strictly to control black marketeering. We are endangering future cooperation with a major foreign power with our suspicion. What are we thinking? These people are not like the Nazis. They want to make a better world. Even that fool cowboy Cole said so." He fidgeted with barely contained rage. He had to do something with Major Cole, he had to control Cole.

0840 Hours

Major Aalpeter left the Ambassador's museum with a briefcase full of documents. Classified messages were piling up. Ordinarily, some clerk in a classified document storage vault would have reviewed these intercepted messages but with personnel losses right and left, there were few clerks left to analyze and prioritize the flood of paperwork from field agents. All around him the organization was collapsing in on itself.

He needed to spend time researching the papers Mrs. Parks had given him on the Russian major instead of doing the Ambassador's busy work. First, however, he needed to visit Herr Rolf, the counterfeit document artist.

They met in the alley behind the shop. Aalpeter didn't like to be seen in uniform. "I have two copies of valid United States visas. Can you make duplicates for the German men's passports?"

Rolf took the folded papers and scrutinized them as carefully as a diamond cutter. He nodded more and more vigorously. "Yes, yes I can use these. They are like gold. I will have them ready in four days. I'm sure they will pass inspection. Unfortunately, I will have to use false numbers. Every visa is numbered. If anyone checks the embassy log, the forgery will be discovered."

Mason broke into a grin. "I went to the embassy and told them I was checking on a fake passport. They let me look at the log. The last visa given was numbered 7322. They issue no more than 20 a day. If you use numbers above 7400, they will not be able to find a conflict. It takes a while to get new lists to the border inspectors so they will assume these are new visas."

Rolf raised eyebrows and shook his head in approval. This could work.

0955 Hours

Sherry White misted the onion skin with lemon juice and heated the paper perilously close to its flash point. It was working. Slowly the letters on the page began to darken. She kept the paper moving over her small hot plate to avoid hot spots. Finally, it looked legible. Satisfied, she blew to cool the paper and laid it beneath a goose necked lamp. Using a magnifying glass to pick out details, she read.

"My dearest Alexi, I cannot tell you how much I miss your company and the strength of your body against mine. Without you, I am like a lioness in a great empty jungle. I hope to join you soon. But now, my heart is heavy as I tell you what you have asked. Colonel Lushka, three times Hero of the Soviet Union, has served our country with nobility and great courage. I admire and honor him but I must sadly tell you that his many wounds of war have begun to degrade his ability. He forgets what he is saying sometimes and becomes confused. His loyalty and his love of country cannot be questioned but he has become unpredictable. It is my opinion that he should be replaced if you so choose."

Then a handwritten note read, "With all my love, your Svetlana."

She said aloud, "Wow, I hope Lushka never finds out she wrote this. Even her General Colonel boyfriend won't be able to save her from that maniac."

Setting that letter aside, she went to the next. It was a letter from Colonel Lushka but she could not read the name of the person to whom it was addressed. Lushka asked what to do with his political prisoner after interrogation has exhausted his value. "Wow, again," she said taking a deep breath. "There is a lot going on with our Russian buddies."

CHAPTER FOUR-DECEMBER

December 2, 1500 Hours

"Hero of the Soviet Union, that is a very impressive medal."

Sergei Zelenkov continued walking through the snowy park but slowed his pace. He looked straight ahead while eating from a small paper cone of *Mandeln,* the honey roasted almonds whose sweet smell marked the coming of the Christmas season in Austria.

The voice had come from a pudgy man seated at a park bench who spoke Russian with a foreign accent. "Most people assume your fine medal is from Stalingrad but it's not, is it Major Zelenkov?" Now, the Russian major stopped and seemed to concentrate on selecting his next nut. The voice continued. "Actually, you earned your award at Katyn and Croatia and maybe other places. You were an executioner, a mass executioner."

Now Sergei turned and faced the small, plump man with spectacles and intense eyes. "You are an American, yes? And not in uniform, you could be arrested here in the Soviet Zone."

Major Aalpeter, or sometimes James Mason, smirked and replied, "Yes, you could shoot me on the spot. Then, however, you would not hear my message and you need to hear me."

Sergei said nothing as the American stood to face him. "This time of year in Austria *Santaklausen* visits children but he is always accompanied by the evil demon *Knect Ruprecht*. You may have to choose between them. Will it be candy or switches?" Sergei waited for the message.

"You know there has been an attempt to kill Joseph Stalin. The Army is blamed for poisoning him. There will certainly be another purge of Army officers and you are in great danger. Even if you survive the purge, eventually the massacres of Katyn will become public. You cannot hide the bodies of so many people forever. The Soviets will blame Hitler but the truth will come out. You, Major Zelenkov, will become an embarrassment."

Sergei gave no hint of emotion except in the muscles of his jaw. "You cannot know this. You are making a guess."

"No Major Zelenkov, you are the man who pulled the trigger. I understand that you were just a soldier following orders but others will not be so forgiving. How many did you kill? I have heard 20,000 at Katyn alone. Then there were the Croats and the Cossacks. Too many to count I imagine. I have heard that at Katyn Forest they brought busloads of Polish officers for you. One at a time, they were dragged into your shed and made to kneel before you. You shot them in the back of the head and they fell down a slide into a waiting truck to be dumped into mass graves."

Sergei's neck knotted visibly. "You know nothing. You are just telling stories. I was a good soldier."

"Ah yes, you were a good soldier. I understand you used a Russian revolver at first but it was too heavy and your hand became tired. So, you changed to a German P38 automatic pistol. Two conscripts loaded your clips as you stood and killed. All day long, you stood and killed. It must have been difficult. Did you stop for a noon meal? Did you take toilet breaks? How many days did you stand and shoot men in the back of the head?"

Sergei crushed the Mandeln bag in his fist. "Bastard, I am a soldier. I serve my nation and my people. I will shoot you now."

"Major Zelenkov, the flowers of spring will bloom over your grave unless you run. You know how it will be. You will quietly disappear and next your wife and son will get the knock on the door. All record of your life will evaporate. The Soviet Union does not let its dirty laundry hang in the sun. No Major, you must run. I can help you."

"You?" Sergei sneered, "You are a fat little American. How can you do anything? And your Russian is terrible. I speak little English so let us use German. You do speak German?"

James Mason suppressed a grin. The negotiating had begun.

December 31, 1900 Hours

Vienna had always been famous for grand balls. No place else in the world could match the opulence of its venues, the artistry of its musicians and the enthusiasm of its aristocrats. But the city's great halls and palaces had stood silent for six long years of war. Now, the Allies wanted to restore normalcy and that meant restoring the great balls.

Traditionally the ball season began with Sylvester, the New Year's celebration. It had always been the largest and most exclusive of the social events, but this year things would be a little different. Instead of Dukes and Counts in regal uniforms with sashes and ostrich plumes, the men of the occupation powers would wear ordinary military uniforms. The women, however, could still parade in the finest gowns available in austere post-war Europe.

Instead of the Austrian nobility, Allied generals represented the power elite and acted accordingly. The Russians volunteered to host the gala and chose as their site, the enormous Hofburg Palace. It occupied more than a city block surrounding the gardens and statues of Heldenplatz, the "Heroes Square."

James Cole arranged to use the Nazi limo for the night to Deb's delight. She, however, delayed their departure fifteen minutes while she practiced making her exit from the car in a billowing gown that would have been perfect for a cotillion. When finally satisfied, she settled in to the back seat and beamed with childlike excitement. Not only did she live in a palace, she was going to a grand ball. How magical was that?

They drove past Sigmund Freud Park into three blocks of traffic queued up for arrival at the curved Hofburg which spanned the full width of the plaza. Hundreds of cars inched forward to the Neue Burg entrance, the same place Hitler had stood to announce Austria's annexation.

When the Coles finally pulled up, a tall man in a bellman's uniform with gold shoulder braid opened the door for Deb and held her gloved hand as she emerged with beauty pageant composure. James came around the car and took her arm. She had no wrap against the cold but she didn't seem to care. This was the high point of her life.

Inside, the service staff wore elaborate outfits from the golden age of Austria. Powdered wigs, brocade waistcoats, silk knee breeches and square toed buckle shoes seemed to match the setting. James stepped up to the reception table and announced, "Major and Mrs. James Cole, United States Army."

Lists were checked and notes made. A boy in a page outfit spoke in English. "Please follow," and led them down a great marbled hall flanked with statues and oversized paintings. Reaching the ballroom steps, he presented a card to the Master who inspected the couple and then turned to a room already filled with hundreds. He raised a huge baton topped with a gold ball, tapped it twice and boomed, "Herr Major und Frau Cole."

Deb seemed to grow several inches as she swept by the announcer and bowed to the crowd, delicate as a ballerina. A handful of people applauded. The page then led them to an elaborate table for twelve laid out in linen, crystal, silver and china—extravagant fare. Before they could take a seat, a server presented flutes of champagne, again with a bow. James smiled and silently toasted Deb. She grinned, tilted her head and tipped her glass back at him.

2200 Hours

Far across the room sat a solitary man. Major Horatio Aalpeter, the Monuments Group Comptroller, otherwise known as James Mason, sat unnoticed and unremarkable. He considered anonymity his greatest strength. Short and heavy-set, he was utterly forgettable behind round spectacles. Most men wore their medals proudly. Horatio wore none.

He wove his way adroitly through crowds without eye contact or jostling. No one noticed him but he noticed and remembered everyone and everything. For him, this ball was an opportunity. He could watch and eavesdrop on people he could never have approached otherwise. He sipped water in a wine glass and soaked up conversation.

Scanning the crowd, he spied James and Deb Cole who seemed to be enjoying themselves. Their table included Colonel Mather and an assortment of other American officers. Mrs. Mather, the only other woman, was dressed plain as a Vicar's wife, in a gray silk gown. Deb, cute and breezy, flitted around the table like a celebrity, loving every bit of male attention. One man was particularly attentive. Aalpeter searched his memory. He knew this fellow but couldn't quite place him.

Then it came; Captain Woods, the idiot who wandered around the Soviet Zone dressed like a dime novel detective. Mason's eyes narrowed like a stalking weasel. Woods was a tipsy suitor, hovering and hanging on Deb's words. She, on the other hand, pretended not to notice him. But as he went to the bar she momentarily ignored the chatter of other men clamoring for her attention to watch him.

Woods was a strikingly handsome man; such men are always useful. A plan began to take shape in Mason's mind. It was a devious plan, an immoral plan; he liked it.

2315 Hours

A world class orchestra played waltzes and other classical pieces. The ballroom floor filled with bejeweled women in fine gowns who swirled and glided with their military partners. No one paid much attention when the Master announced, "Oberst und Frau Lushka."

Lushka's uniform bristled so thick with medals it looked like brightly colored armor. Svetlana, on the other hand, wore a plain, unadorned uniform with a skirt and shoes instead of her usual jodhpurs and boots. She had, however, abandoned her braids for a stylish hairdo. It made her seem more feminine, more human.

Belcher leaned across the table to James Cole and whispered, "My God, did I just climb the beanstalk? Look at the size of that monster." Lushka spread his arms, or at least, one and a half arms, and bellowed loud enough to make the orchestra stop playing in mid note. Colonel Mather rushed to Cole's side. "What's that man saying?"

Cole listened and translated, "He is welcoming us on behalf of the Soviet Forces." He listened a little more. "The man sounds really drunk. He says he wants us all to give thanks for the sacrifices of the Russian people." Cole frowned. "He is also calling for the proletariat to rise up and defeat their capitalist oppressors. He wishes us all… something… maybe a joyous life and pledges complete support to the forces of revolution worldwide. Now, he's singing something I can't understand. It might be the Russian national anthem. I can't tell."

Mather screwed up his face. "I never understood this communist crap. What is this proletariat stuff anyway?"

"The proletariat are the workers, the producers of goods. The bourgeoisie are the capitalists, the owners. The basic idea behind communism is that everything should be owned by the workers. There is no need for capitalists. Unfortunately, that means that the state owns everything in the name of the workers. The 'dictatorship of the proletariat' turns out to be just plain old dictatorship."

Mather slugged back his bourbon and grimaced. "That's actually a little more than I needed to know." Just then, Lushka started back up. "Now, what's he saying?"

Cole's mouth dropped. "This fool is bragging, taking credit for everything that has been accomplished by the Soviet occupation forces." His voice grew serious. "Oh boy, just look over there at the head tables." Mather turned to the far end of the room. Four tables sat on an elevated platform. One for General Mark Clark was decked in American flags. The next, for the staff of General Bethouart was festooned with French tri-color bunting. The British table for General McCreery was less ornate with only a few Union Jack flags. The final table was done in solid red with a giant gold hammer and sickle hanging behind. At this table, a furious looking Marshall Konev stood stiffly clutching a drink and glowering down at Lushka.

Svetlana finally calmed Lushka enough to wrestle him to his own table. There, she patted him like a child and spoke softly in his ear. The Russian colonel's sideshow over, the orchestra resumed playing and the dance floor filled. No one noticed when Lushka was quietly escorted out a side door by six large men. Svetlana went meekly to Marshall Konev's table and appeared to be pleading Lushka's case.

A Russian wearing gold shoulder boards approached and gave Colonel Mather a solid handshake. Colonel Bukinev was a handsome man with unnaturally blue eyes, chiseled features and gray hair at the temples. He had a professor's look, the kind of professor girls remembered with a crush. Most English speaking Russians had a distinct British accent. Bukinev's grammar was perfect but his accent was American, maybe even

New York. He chatted with Mather for a moment and then took Mrs. Mather's hand and kissed it with an elegant bow.

Horatio Aalpeter watched all this with keen interest. Colonel Bukinev had just made it a point to mark Colonel Mather. Everyone now understood these two had some sort of relationship. Interesting, he thought. That might be useful in the future. Then he turned his attention back to Major Cole. Grabbing a waiter, he pressed several bills into the man's hand, pointed out Cole and whispered.

So many things were working out. His plan was falling right into place.

2355 Hours

Just before the stroke of midnight, the conductor rapped his baton and shouted, "Attention, your attention please." Then growing irritated, "Silence." He was, after all, still Viennese and the Viennese cannot stand disorder. He spoke in elegant German. "Ladies and gentlemen, for more than 250 years the New Year was rung in by *Pummerin*, the great bell of St. Stephan's Cathedral. Unfortunately, the Cathedral was burned and the great bell destroyed." He shot a glance toward the Russian head table silently reminding everyone of the looting and destruction by invaders. "No matter, smaller bells will ring deep and clear. A new year is about to begin, a year without war." His voice filled with pride as he shouted, "And now, ladies and gentlemen, the Vienna Waltz."

The orchestra began to play their city's virtual anthem. Americans and British stood and launched into a drunken version of "Auld Lang Syne." The Russians sang, or shouted, the Soviet Army song. The French, after a few uncomfortable moments, felt obliged to sing something so they bellowed their national anthem and tried to drown out the others. The conductor glowered at the room full of barbarians disrespecting his fine music.

Americans put on their party hats and honked noisemakers. British snapped Holiday crackers, small decorative tubes with a popper in the center that opened to reveal party hats and small toys. The French toasted the Russians with Wine. The Russians returned the toast in Vodka.

At the Cole's table, one or two of her tablemates made a polite effort to give Mrs. Mather a peck on the cheek to welcome in 1946. Men lined up to kiss Deb with varying degrees of enthusiasm. Charley Woods went through the line twice and received a punch on the shoulder for his second trip. Still, he got what he came for, a second kiss, much longer and wetter than the first.

James Cole found it all quite amusing. He didn't realize that, at Aalpeter's request, the waiter had been bringing him increasingly stronger and stronger drinks. He was now quite drunk and quite cheerful. He toasted Colonel Mather and several others with slurred speech and an unsteady hand.

Aalpeter found Belcher in the crowd and handed him a note as he whispered to the slightly tipsy captain. "Colonel Mather wants you to take Major Cole home. Do it discreetly. We don't want to embarrass him, after all. And while you're at it, ask Mrs. Cole to meet me at the bar over there."

Belcher took the note and read the printed address. He raised his eyebrows and gave the matter the serious consideration of a drunk, but didn't bother to question who was asking him to be Major Cole's keeper. With a shrug, he lumbered off to pass the message to Deb and gather up his boss.

Deb Cole was giggly drunk but still holding court. She broke away and floated over to Horatio Aalpeter's bar expecting to meet another admirer. As she drew herself up with a self-satisfied breath, he handed her champagne and ginger ale. He had watched all night and knew what she drank.

"Thank you for honoring me Mrs. Cole. I won't take much of your time. I need your help and I think you will find it quite easy to accommodate me. You see, I want you to seduce

Captain Woods." He paused and sipped his wine glass filled with water. She seemed not to understand.

"I am a married woman. Why on earth should I do that?"

He smiled. "Because that's what you want... and because I will tell your husband about the abortion if you don't."

She still didn't seem to comprehend. "What? You don't know what you're talking about. Thanks for the drink but I'm leaving."

He leaned on the bar and spoke to the mirror. "You had to travel all the way to New Jersey for the operation. Your mother loaned you the money. You were three months pregnant and your husband had been away at war for eight. It would have been very awkward. I don't blame you but please, don't play the innocent. You want to sleep with Prince Charming and I want to blackmail him. You can make both of us happy."

She tried to answer but no words came. Finally she managed a whisper. "My husband's here. I can't just..."

"Your husband is being driven home. He's too drunk to remember anything. Here is a key to room 708 at the Hotel Astoria. Woods knows where it is. Just tell him you need someone to walk you there. He'll be a gentleman. He'll be more than a gentleman."

He handed her the key and slid away from the bar. She stood for a long time just staring at the object in her hand. Then, snapping out of it, she stood erect, took a deep, uncertain breath and scanned the room looking for Charley Woods.

CHAPTER FIVE-
JANUARY 1946

January 4, 2030 Hours

Major Horatio Aalpeter, had Sergeant Richardson set up an 8-millimeter projector inside the office at the Monuments Group warehouse. Horatio had a pair of ceramic-capped half liter bottles of local beer and a waxed paper bag of fresh pretzels with mustard. He took off his tie, slipped off his shoes and settled comfortably into his reclining desk chair.

This was going to be a one man party, his own personal little porn show. He loved the power that derived from his position... and from his cunning. He turned off all lights and flicked on the projector master switch, carefully reciting his instructions. "Wait three seconds and turn on the bulb. Not too soon or the heat will burn through slow moving film."

The projector began clicking and the image on the wall flashed with leader numbers; four, three, two, one. The scene that appeared next was an empty hotel room. Horatio knew the camera had been activated by the room's light switch. In a few seconds, Deb Cole stepped into the picture. She had a heavy man's overcoat draped over her shoulders. "How considerate Captain Woods."

Horatio chomped on a pretzel and grinned at the image. He rocked back in his chair like a child at a Saturday matinee. This was going to be great, just great. Charley Woods entered the picture and carefully removed the overcoat from Deb's shoulders. She looked small and frightened as a kitten. She clutched her hands before her chest and looked down.

Woods approached and took her chin in his hand. She said something. What a shame there was no audio. Woods took her in his arms and she dug her head deep into his chest. She looked so young and fragile. Woods smoothed her hair and whispered as though comforting her. This wasn't the erotic show Horatio expected. He popped a beer and sat forward.

Slowly, Woods began kissing her neck. His hands began to explore while pressing her hard against him. She was shaking now and, damn, she started to cry. Horatio clearly saw the fear in her watery eyes. It was fear mixed with a touch of lust, but mostly, it looked like shame.

Horatio put his beer bottle down and sagged back in the chair as he wiped his lips. It wasn't supposed to be like this. This was supposed to be an orgy of wild abandon. She was supposed to be a slut. Sluts don't cry—and he wasn't supposed to feel like some slimy voyeur.

He reached for the projector switch. No wait, get the light first. Where was the damned light switch? It went completely black in the room and a stench of burnt celluloid stung his eyes.

January 5, 2030 Hours

Sergei motioned to an Austrian waiter in a white linen jacket with a towel over his arm. "We need a glass of milk for the boy." The waiter nodded and was off to the kitchen.

The "Unter den Linden" restaurant was a marvelous place. Built during the reign of Maria Teresa, it reeked of colonial grandeur. Polished marble pillars rose several stories to ornately sculpted ceilings with Renaissance paintings, most of mythological figures. Tables were cloaked in heavy Irish linen with Czech crystal and Spanish silver. Somewhere a violinist played softly. This was the good life he wanted.

"Sonya, my dear, if you could live anywhere in the world where would it be?" She was a small, fine boned woman, not yet accustomed to finery and manners. Even dining in a restaurant made her uneasy. She knew that her husband was important and that no one would ever dare criticize, but still, she didn't want to appear low class.

"Oh Sergei, how could any place be finer than this. Little Yuri loves it. He goes often to the Prater amusement park and plays in the lake behind our apartment. There are fine buildings and trees everywhere. Why would I want to go anywhere else?"

Sergei stretched his leg under the table. An old injury bothered him. "Many things are happening. We may have to relocate. I might have choices about our new home. Is there any place you like? She thought and the thinking seemed to take great energy. She scowled and twisted her lips. "I don't want to go to America. They have capitalists and wild Indians. I would be afraid of both."

Sergei smiled at his childlike wife. "I promise we will not go anywhere there are wild Indians. Do you like warm weather?"

She once again screwed up her face. "I don't know. I've never been anywhere that was warm. I would need new clothes."

Sergei said nothing but thought, "We'll all need new clothes, new identities and new nationalities. How will it be for my little boy growing up outside Russia? Will he forget Mother Russia or will he become a lonely foreigner in a strange land?" But then a sigh, "He's still young. He will adapt."

The waiter brought a tall glass of milk, a precious commodity in starving Austria. Sergei favored him with a momentary flash of a smile. Then, staring back at his family, he tried to imagine them in different settings. His wife was meek and pliable; she could manage. The boy was a story not yet written. There was no way to predict how he would react. So much was changing.

January 10, 0900 Hours

The January morning air was dank and heavy. Sergei wore an ankle length bearskin coat and cap with a red hammer and sickle emblem. He wore no rank yet no one challenged him. Soldiers stepped back out of his way. Something about his bearing told them who and what he was. He entered the bombed out church and inspected the set up. A window had been broken out and fitted with a slide down into a waiting truck. Tables and racks were prepared.

Sergei removed his right glove and looked at his fingers as he stretched them. He pulled his P38 pistol from under his coat, popped out the clip and inspected it. Satisfied, he snapped it back and cocked the gun. Turning to one of his aides, he said, "I am ready. Bring in the first man."

A grizzled, dirty man without a coat was wrestled through the door. His arms were tied behind his back and his legs hobbled with a cord. Two guards threw him to the ground and one read from a clipboard. "Anatoli Burdeyen, Army officer and enemy of the people of the Soviet people."

"Position him," commanded Sergei. The guards forced the man to kneel facing the window. He twisted around to look Sergei in the eye. "I am a loyal Communist. I have always obeyed my orders."

"I know," said Sergei softly. "I am sorry." Then, without hesitation, he touched the gun to the man's head and fired. There was remarkably little reaction. The man's head drooped and he fell against the window frame to twitch just once. There was hardly any blood. Sergei made a motion with his chin and the guards pushed the body out onto the slide.

Neither guard had ever seen a man executed before. Both were ashen and fearful as they looked at the cold, calm of the executioner. They must have understood that they could easily be the ones kneeling and he would be as heartless with them as this poor dead bastard.

Sergei saw their shock. He had seen it before, more times than he wanted to remember. By afternoon, they would be accustomed. It could be routine. Horror slowly drains away with repetition. With enough repetition, anything can become bearable, even acceptable. He sounded completely businesslike as he commanded, "Next man."

Three more were dispatched in the same way but then there was a commotion outside. Sergei showed no interest. He simply waited. Finally, a total of six guards succeeded in pushing a giant through the door. It was Lushka.

Sergei stepped back overwhelmed. "My colonel, this cannot be. I will not be the one..."

Lushka wrenched left and right until his attackers all lay on the floor. He laughed, "Not bad for a one armed man, eh?" It was Lushka, irascible as ever. The guards were clamoring to their feet when Sergei ordered. "Let him stand. No one is to touch this man."

Lushka bellowed, "What will you do, comrade? Will you let me go? I don't think so. Here is my request, my friend. I want to die fighting. Let me stand, facing you. I count to three and then, I attack. You kill me or I kill you. Do you understand that? I *will* kill you. I will die a warrior or a murderer. Either way, I have dignity."

"No, my colonel, I will not shoot you."

Lushka looked devilish as he shouted, "One."

"No, it cannot be so."

"Two."

"No, do not do this thing."

Lushka bellowed like a bull, "Three." He lowered his head and charged with arms flailing. Sergei stood and popped off three shots through watering eyes. Three wasn't enough. Lushka hit him like a truck, slamming Sergei back against a far wall. The big man drew back his good arm and pounded Sergei with a sledge hammer punch to the face. Stunned, Sergei struggled under the weight. His vision blurred and his gun hand was trapped between his chest and Lushka's.

But Lushka was also entangled. He had to lean back to free himself and when he did, Sergei's reflexes took over. He tilted the pistol against Lushka's chest and fired five more shots. The big man stumbled back, looked down at his tunic. Hot red blood steamed in the cold air. He raised his arms and shouted to the world.

"Now dies Lushka, who feared none but was feared by many."

His face was wild until he began to wobble. Slowly, his balance gave way and he fell like a statue thumping against the floor in a cloud of dust. The guards were slow to approach as though fearing Lushka might suddenly come back to life. One finally mustered the courage to ask, "Should we try to fit him through the window?"

"No," said Sergei. He could feel the side of his face swelling already and he struggled to regain his breath. "Place his body in the truck. He will be buried in the Central Cemetery alongside Strauss, Beethoven, Brahms and Schubert. Few knew how much he loved their music. I will arrange a marker.

January 14, 1400 Hours

Major Horatio Aalpeter rose to welcome Captain Woods to the warehouse office. "Thanks for coming and I appreciate you not telling your boss about our meeting."

Woods sat with some hesitation. "What's this about? Why shouldn't I tell Major Cole?"

"Oh, we'll get to that. First, are you aware that under the code of military justice adultery is considered a crime, a fairly serious crime?"

Woods shifted uncomfortably. "What does that have to do with me?"

Aalpeter smiled and continued. "Punishments vary from reduction in rank and forfeiture of pay to several years at hard labor. The most severe sentences are given when an officer is found guilty of an adulterous relationship with the wife of a superior. Recently, a lieutenant found sleeping with his commander's wife was busted to private and given six years hard labor. Let's see, your commander is Major Cole, correct?"

Woods was shaken but still tried to protest with as much conviction as he could muster. Aalpeter folded his hands and rocked back in his chair until Woods seemed to be running out of steam. Then the major commanded with a voice of cold authority. "Get the light switch."

"What?"

"Turn off the lights. The switch is there on the wall."

Woods rose and went to the wall. He put a finger on the light switch but hesitated. His brow was damp and he felt his stomach clench. He didn't know what was coming but he knew he wasn't going to like it.

"Go ahead, turn off the lights."

The room went dark just as the projector began to click and whir. Woods heard the major count to three and then a bright light flooded the far wall. Numbers counted down and the image of a hotel room appeared.

Woods sagged almost sliding down the wall. His finger felt the light switch and flipped it back on. "Turn it off. You made your point. Turn off the projector. Just tell me what you want."

Aalpeter carefully shut down the projector. "Well, now you see why I asked you not to tell Major Cole about our meeting." He leaned forward looking over his glasses. "You know he's killed over a dozen men, some with his bare hands. No reason to invite difficulty is there?"

Woods slumped into a chair and buried his face in his hands. Aalpeter continued. "You have a way with women. You know you do. There is a Russian woman I want you to seduce. That part will be easy. The hard part will be gaining her confidence. But, we'll start with the seduction. Her name is Commissar Svetlana Borsky."

January 15, 1900 Hours

Colonel Mather ordered a cocktail party be held at the new Vienna Officer's Group club. The VOG Villa, as it was called, was a mansion once owned by an Austrian general. It still had minor bomb damage but the partial repairs actually gave it an interesting if macabre atmosphere. Here the victors could enjoy the fruits of their conquest as the vanquished Austrian servants in starched white coats served martinis and hors d'oeuvres.

The Americans were not alone. Mather, still hoping to establish cordial relations, invited British, French and, of course, Russian officers and their wives. They gathered in groups by nationality, eyeing each other suspiciously over drinks. Few spoke any other's languages and those who did were assumed to be spies. Captain Charley Woods lived up to their expectations.

With his All-American grin, he marched over to the cluster of Russians. They looked uncomfortable in coarse, ill-fitting civilian suits instead of their usual uniforms. The Occupation Authority had granted an exemption to the uniform policy for this party. Charley, however, looked suave in his tweed hunter's jacket with leather pads on the elbows and gun shoulder. He left a trail of pipe smoke as he cruised into the crowd looking for a special woman.

Svetlana wasn't hard to find. She was taller than many of the men and her regal bearing made her a stand-out in any crowd. Charley walked directly to her and offered a stiff arm handshake. He spoke in German, the most common language in use. *"Guten tag, Ich bin Charley Woods."*

Svetlana smirked at him and grabbed his hand in a crushing grip. "Hello, Charley. I don't speak German."

He kept the smile even as his hand was being mangled. "English, you speak English. Not many of your countrymen speak English."

She released his hand and he resisted the urge to shake it out. Svetlana raised her tumbler of vodka and took a slug. "Yes, we were given a choice of learning English or German before the Berlin Olympics. I hated the Germans so I chose English."

Charley looked genuinely impressed. "The Olympics, you were in the Olympics? What was your sport?"

She crossed her arms still holding her glass and looked him up and down with an amused smile. "Javelin, I was a javelin thrower. I was disqualified but I am still proud that I did my best throw ever. They gave medals to two Nazi women and a Pole."

Charley took a step back and took in her full length. With an approving look, he bit his lower lip and gave her a devilish look. "I can see that. You have the body of an athlete. No, you have the body of a goddess. I wish I could have seen you compete."

She tossed her head and suppressed a chuckle. "You would have been a child in 1936."

He looked down at his feet, smiled and lifted only his eyes. "I am not a child now."

Svetlana burst out laughing. "You are funny, American Charley Woods. So, I am thinking you are a spy, yes? And you want to sex me and get secrets. Is this so, Charley?"

Woods flashed his best, heart-melting smile. "Yes."

"So, we make deal. You sex me and I give you a secret, then you give me a secret. Is this a good trade for you?"

"A trade, one secret for another? Sounds good to me. Now, let's get to the sex part."

January 16, 0800 Hours

Aalpeter listened to Woods's report without a snicker as the younger man recounted his night with Svetlana. He rushed through the carnal details to cover the exchange of secrets.

"I figured they must already know about the U-Bahn tunnel under Major Cole's house since they sent Russian soldiers down there to capture the SS men. So I told her we have a small entrance that we use to sneak in and out."

Aalpeter's face tightened. "Did she know about the listening post?"

"Gosh, I didn't think about that. She didn't seem surprised at all. I guess she already knew all about it."

"What secret did she tell you?"

Woods beamed and leaned forward. "She said they have some spy named Phyllis and they will trade her if we have something important enough."

"Did she say what would be important enough?"

"Naw, and she kept calling this Phyllis 'he' as though it was a guy."

Aalpeter went quiet and tapped his pen on the desk.

January 17, 1130 Hours

Cole had once again been summoned to Colonel Mather's office. He wasn't sure what to expect but Fraulein Gint looked tense as he reported. She whispered, "Something is happening. I don't know what, but the colonel asked me to get a copy of the personnel records for all your people. He has been calling all office chiefs in the G-2 directorate. He is more excited than I have ever seen him. Please to be careful what you say. I know sometimes you speak more than is really good for you."

He smiled at her. "Thanks, I appreciate the warning. I'll try not to irritate the old man."

She gave him her very best, "You know I'm still available," smile. Cole wound his way back to Mather's office, knocked and entered. Colonel Mather sat with his hands folded wearing a smug catbird smile. He ignored Cole's snappy heel click to a position of attention and leaned back in his chair as if to relish the moment.

"Major Cole, Major James Cole, Detachment Eight commander and chief cowboy. I'm afraid your rodeo is just about over." He paused to let the statement sink in. Then, trying to suppress a smirk, "Your group has been deactivated."

Cole said nothing.

"You are all being reassigned. Johnson and McMahan will go to the records section. Belcher and Ryan will still be under you but it will be in your capacity as acting Chief of Intelligence for Denazification."

Mather allowed a tight grin. "You will be working directly under me, directly under me, no one else."

Cole remained stoic, allowing no trace of emotion. He still stood at attention, eyes focused on the wall over Mather's head. "Where will I be working, Sir?"

The colonel thought for a second. "We'll have to iron that out. Things are pretty crowded in this building. Never mind, though. You need to go and let your people know. And be sure to tell them there will be no more harassment of our Russian allies. No more gunfights on the Ringstrasse. We're here to catch Nazis. So, run along now and give the good news to your people."

He made a wave of dismissal and Cole pivoted to leave. Back at the reception desk, he bent to Fraulein Gint's ear. "The colonel just told me all my detachment is being deactivated and we're all reassigned. Do you remember the personnel records you gave him? How many were there?"

She beamed. Leaning close enough he could feel the brush of her hair she whispered, "Only four officers are shown on your detachment Table of Allowances. The others are off the books."

Drawing even closer, Cole's face tightened, "What does that mean, 'off the books'?"

She sat tall and very pleased with herself. "I worked with Major Aalpeter to set up your detachment. We were given only four people available from personnel. The others are actually shown on paper as being assigned to the Monuments Group. They don't know it. The colonel doesn't know it. Only Major Aalpeter and I know it." Then with a coy wink, "And now you know. If you keep things quiet, you can keep both your staff and your offices. Col. Mather doesn't even know where you're located."

Cole nodded as he thought. "But, just who is this Aalpeter?"

She beamed, "You know him well but you call him James Mason."

Cole remembered the night they were drinking in the American Bar. Mason said something about hating his real name. The kids in school always made fun of him.

So, this disbanding was going to be a sham. But now, Cole would have to be even more careful. His support was all but gone. First the Pond, now his legitimate Army support; everything was gone except his connection to Mason, or Aalpeter or whatever he wanted to be called.

He started to leave but then turned and gave Fraulein Gint a 'Father Knows Best' look of affection. "Thank you for all you have done. I appreciate it. You are a great friend. We all appreciate it." She held a folder in front of her face to hide the blush.

1430 Hours

Billy Connors drove slowly through the wasteland of bombed out factory buildings. He was the only one who knew where the Monuments Group was located. Cole was impressed. What better place to locate a high value operation than in an abandoned dump where no visitor went unnoticed? The warehouse itself was unremarkable. Dark and rusted, there was no sign of life. Cole got out of the car but saw no entrance.

In time, a civilian guard in a black uniform came out and asked in German what the American major wanted. After a check of Cole's identification, he was escorted inside to the cavernous storehouse. Major Horatio Aalpeter sat waiting in his office. He half rose and offered a seat and a cup of coffee.

"I'm sorry I didn't tell you more about myself. It was an oversight. Fraulein Gint has informed me of the announcement of your unit's deactivation. She works closely with Mrs. Parks who, by the way, still keeps close contacts with British MI-6. That's where she gets much of her research information. Now to deal with your new status, we have more problems than you know."

Cole stared without comment. Aalpeter moved papers across his desk and grimaced. "My group is being moved to Salzburg. We have reduced our holdings to the point we can consolidate everything there. My position is being eliminated as well. There doesn't seem to be anyone left with the power to keep me here. I am being reassigned to Munich."

Cole set his coffee down. "You're saying that I'm on my own?"

Aalpeter shrugged. "I can still provide some limited help from afar. Today, I will give you a crate of money. It should be enough to last you for quite a while. Be careful though, some of it is counterfeit. I don't even know which. I'll give you a list of contacts. Of course, you realize that these names must be protected at all costs."

"Of course. How long before you leave?"

"Three weeks at the most. We must clean up loose ends. I don't want to leave you with more problems."

"You mean my scientists waiting in Salzburg?"

"Yes, but there are others as well. I'll tell you more in a couple of days."

January 19, 1000 Hours

Deb Cole marched into the headquarters building and breezed right by Fraulein Gint who stood and motioned for her to stop. High heels clicking like a jackhammer, Deb was intent and paid no mind to anyone in her way. In a wide-shouldered wool overcoat with matching hat and pheasant feather she looked every bit the society swell.

At the far end of an enormous hallway she flung open a twelve foot door and marched in boldly. A young captain with gel-slicked hair and a starched khaki uniform jumped in front of her with his arms outstretched. "Whoa, whoa, whoa, just slow it down, Missy. You can't be in here."

She clutched her purse in crossed arms and gave him a haughty look. "I am looking for a lawyer. Are you a lawyer?"

"Yes, but I am a Staff Judge Advocate lawyer and we don't do work for civilians. We are here to handle military issues."

Deb was not impressed. "This is a military issue. I want to know my options if, and I'm not saying for sure, but if I were to seek a divorce."

The captain lost his cool look and bit his lip. He looked left and right. "Listen, step over here for a minute. I'm not supposed to give you advice but I can, at least tell you where you stand." He took her arm and pulled her into a small waiting room.

He measured his words, "The Occupation Authority brought you wives over here before we had any policies or regulations to cover your legal rights and obligations. As it stands now, you have no official status except as a dependent of your husband. He has rights. You do not. You cannot divorce him here. You can go back to the States and file there. You could also hire an Austrian lawyer but we don't even know what the final version of their government will look like. In any event, the ruling of an Austrian judge will have no merit against an American military man. It probably won't be recognized by any American court."

He tried to look compassionate. "Listen, your best course of action is to patch things up and make the best of it. If that's completely out of the question, then have him get you transportation back stateside and file there. Whatever you do, don't announce to anyone what you are considering. I don't know who your husband is and I don't want to know. But if he gets angry and throws you out, you have no legal status. You won't be able to get a visa or cross a border. It could become a nightmare."

Deb's face tightened and she shook her head slightly. "Thank you. I was just curious. I appreciate your advice. She held out a hand and he took it cautiously. Then she was gone but her clicking heels had lost their strident pace.

January 20, 0800 Hours

James Cole arrived at the Café Museum breathing clouds of icy breath. January had turned bitter. Slushy snow refroze into ugly piles tinged with coal ash. James Mason had already ordered two Schlagobers, strong black coffees with whipped cream. He seemed on edge during his last days in Vienna.

"You're late."

Cole checked his watch. "I show myself right on time. What is so important that I had to sneak out from under Mather's nose? He monitors my every move, or thinks he does anyway."

Mason leaned forward to whisper. Cole had never seen him do that. "You know the Russian Zelenkov sees you as his nemesis. You have defeated him at every turn and made him lose face. He wants to meet you in person."

Cole's brow wrinkled. "For what purpose? Do I need to be concerned for my safety?"

Mason sat back and sipped his coffee. His eyes darted left and right. "I've been courting him for weeks. I think he's ready to defect. He hasn't committed yet but he doesn't have much choice. If he stays in the Red Army, he'll be killed."

Cole thought it over as he removed his frosty overcoat and settled in. "Okay, but why me? I don't see what he wants from me. You've done all the coordinating. You're the one who should be his handler."

Mason shrugged from behind his steamy cup. "It must be personal, perhaps even symbolic to him. I'll brief you on everything we have set up. You should understand, however, he won't turn. Don't expect him to work against the Soviets. He's still a loyal Communist. He just wants to save his family. We have set up an identity for him in Switzerland working for the new United Nations organization. We'll have new documents from Rolf in a few days. Soviet Major Sergei Zelenkov will become Johann Sweitzer, an Austrian labor organizer who fled the Nazis and found asylum in Switzerland. He speaks German well enough to pass but I worry about his wife and son."

Cole cupped his coffee in both hands for warmth. "I don't understand. If he won't turn on the Soviets, why are we willing to help him? He'll still be an enemy, worse he'll be an enemy on our payroll."

Mason seemed smug. "I have a plan that won't require his cooperation."

Cole wasn't satisfied. "This doesn't feel right to me. Why specifically ask for me?" Mason shook his head as if to say, "Who knows."

1415 Hours

That afternoon Cole swung by the Astoria Hotel for his daily check. Lidia saw him coming and withdrew an envelope from the key slots. It was on formal looking cream colored paper addressed in elegant script to "Hernando." Inside, a small note read only, "FKK Park, 10:30." Cole asked Lidia if she knew the place. She shook her head no but pulled a worn phone book and quickly found an address.

January 21, 1000 Hours

Cole reviewed the plan in his mind remembering Mason's advice from their first meeting, "Trust no one and always carry a gun." He checked out his compact Walther. Seven shells in the clip and one in the chamber, he was as ready as he could be.

McMahan drove Major Cole with Belcher and Ryan following for backup. It took a bit of circling on back streets before they saw a small, easily overlooked sign to the FKK Park.

It turned out to be, not a park but a huge building, probably an old Victorian era greenhouse. A great dome of glass panels rose over walls of carved stone. Ornate iron statues guarded the entrance. Cole gathered his crew. "Okay, I don't have a clue what to expect. McMahan, you stay and keep an eye on the cars. Belcher, Ryan, give me a few minutes and then slip inside in case I need help. Keep your heads clear and be ready to deal with anything."

With that, he turned and climbed steps under a sign that read "Naturistenpark." God, he hated uncertainty. Inside eight-foot high doors, a tiny anteroom held only a desk. Wood paneling black with age made it seem close, suffocating. The clerk, or guard or whatever, asked in surly, working class German if Cole was a member. Receiving a no, he demanded five Reichsmarks. Cole thought that excessive. He could have had a decent meal and two beers for the price of admission to this... whatever it was.

The guard handed him a small key, a locker key with a numbered medallion on a leather strap, and pointed to a single door. Cole took a breath and stepped into a fancy room of oak paneled walls and long rows of furniture quality wooden locker doors. He walked toward sunlight at the far end of the room but a man on a stool blocked his way. The man wore a gray turtleneck sweater and a furrowed look that suggested he meant business.

"No clothes outside," he commanded in curt German.

"No clothes?" Cole repeated without understanding.

"Natural only," gray sweater shot back. Cole leaned forward to see out into the glass roofed building. Everyone was nude. "Oh my God," he exhaled. "It's a nudist colony." He turned and walked back down the rows of lockers looking for his number but unsure just what to do.

Then it came to him. It made perfect sense. No reason to worry about weapons or listening devices if everyone is nude. Clever, but could he do it? Could he walk out into the sunlight completely nude and surrounded by other nude people? Certainly, he had done worse, hadn't he? James Cole could feel his breath quicken.

He found his locker and began undressing with tentative hands and a look of controlled panic. He folded his pistol and wallet inside his uniform shirt. What lay ahead? What would Major Zelenkov be planning? Removing his shorts, he stood naked and leaned forward on the locker wall to let his head sink below outstretched arms as he fought to control his pulse. He gazed down to bean-pole skinny legs so white they had a bluish cast. His knees were boney knobs; his belly, soft and hairy. This was going to be humiliating.

He slammed the locker door, removed his key and sucked in a hard breath. "God and country, here we go."

At the door, gray sweater grabbed Cole's wrist, scowled and pointed at the key. Cole obligingly put the strap around his wrist. Sweater nodded approval and handed him a scratchy towel. Then James Cole, Major in the United States Army, stepped boldly out into a bright sunny day. Other than a forced smile, he was completely buck ass naked.

All around him, dozens of people laughed and played outdoor games. Two couples, well over sixty, played badminton mindless of breasts and penises that flapped wildly as they ran and jumped. Cole felt almost light headed. He tried to think of an appropriate role to play in this situation. Nothing came. How could anyone act normal? He was naked, completely exposed and vulnerable. Not just his body, his whole self, seemed to have been laid open for inspection.

He surveyed the crowd. There were many women. Most were matronly and plain but a few were downright good looking. Somehow, there seemed absolutely nothing sexual about their nakedness, nothing at all. But with the men, he could not help himself from comparing penis size. The variety was amazing. He had always been uncomfortable in gang showers and took pains not to look at other men. Now, it was unavoidable.

He felt a minor panic when he realized his own penis had retracted to the size of a thumb, and only a thumb down to the joint. Perhaps it was the cold. The glass dome overhead was, after all, covered in patchy ice and snow. No, in reality, steam vented from heaters all around actually kept it a hothouse. No one else was having a problem with "shrinkage." Unconsciously, he moved the towel in front of him.

Several small children ran by laughing and shouting. Two bumped against him, the giant, gangly, naked man. Their touch made him recoil. It just didn't seem right for little kids, boys and girls, to be so carefree without a stitch on. He felt like a deviant but the children were completely indifferent to his nakedness. He walked quickly, hoping activity would calm him. He still had no role that fit his situation, no persona to hide behind.

Nearby, a group of men gathered, laughing and talking. They had wine glasses. He could really use a drink but he had no wallet. But then, they couldn't have wallets either. There were at least four burly, rough looking men but they had wine. He tried not to notice that they were all proudly displaying their equipment. He continued to hold his towel strategically.

As he approached, the crowd parted and a single man stood alone. He was a handsome fellow with a gymnast's body and a boyish face. James Cole always looked first at the eyes. This man's were hard and steady. The handsome man spoke in Russian and the others all slugged their wine and walked away.

"You are Hernando, yes?"

Cole nodded cautiously.

"We will speak in German. None of my people speak German. I am Sergei Ilyich Zelenkov. You know of me, yes?"

Again Cole nodded. He expected someone taller, tougher looking. Zelenkov had the trim bearing of a staff officer, someone used to order and rules. He was younger and better looking than anyone would expect of an undercover operator, an executioner, a loyal servant of the brutal Colonel Lushka.

"I am happy to meet you Americanski." The naked Russian smirked and shook a finger. "You have been a great aggravation to me. I respect what you have done but I must tell you, it caused me great trouble. Now, I expect you to make up for it. What can you offer?"

Cole relaxed just a little. He looked around and, seeing no one within earshot, began. "On Sunday you must take your wife and son to the Prater Amusement Park at 1100 hours. Bring only what your wife can fit inside her bag. Dress normally. You will be given everything new. Just beyond the giant Ferris wheel is a row of booths. One is a ..." He stumbled for a word... "a *freak show* we call it in English. The sign outside has a picture of a woman with a beard. Take your family inside. We will pretend to kidnap you."

Sergei interrupted, "Will you frighten my wife and son?"

"I cannot promise. The men who will take you are instructed that they are not to be harmed. You will be driven into the American Zone just a few minutes away. There, you will spend the night in a hotel room, a very nice hotel room. We will give you money and new clothes. In the very early morning hours, you will travel to the Schonbrunn Palace gardens. We will have a small airplane that can operate off the great lawn. It will take you to Salzburg in the American Sector. This must be done in the darkness to avoid detection. If the weather is not good, you will stay in the hotel until it is safe."

Sergei didn't look pleased. He walked with hands clasped behind his back while Cole tried to keep up beside him. Their path wound to a large oak tree inside the huge arboretum and beneath the tree was a small stand. Here a man wearing nothing but an apron dispensed wine without charge. Sergei ordered two.

As they walked and sipped, he made his deal. "I will not have my family handled like prisoners. We will go to the Prater Park and enter the tent as you described. Then I want you to create a disturbance. Have a man in a Soviet uniform along with a woman and child who take part in a mock kidnapping, a very noisy kidnapping. Meanwhile, I will change clothes and we will leave in a car. I will select the hotel and I will make my own travel arrangements. You must send believable teletype messages about my capture for the KGB to intercept. I must not be accused of cooperation. After a period of time, you shall announce that I have been killed. Do you understand?"

For a moment, Cole forgot about his nakedness. "I must present your proposal to my superiors and…"

"No, you do not need to speak to anyone, not Mason or your Colonel Mather or even Ambassador Winters. You make the arrangements. You are the only one I trust. I will come over to the West only if you are my handler, my only handler. Do you understand?"

Cole made a face. "Why me? Others have more power."

Sergei tightened his lips. "Because you work alone. You have outsmarted me and you can outsmart your own people. I will only feel safe if you handle my defection. Only you, Hernando—no one else."

Sergei saluted with his wine glass and turned away. His gang of thugs quickly reformed around him. Cole felt an overpowering urge to get out of there. He walked quickly, clenching his teeth. He wanted clothes. He wanted out of this zoo. He wanted to breathe air that wasn't damp from steam vents. He didn't want to bump into a naked Belcher but there he was.

Thick and hairy, Belcher looked more ape than human. Cole fairly hissed the words, "What in hell are you doing?"

"Just following orders, Sir. You said to wait a few minutes and then follow you, so here we are."

"We? You're not saying Ryan is in here?"

"Right behind you, Sir." Her voice was cheery as a morning bird song. Cole spun to face the small, girlish and completely naked body of Cynthia Ryan. She gave him an impish grin. "We do follow orders."

Cole couldn't get any air. His words trailed off. "Sweet mother of God, what were you..."

"We were just providing backup, Sir." She seemed incredibly pleased with herself as she stood feet slightly apart, hands on hips and head high. He couldn't help thinking of Peter Pan in the buff. Cole tried not to look but his eyes keep flickering back to her body.

Belcher chimed in. "I tried to send her back to the car when we realized it was a nudist facility but she wouldn't have it. You know how stubborn..."

Cynthia let out a little giggle. "Why Major, are you paying me a compliment?"

Cole felt his cheeks go hot as he realized that his third "thumb" had just become a bratwurst. "Get out. Both of you get out now. I'll talk to you in the car." He repositioned his towel and hurried away in a slightly bent posture as he looked back at the Russians.

Sergei watched from the shade of an indoor tree and muttered, "This is the man who outsmarted me?" He shook his head and sipped wine.

January 22, 1400 Hours

It was early afternoon when James Cole gathered the detachment for his announcement. He wanted to be empathetic but with sincerity and strength. Remembering a Henry Fonda movie, he quietly became that character.

He was doing better with groups these days and felt only a slight ripple of anxiety as he stood before the assembled crowd. Without realizing it, he avoided eye contact with Belcher and Ryan. Putting the memories of the nudist park out of mind, he stood tall and cool as he began.

"As you all know, these are difficult times. There are major reorganizations and cuts throughout USFA. As part of those cuts, Detachment Eight has been dissolved."

There was a collective gasp. He allowed a slight smile. "That was the bad news. The good news is that we're not going away. We have been working on the fringe of legality all along. Well actually, we have gone well beyond the fringe, but now, we are going completely undercover. Our detachment may have been taken off the books but we haven't been taken out of the fight."

He leaned forward resting his knuckles on the conference table. "We will continue as a shadow organization right under Colonel Mather's nose. Belcher and Ryan are being reassigned to G-2 DeNazification along with me. The truth is, even before we Americans arrived in Vienna, the Russian NKVD had 2300 agents comb the city. They weeded out virtually all the sympathizers. There isn't much left for us to do. We'll dummy up reports from time to time showing interview counts and statistics but otherwise, we'll go on doing what we need to do."

Cole let that sink in. Every face still looked taut. "Johnson and McMahan will be reassigned to G-2 Records. No one says you have to physically be present in the records section of the headquarters building. In fact, there's no room for you. You'll stay here." Both men gave somber nods of understanding.

"Roland, Woods, White and Richardson: you don't appear on anyone's table of allowances. You will remain..." Cole looked around. Where are White and Richardson?"

Cynthia Ryan responded, "Sherry often comes in late after working her night shift in the listening booth but she's always here by this time." There was a long moment of silence. Ryan came back, "She lives in the apartment two doors down. I'll run and check on her."

Cole indicated approval and went on, "Continuing operations against orders is a risky move but I see no alternative. Our leadership is blind to the growing Russian threat. They are so consumed with the hope of gaining cooperation they ignore the blatant transgressions of our Soviet adversaries." His group wasn't listening. They were watching the door, waiting for Ryan's return. It didn't take long.

Ryan burst back into the room breathless. "Her bed doesn't look slept in. There's no sign of Richardson either." They all turned to Cole.

He stood straight and stern. "Full combat gear, we're going into the tunnel."

1530 Hours

Deb wasn't home when the gaggle arrived. Three vehicles skidded to stops before the Cole mansion and the odd looking group piled out. They wore gabardine uniforms with neckties and polished shoes. Canvas ammo belts slung over their shoulders, they carried pistols, Thompson machine guns, rifles and even a grenade launcher. A few wore helmets. They streamed in the front door, down into the wine cellar and onto the wooden stairs. Cole opened the fake rock door that protected the tunnel entrance.

Once inside, it was dark, cold and solemn. Breath steamed and everyone listened to the heavy silence. Cole voiced what they were all thinking. "The red lights are still on. Sherry would never have left without turning them off."

They began walking along the dimly lit tracks. These weren't trained combat soldiers. Only Cole had ever been in a legitimate fire fight. Even their running battle with the Russians in staff cars couldn't be considered much of a fight. Now they stumbled along, loosely line abreast. It was a tense, nervous silence punctuated only by heavy breathing. With every step, Cole's stride increased and his chest thrust forward. He was becoming more and more John Wayne.

As they approached, the control booth ahead was dark. Flashlight beams slashed across the subway walls until settling on the booth's glass windows. No one spoke. The glass was full of bullet holes. Cole broke the trance, "Spread out and look for… well, anything you can find."

It wasn't a minute before Roland shouted from the dark tracks, "Body, I see a body." He was quickly joined by McMahan who called back, "It's Richardson. He's full of bullet holes." Cole tromped over, pushing McMahan out of the way to stand over the dead man. He ran his flashlight up and down the body before speaking.

"His holster is empty. His hand is extended. He died fighting, probably trying to protect Sherry." Cole turned and shouted, "Any sign of her?"

Ryan had climbed up into the control booth. She shouted down in a shrill voice, "Nothing up here, Sir. The telephone console has been destroyed, blasted by bullets." She paused for a second and added, "There's no blood." Then she turned and walked out onto the subway platform scanning as she went. "The steps out here are thick with dust and grime. There are footprints of many men and much activity. It looks as though it was quite struggle."

Cole was momentarily silent. His priorities just changed completely. His voice was quiet as he commanded, "Gather

Richardson's body and let's get out of here." It was John Wayne talking, and John was mad.

2045 Hours

Two cars pulled quietly through a darkened alley in a bad section of the French Zone. Cole and Ryan got out and moved into shadows, avoiding the lone street light. The night had taken on a sharp chill and the pair left a halo of steaming breath. "Do you know exactly which room is Honig's?"

"It's the second upstairs window. It will be right at the top of the stairs. The door has an old fashioned lock that can be opened easily with a thin bladed knife," Cynthia Ryan answered.

"Okay, I'll take Belcher and Roland. You stay with McMahan and the cars. If there is a ruckus, start the engines and be ready to run." He sounded much like Gary Cooper.

The back door was unlocked and the three men eased their way up the stairs. Soft footsteps creaked on ancient stair treads. Cole led with his pistol held high. At the landing, they heard a toilet flush and an old man in long underwear waddled out of the community bathroom leaving the door ajar to light the hall. Cole pointed his gun and put a finger to his lips telling the man to be quiet. The old fellow raised his hands in silent surrender.

Roland stood beside Honig's door so his feet could not be seen underneath the gap. He slid a knife down releasing the catch and turned to Cole. The tall major moved quickly to shove the door open, leap into the room and assume a wide firing stance with his gun pointed straight ahead. Honig sat patiently waiting, hands folded with a cigarette still burning in his fingers.

He spoke in English. "I saw your cars arrive." He took a drag. "I knew you would come. It was only a matter of when. I am now alone, defenseless. The French have abandoned me. They think I am a traitor who worked for Devereaux. The Austrian government won't help me. They also think I betrayed them. The Russians say they will give me sanctuary but not my family. The French have taken my wife into custody. She will suffer greatly if I go to Russia. I am lost, nowhere to go."

Even in the dark, Honig seemed stooped and older. He exhaled and coughed. "I am prepared to die. I fought for my beliefs and was always ready to die but this is not the way I expected it to be, shot while hiding in a rundown hostel. You were ready to kill me before, Major. Now, there is nothing to stop you."

Cole was impatient. "Come with us now. Don't waste my time. I need your miserable, lying ass. You will live if you help us save Sherry White."

Back at the detachment, Honig was taken to the interrogation room he knew well. Mrs. Parks brought him coffee but he didn't acknowledge his old friend. Cole plopped into an opposite chair and slapped a yellow pad on the table. He stared right through Honig and the older man tensed ever so slightly.

"Who is Devereaux and who does he work for?"

Honig ran a hand though greasy disheveled hair and took the coffee cup in his hands. He looked as if experiencing great pain. Finally he began, "There is a group…"

"Speak up. I can't hear you." Cole's voice was harsh.

"I said, there is a group in France who seek revolution. They call themselves *Aube Rouge*, 'Red Dawn.' While they are loosely allied with the French Communist Party they, or rather we, want more than representation. We want a new order where common men are valued and rewarded for their labor. We want to sweep away our capitalist masters and make way for justice and real freedom."

"That's all swell," said Cole with heavy sarcasm. "Now tell me about Devereaux."

"Ah Devereaux, he is the clever one. He is listed on the French Embassy staff and therefore, does not appear on the Occupation Registry. He is not officially in the French Army even though he holds a rank of captain as an attaché. He is a master of making others do things for him."

Honig could not keep from smiling. "Just as he made you work for him. The girl Anna, Lushka's secretary, was actually an agent for the Red Dawn. Devereaux did not have the resources to receive her messages so he set you up. You made the contacts. You thought she was your source and you dutifully picked up her messages which I then forwarded to Devereaux. Once we had the microphone installed in your office it was even better. I could hear everything you said and record much of it. Devereaux needed Russian support for our movement so he supplied them with just enough information to keep them happy."

Honig looked serious. "When he let you hear the phone conversation about the Phyllis kidnapping, he was really trying to help you. It is true that he also helps the Russians, but he doesn't trust them. You should have listened to him."

Cole didn't show the discomfort he felt at that statement. "What happened to Anna?"

Honig shrugged, "She's in France. Her family really is White Russian and could never be safe unless they assumed new identities. She is a wonderful girl, brave and careful. I pray for her."

"So you believe in God?"

"Sometimes."

"How can I find Devereaux?"

Honig held up his hands. "He is elusive. He always contacted me. The French Secret Intelligence Service is after him now so he is going deep undercover. I don't know how to contact him."

"Don't lie. There is always a way, a dead drop, a cutout, a message board, something."

Honig squirmed a bit and answered very slowly. "There is a coffee house he likes, the 'Sperl' near the Opera District. A waiter named Bernard used to get messages to him but I doubt it will still work."

"Who else in Vienna is part of this Red Dawn group?"

There was a long sigh. "You ask too much. I will not endanger other patriots. I will say only that none are concerned with you. They seek support in their struggle for a communist France. America will never be our ally but we do not see you as an enemy either. You fought for our freedom from the Nazis. We owe you a great debt. You have nothing to fear from us."

Cole drew close with his elbows on the table. "Sherry White has been kidnapped. Can you help me get her back?"

January 24, 1930 Hours

James Cole sat at the head of a table meant to seat sixteen people. Deb was a few seats away. A single candelabra provided dim light for these two people in a dining room designed for grand parties with many servants, two people who sat in silence. There was no maid, no butler and no other staff. Deb leaned on one elbow and rested her chin in her palm as she clinked her fork noisily fishing around her decorated china plate. James chewed silently with a faraway look.

He dreaded the conversation that must come next. To make things worse, Deb was in one of her teenage-like moods. She swirled her wine glass absently and gave him a hostile stare. Cole folded his napkin and took a deep sigh. Forcing a smile he began.

"Deb, you know the woman who worked downstairs?" His wife stopped fiddling and pursed her lips. She didn't look happy. Cole continued. "Her name is Sherry White and she's been kidnapped. Her companion, Sergeant Richardson, was killed in the tunnel right under our house. It isn't safe for us here anymore."

"What do you mean, it isn't safe? Don't you have soldiers for that kind of thing?" Her voice had a sharp edge.

"Yes, there are several soldiers in the tunnel right now. That's the only reason we're still here." He grimaced and gave her the news. "We must leave this house tomorrow. We'll be in a hotel until they can find us another..."

She stood up knocking her chair over. Her eyes went wide and face forward. Her stiff arms ended with tightly clenched fists. "This is MY house, Do you understand, my house, I shall not leave. I won't."

James Cole looked weary. "We don't have any choice. The Army will find us another place. Certainly it won't be like this but I'm sure it will..."

She snarled at him. "This is my house. Do you understand? I don't care what you have to do. I want to keep my house. Living here is the best thing that ever happened to me. It made being married to you worthwhile. If I can't have the house you gave me then I don't want you either. You've never been a real husband."

Cole stared into the darkness. There was so much he wanted to say but why bother? She was right; their marriage had never really worked. Well, it was okay as long as they were separated, but living together had been a complete disaster. He gulped his wine and grimaced as though tasting vinegar. "If you want a divorce, I won't fight it."

That took the air out of her tantrum. "A divorce, you want a divorce? What would happen to me?" Her voice grew small, maybe frightened.

"I will set up your travel by ship back to the States. Once there, you can go anywhere you want. I will pay you a small monthly allowance until you remarry. It will be enough to live if you are frugal."

Deb let her eyes move over her great room. She began to sob quietly. Crossing her arms tight, she swayed slightly. Tears trickled down both cheeks. She whispered, "My house, my beautiful, magical house," as she inhaled deeply. Then, in a controlled voice, she said "Let me think it over."

January 25, 0900 Hours

Curtis Winters breezed into Col. Mather's office without knocking and sat casually crossing his legs. "Hello Gene, it's been a long time."

Mather hated to be called Gene. He had always demanded the handful of people who knew him on a first name basis call him Eugene. The shortened version sounded childish and trite. Mather lifted his chin and answered. "Hello yourself, Curt," emphasizing the informal use of Winters' first name. "This is an unexpected surprise." That sounded dumb, surprises are always unexpected.

Winters returned an indulgent smile. "Gene, you have established a reputation as the most pro-Soviet officer in USFA. I'm here to change your mind." He paused long enough for that thought to sink in. Winters continued. "This chain of command you have hanging behind you on the wall is broken." He glanced up at the pictures of Truman, General Clark and Colonel Mather.

Mather shot back in a voice that sounded whiny, even to him. "I am a loyal soldier and I follow my orders. You, on the other hand, have always been a radical Republican who hated Roosevelt and now Truman."

"Gene, this isn't about American politics. Well actually, in a way it is, but that's not why I'm here. My visit is purely to save your skinny, self-absorbed ass. You're on the wrong side of history and it's just about to bite you. The Soviet Comintern is at work all around us. They seek world domination, nothing less. Their methods are clear." His voice rose. "All you have to do is listen. Their propaganda makes it clear, they are our enemies."

Mather held up a hand like a crossing guard. He shook his head and looked down at his desk in utter denial. "While it is true there have been several incidents attributed to the Russians, I have a strong personal relationship with Soviet

Colonel Bukinev and he has explained all of them." Mather tried to look Winters in the eye. "They truly want peace. The fence and travel restrictions are solely to control black marketeering. The shootings of Soviet soldiers in American cars were, again, the result of a criminal element involved in the black market. The alleged Soviet raid on Detachment Eight was a fabrication by an out-of-control CIC officer I just fired. "

Now it was Winters who sighed and raised both hands with a disgusted look. "Stop, do you even know who this Russian colonel is?"

Mather seemed rattled and began his ritual pipe cleaning. "Of course, he's my Soviet counterpart in Intelligence."

"No," said Winters, trying to be patient. "He is a political officer whose job it is to con you. We intercept weekly reports in which he mocks you and your people. James Cole, the man you just fired, is the only one on your entire staff who is out there trying to protect you, our people and our nation. The rest of your staff is running around chasing Nazi shadows and pretending the Soviets are our benign allies."

Mather looked as though he could take no more. He glared at his visitor and pointed the stem of his pipe. "And just who the hell are you to make these accusations? You're just one of the leftover spoiled brats of the OSS. Do you know what those of us in the real Army called you Harvard and Yale semi-heroes?" His neck stretched like a turkey. "We said OSS stood for 'Oh So Social.' Did you know that? Did you know how we despised you and your clique? Rich society boys who broke every rule—to you the war was just a big game." His voice tapered off and he stared at the wall until his cheeks cooled.

Winters sat back and waited before he spoke. "You're partly right. Many of us had connections that allowed us to bypass rules and petty bureaucrats to get things done. I still have those connections. Do you know that I appointed myself 'Ambassador for Cultural Affairs' and set up shop here in Vienna? I simply showed up and presented a letter of introduction to the interim Austrian government."

Mather grumbled, "Just what I would expect of you."

"Well, here's something else you should know. Even though Truman has dismantled America's intelligence capability, a handful of us can see the future threat and we aren't going to stand by and watch our country subverted. A group of senators, along with many of our nation's highest leaders, are preparing to fight back. They will soon begin investigating un-American activities and rooting out Communist sympathizers. My group will help find imbedded spies and neutralize them. You, Gene, are walking on very thin ice as a Soviet supporter. As I said before, wrong side of history."

Mather sank lower in his seat and fiddled with his pipe. "General Clark will not tolerate your interference."

Winters flashed a quick smile. "General Mark Clark is a good soldier. He will not oppose his president. But he is also a good American and he will not tolerate conspiring with our enemies."

Winters leaned in for his most earnest pitch. "I am here today to give you new marching orders. Do not question where they come from. Do not presume to ignore what I say. We are entering desperate times and we are prepared to use desperate measures. You, your career, even your life, are less important than our cause. We will not hesitate to eliminate obstacles. Don't be one."

Mather's temples pulsed. "Are you threatening me?"

"I am here as a friend advising you that the rules have changed. You must also change, and the first thing you must do is abandon your harassment of Major Cole. Tomorrow, he will do a prisoner exchange. He has set it all up but I want you to be there to show that our Army is united in the struggle against the Red Menace. We cannot have Army colonels who are soft on Communism. If you try to contact anyone higher up in the chain of command to report what I have just said, it will only serve to identify you as one of those obstacles that must be eliminated."

With that, Winters stood, straightened his London-tailored jacket and left. His voice trailed after him. "Good to see you again, Gene."

Colonel Eugene Mather pursed his lips and his hands began to tremble.

1030 Hours

Mather burst into the American Military Governor's office red faced and breathless. "I need to speak to General Clark immediately."

The civilian secretary was a pleasant grandmotherly type. "I'm so sorry, I'm afraid that's not possible just now."

Mather's voice was shrill. "It bloody well is possible and I demand to see the general now."

From an adjacent office, a uniformed man the size of a phone booth heard the commotion and stepped out. He looked like an ex-football player gone completely to flesh. A raging tiger might tuck its tail and slink from this monster. Between hog jowls, a stub of cigar seemed a permanent fixture. This was Major General Berringer.

"Colonel," the giant thundered, "Have you ever heard of a chain of command. You have no business here unless invited."

Mather stammered, "National security, Sir. I am here on an urgent matter. I have just been threatened by a civilian who claims to represent a subversive group within our command structure. He says I must defer to a major in my command. I must report..."

Berringer bit his cigar. "Yes, yes, you feel you must report this cock and bull story to the Governor General without substantiation. You're a brave man, Gene, taking such a big risk."

Mather froze. This general could never have known his first name. Winters must have already been here. This two-star general was one of them. He was part of the conspiracy. Mather took a wary step back and his mouth fell open slightly.

Now Berringer glowered, "Colonel, I think you may have just misunderstood what you were told. The question is not whether you work for one of your subordinates but rather whether you work for the good of the United States Army. You must understand that your loyalty is under close scrutiny and, if I were you, I would reconsider this crusade you seem determined to pursue. It is a fool's errand and you could very easily become the victim of your own misguided zeal."

Mather tightened noticeably. The big general lumbered toward him drawing close enough to share the smell of his cigar. "Now, I think this would be a good time to apologize and leave quietly. If you were to do that, I might find it in my heart to forget this breach of etiquette. Otherwise, I might just consider insubordination charges." He leaned close with his huge head right in Mather's face. "You decide. I can go either way."

1500 Hours

The funeral for Sergeant Richardson was small and awkward. He was a devout Baptist but not pushy about his religion. Since the Army would not pay to ship the body back to the States, he was buried in the city cemetery. There, it was mandatory that a Catholic priest perform the ceremony.

Cole thought the Austrian priest looked theatrical dressed in his medieval garb, chanting in Latin as he waved a little incense thing on a chain as he sprinkled what Cole assumed was holy water. No one else seemed to find it strange, this Catholic ceremony for a Baptist man.

The crowd was a strange mix of officers who mistakenly thought the dead sergeant worked for them and people from the 'disbanded' Detachment Eight. There were several Austrians in civilian clothes but no one seemed to know who they were.

When it was over and laborers began shoveling dirt, Mather pulled Cole aside. "This whole thing is a disaster." He licked his lips in the bitter cold. "I don't really don't know what's gone on but I have to believe you have some responsibility for this man's death. You claim it was the Russians but you have no proof. You are full of stories of Russian misconduct but these things only happen when you are there with no one to verify. How do you explain that?"

Cole ignored the question. "We will meet tomorrow morning at eleven for the spy exchange, Sir."

"What? How do you dare...What makes you think...?" Mather almost sputtered. "Madness, this is madness. I have worked with Russians at the highest level. They are not the wild, criminals you describe. And just who is directing this madness? Who is in charge?"

Cole grimaced and looked at the grave now being filled. "You will meet him soon. First, we must see to the defection of a high ranking Soviet officer, an executioner with more blood on his hands than any Nazi."

"We, we, we, who the hell is this we? I do not work for you and your cowboys. You work for me."

"Colonel, we both work for the same team. You will see that soon. I promise everything that will transpire is in the best interest of our country. You'll see."

January 26, 1040 Hours

Herr Honig sat glum and slumping in the backseat of an Army staff car. Outside, wind whipped the Friedensbrucke Bridge as a small crowd of American officers and Military Police assembled. The bridge had been closed to all traffic in anticipation of the prisoner exchange. Eleven o'clock came and went with no sign of the Soviets. Through the cold-fogged car window, he watched Colonel Mather pace, hissing clouds of cold vapor as he berated Major Cole.

"I wasn't told of the kidnapping. I didn't even know this Sherry White person existed. I wasn't told of the deal to exchange prisoners. Now, I find myself responsible for this whole damned carnival show." Mather paused to slow his breathing. "Will you never stop your insubordination? If this thing goes sour, I'll have you shot. Do you understand? I'll have you shot."

Cole suffered the outburst calmly with a pained expression. He looked away and spoke softly despite Mather's rage. "I see vehicles approaching. The Russians are always late just to show they're in control."

Honig turned to see the convoy of dirt brown trucks gathering at the far end of the bridge. A line of Soviet riflemen promptly lined up behind a wall that guarded the bridge entrance. He counted more than a dozen. A Soviet officer wearing a huge wheel hat and gold braid on his shoulder boards paced back and forth staring across to the Americans.

Honig had no restraints. Why should he? There was nowhere for him to run. He stepped out of the car to hear Cole whisper to Mather, "I think we should display Honig. They won't do anything until they see him." In his own way, he had always liked Cole. The American was a complicated man on the outside but inside very different, very childlike.

Colonel Mather fumed. "Don't tell me how to do my business." Then the colonel turned and shouted, "Bring the prisoner forward and stand him beside that statue of a horseman. I want some MPs with rifles to aim at the Russians. We need to look tough."

Honig was marched out into the open wind. He wore no coat, just an old suit with an open-collar shirt. The chill wind made him huddle his shoulders and neck but he stood patiently. He had been told exactly how the drill would unfold. He had only to wait.

After a brief delay, Sherry White appeared on the far end of the bridge. Two Soviet soldiers shoved her out into the open. Even from such a distance she looked ragged and tired. She wore only a plain cotton prison dress and clunky shoes. Honig had never seen her without makeup and shoulder pads. Her face was eggshell white. For ten long minutes he and Sherry White stood at opposite ends of the bridge shivering and staring at each other.

Then the Russian with gold braid gave a harsh shout. At that cue, Honig took a deep breath and began walking, but slowly. He held himself erect with as much dignity as he could muster. At the far end, Russians prodded Sherry and she too began a halting march forward. It took several tense minutes for the two to pass in the middle of the long bridge.

Honig kept his eyes straight ahead as he spoke out of the side of his mouth. "Keep walking at a steady pace. Say nothing and do not look back. Once you reach the Americans, take immediate cover but don't run. Don't give anyone a reason to become impulsive and start shooting."

Sherry nodded and continued her deliberate pace. Tears streaked her face and she sucked in a jagged breath. He knew it must be hard for her not to break into a run. As he neared the far end of the span, Honig deliberately slowed his pace. He had been instructed that he must not arrive first. The Russians could easily shoot Sherry from that distance and claim a victory saying they got their spy and deprived the Americans of theirs.

Finally reaching the Russian side, Honig was shoved into a Russian truck. He sighed and looked back to see American Military Policemen swarming to protect Sherry. Good for her, safely home.

Now he contemplated his own future. He had no great love for Russia but after learning of his wife's death in a French prison, he lost all desire to return to his native country. They said it was a heart attack. Who knows how she really died. She survived the Nazis only to die in the hands of de Gaulle's stooges. Maybe he could still do something of value for the socialist cause. The open truck rattled away as Honig stared like a lost child on the first day of school.

1700 Hours

Sherry had showered and changed into a thick sweater and wool slacks. Her hair was straight and damp. Without makeup, her face seemed drawn and pale as she sucked hard on a cigarette.

Cole knew this was going to be tough. He tried on a Gregory Peck persona, cool but not distant, as he took a seat opposite her in the interrogation room and made solid eye contact. He cleared his throat and sounded professional.

"Sherry, what happened? How were you captured?"

She shifted and looked away as she described the sudden assault by Soviet soldiers. "They came with a lot of noise. Laughing and shouting, they seemed like teenagers out for a good time. No one seemed to be in charge. I think they were a bunch of conscripts just looking for an out-of-the-way place to party. We turned the booth lights off and tried to sneak down the ladder to the subway tracks. Richardson went first but they saw him and trained their flashlight beams on him. He was blinded and held his left hand in front of his face as he drew his pistol. They started shooting. It was uncoordinated fire with most bullets going wild. Richardson got off three shots and hit at least one Russian who screamed and danced around in pain. The others settled down and riddled Richardson with rifle bullets, dozens of bullets."

She took a long draw on her cigarette and blew smoke through her nose. Her eyes were focused far away, obviously reliving the moment.

After a brief silence, she resumed. Cole didn't interrupt. "I tried to run but they tackled me. They held me down on the ground and searched my body, every inch of my body. Once they were sure I had no weapons, the search became a game.

The boys took turns, laughing and probing, holding my arms above my head. I tried to fight back but there were so many I could hardly move."

"Were you raped?"

"Well no." She blew a long tight stream of smoke. "I wasn't raped, at least not technically." He paused and let her take her time. "I was, apparently, a source of great amusement to the young soldiers, like a girl prisoner in a boys' high school locker room."

Cole tried to hide his concern. "After that, what happened? Were you interrogated?"

"Oh yes. They took me to some sort of jail. There, I was questioned for about two days. There were two of them working in shifts, a Soviet captain and another man in a suit. They were surprised I spoke Russian. They asked silly questions. I laughed once. That earned me a punch in the face. I didn't laugh after that."

"What kind of silly questions?"

"Oh, you know the kind of stuff they always ask. What is our 'order of battle'? What is our force strength? What were our future plans regarding the Soviets? It went on like that. Eventually, I convinced them I was little more than a secretary and had no knowledge of such things."

She coughed and turned to Cole with a weak smile. "When they were done, I was left alone, utterly alone. Food came through a slot. No one picked up the dirty plates. I had a stinking toilet bucket that was never emptied. I lost track of time. There was no sound, no movement. God, did I need a cigarette. I paced and talked to myself. I felt lost."

Cole abandoned his dispassionate interview and leaned forward. She seemed to snap out of her reverie and looked at him.

"Sherry, I am so sorry this happened. I feel personally responsible for not protecting you and Sergeant Richardson. This was just too much to ask of you."

She was fidgety, taking quick shallow drags on her cigarette and tapping her free hand on the chair arm. She looked at a blank wall. "Do you know what I thought about as I paced in my cell? I thought I was going to die and wondered how they would kill me. But, even more than that, I thought of..." She looked at him earnestly. "I thought of you."

James Cole leaned back with a completely blank face. "Me?"

She nodded, a bit too vigorously. "Yes, I thought of you. I have known many men in my life but none of them ever made me feel safe. None of them ever made me feel confident in myself. None of them made me feel that I mattered to them."

After a long, awkward silence she stood. Moving quietly around the table, she approached the confused James Cole. She paused for a moment and then bent to wrap both arms around his neck before settling into his lap. She nestled her head deep into the hollow of his shoulder. At five foot, ten, she was taller than most men but her size was in perfect proportion to the lanky major. They fit together.

Cole looked stricken and helpless. While his mind was paralyzed, his left hand moved on its own volition to find the small of her back. He dropped his pen and allowed his other hand to settle between her shoulder blades and press her to him. It was an awkward embrace, but it felt right to both of them. Silently, they held each other without speaking. James began to rock ever so slightly and moved his hand to stroke her hair.

In the darkened observation room, Lieutenant Cynthia Ryan rose from her chair to stand before the one-way mirror. Mrs. Parks, Captain Belcher and Captain Roland looked at her as she whispered. "The debrief is over. Let's get out of here. Go quietly so we don't disturb them." The others nodded, gathered their paperwork and tip-toed out into the hall. Even there, no one spoke.

1815 Hours

When she had calmed and her breathing settled to a peaceful rhythm, James whispered, "Let me walk you back to your place. You need rest."

She pulled away from her nesting position on his lap but reluctantly. Her mouth made a quick effort at a smile, almost an apologetic look. Before she was quite standing, he pulled her close and gave her a soft clumsy kiss on the cheek, just a peck. She tucked her head and blushed as she stood and turned to leave.

She had no coat and the night was stinging cold. He put his arm around her and walked her to the steps of her apartment. "You must rest. I will check on you tomorrow but not before ten. Tonight, it is important you rest."

She took his hand in both of hers and clutched it to her chest. Her voice was so quiet he wasn't sure he heard the words. "Thank you. Thank you for caring." Then an awkward pause before she whispered, "I love you."

Sherry turned and went inside leaving Cole a statue on her steps. In his entire life, no one had said those three words to him, no one. A cold tear ran down the contour of his face. He gathered his collar, took a deep breath and walked back into the darkness.

January 30, 1100 Hours

Wednesday came bitter and damp. Heavy clouds lumbered across the sky threatening to unload any second. Sergei's wife and son were bundled in wool coats and scarves. He wore the same black fur coat and hat with a red star he had worn at Lushka's execution. They were just about the only visitors at the Prater amusement park. Stepping carefully around icy puddles they maneuvered under the Ferris wheel toward a long row of tents. One had a picture of a bearded woman. Standing before it, Mrs. Zelenkov looked frightened. The boy held his mother's hand and twisted back and forth as he played with fingers in his mouth. Sergei forced a brave face and pulled back the tent flap. The family ducked and entered a dark new world.

Inside the tent, the light was dim and the smell of cold damp canvas oppressive. The side show crew was gone. In their place, a small crowd of uniformed American soldiers stood waiting beside a huge black limousine. Sergei's wife began to cry. Major Cole stepped up and spoke to her in his best Russian. "Please Madam, you have nothing to fear. We want only to protect you. Come, I have a car to take you…"

Sergei interrupted, "We go nowhere until I have the passports and the money you promised."

"Of course, of course, but they are at our office building. It would have been foolish to bring them here."

Sergei's hand went to his holster but he did not pull his gun. "No tricks," he demanded.

Cole nodded with all the sincerity of a salesman, "No tricks, I promise."

Sergei walked to the car and inspected it. He wasn't sure exactly what he was looking for but he smelled deception and he intended to be careful. Eventually he motioned and his family nervously entered the back seat. When everyone was loaded, Cole asked them to lower window shades built into the doors.

Tent flaps parted and the limousine roared out. Merging into traffic, two almost identical cars fell in behind. They stayed in formation until coming to a rotary where five roads met at a statue fountain. The three cars made multiple circuits around the circular roadway during which they passed each other repeatedly speeding, weaving and jockeying positions to confuse anyone following. Finally, each turned off onto a different road.

After a tortuous trip through alleys and back streets they arrived at the Detachment building. Cole opened the car door for Mrs. Zelenkov and acted the perfect gentleman. She looked at Sergei for approval and then exited one tenuous step at a time. Her hand lingered in his until her fingers were drawn away.

"Please Madam, come inside for some tea while your husband and I work out some details," said Cole. She took the squirming boy by his shoulder and followed Lieutenant Cynthia Ryan with quick glances back over her shoulder.

Cole smiled, "My men are bringing down suitcases with new clothes. I guessed the sizes. And your documents, Swiss passports with Austrian entry stamps, Swiss driver's certificates with several renewal stamps, immunization cards, health care cards, keys and ownership documents for an apartment in Geneva."

Sergei had been silent for a long time. But now he brought hard eyes to bear on Cole. "And the money?"

"A briefcase containing a small amount of Austrian Military Schillings, 200,000 French Francs and 500,000 Swiss Francs will be brought in a moment. That should cover you for several years. At your apartment, you will find all the paperwork to start a new job for the United Nations. I don't know details but you will work it out."

Sergei nodded slowly, still suspicious. "Will I have an American contact in Geneva?"

Cole shrugged. "No, you'll be completely on your own. Frankly, I doubt you would ever trust an American. You'll be free to build whatever new life you want. We won't bother you. All we ask is a picture. We need a photograph to convince the Russians we have you. Ah, here comes my delightful superior, Colonel Mather, as well as the man you worked with before, Major Aalpeter."

Sergei didn't like any of this. It wasn't going as he had demanded. He smelled a trap and kept his holster flap unbuttoned as the men approached. Colonel Mather wore a trench coat and a distrusting look. Small, hawk nosed and fidgety as a pickpocket, Sergei knew of Colonel Mather but had never seen him in person. Major Aalpeter, on the other hand, he recognized from previous meetings.

No one spoke as they lined up against a damaged brick wall. Cole leaned to Sergei and whispered. "I'm sure your former bosses will recognize this place. This is the parking lot where your failed raid occurred. When they see all the Americans around you, they will not doubt your captive status."

Two American MPs knelt before them and a photographer with a huge camera snapped several pictures. Sergei did his best to keep a blank expression. He had seen thousands of prisoners in his time and they all wore the same empty, melancholy stare of hopelessness he now imitated. The pose could have been a family photo, of a very dysfunctional family. Pictures over, the crowd broke up. Colonel Mather extended a handshake but Sergei ignored him. Embarrassed, the colonel withdrew his hand and sulked away. Aalpeter nodded farewell and left.

A nondescript car, much smaller than the limousine, pulled up and an MP opened the trunk. The suitcases were already loaded. Captain Belcher opened a briefcase to display documents and neat banded packs of money in several currencies. Sergei looked carefully and selected one pack to thumb through. Satisfied, he tossed it back. Belcher added the briefcase to the trunk and closed it. Everything was ready.

In short order, Major Zelenkov, flanked by two MPs, squeezed in the back seat with his wife and son up front. The driver, Billy Connors, set off toward the Belleview Hotel. Billy used small side streets and checked his rearview mirror constantly.

At a small intersection, an Austrian policeman held up a white glove and tooted a whistle on a cord. Billy rolled down the window and shouted, "What's the problem?" The policeman answered in German. Billy shrugged to indicate he didn't understand. Sergei translated from the back seat but his English was terrible. "He says accident is ahead. You must go for right, one block only."

Billy waved to the policeman and cranked the steering wheel. The MPs in the back seat looked concerned but said nothing. Halfway down a narrow side street jammed with haphazardly parked cars, two men in French Army uniforms struggled to push a small Citroen. Billy honked and leaned out the window to shout, "Hey, get that thing out of the way."

One of the men, a French captain, stepped to Billy's window. "*Pardonez mois*, we have a broken auto. Could you please to help us to move it a bit?"

Billy shut off the motor and set his parking brake. He turned to the MPs. "There's a car behind me so I can't back up. I'd better help or we'll be stuck here. I'll be right back." But he didn't come right back. Billy and the Frenchmen struggled but the small car would not go up over the curb and there was no room to pass. Billy motioned for the MPs to help. They were hefty fellows. All members of the 202nd Military Police were required to be over six feet tall and athletic so they would appear intimidating to the other four-power police.

Exasperated, one of the guards threw open his door and jumped out leaning back to his companion. "Stay here; I'll give these bozos a hand. You watch the Commie." He joined the pushers by turning his back to the stalled car and using his fingers to grab under the bumper. He strained to lift but in the midst of a grunting push, he realized the others weren't helping. Billy Conner had his hands raised as if in a stage coach robbery. The other MP was out of the car now standing at gunpoint before two Austrian men.

The French captain held a pistol and smiled at the Military Policeman. His English was suddenly much improved. "Sorry for the inconvenience old man, but we must now relieve you of your prisoners. Once again, you Americans have done the difficult work for me but I shall take home the prize. Don't even consider going for your gun. These Austrian thugs will get a bonus if they kill you. Please don't cost me the extra money." He tilted his head and raised eyebrows in a questioning way.

Sergei was out of the car helping his wife and son. For the first time since defecting, he allowed a slight smile. "Come my dear, we have a slight change of plans. We will not go to the American hotel. I have better accommodations arranged for us."

The Americans were quickly disarmed and tied up. As the Frenchmen tightened ropes around Billy Connors, Captain Devereaux slid a roll of bills into his shirt pocket without a hint of recognition. Then the other French soldier started the Citroen and they drove off. Devereaux took the wheel of the American-provided car and the two Austrians followed. Billy Connors and the two American MPs were left on a curb hobbled by tight ropes. They didn't look happy.

In the Citroen, Sergei sat back with a much relaxed posture. They drove south through the bombed out Miriahlf neighborhood and into the unguarded French Zone. Twenty minutes later, they were deep in French territory and safe from American eyes. There, they parked at a small hotel overlooking a rail yard. Devereaux arrived close behind. Once inside, Sergei's wife took their son aside and left the men to talk.

"So, my friend Devereaux, I am quite happy to see you." They chatted in their silly style with Devereaux speaking very bad Russian and former Soviet Major Sergei Zelenkov speaking first-year student French. Sergei's wife looked from one to the other in confusion.

"Tonight," said Devereaux, "you will board a diplomatic Pullman car on the French train. The other Allies cannot inspect it. You will be the only ones in the car. I used my position in the embassy to set it up but I'm afraid that may be just about my last opportunity to help. Once you arrive in Lienz, you must find your own way. I am going to Salzburg to follow up on a lead. I pray you good fortune in your quest." He made his silly windmill salute and was gone.

2000 Hours

Svetlana agreed to meet Captain Charley Woods but only if he came over to the Soviet Zone. He was happy enough to comply and made a grand entrance to the small restaurant with a wave and a wide grin. Charley shook a few snowflakes from his heavy belted wool uniform overcoat and rushed to her table where he startled her with two quick kisses on the cheek in the French style.

She pushed him back with a smile. In English she said, "You always surprise me American. I am used to being the one to make passes. No Russian man has ever been so bold."

Charley rubbed his hands and blew onto them. "Then your Russian men are fools. I have never known a woman so beautiful and appealing."

"But you say this to all women you want to sex, no?"

He appeared to give the matter some thought. "No, only the ones I want to spy on."

A waiter appeared and seemed embarrassed. He spoke softly in Russian and Svetlana shrugged before responding. She spoke to Charley in an off-hand way. "There's no meat again tonight but the Goulash is also good without. I ordered for us."

"No problem," said Charley, "It isn't the food I am looking forward to."

She let out a belly laugh that seemed to frighten the other patrons. Laying a hand on his shoulder she drew him a little closer. He seemed to enjoy it. "So, my American, shall we spy on each other again tonight."

He grinned like a prom king. "Oh, I really do hope so."

And so, as the night wore on, arrangements were made for another spy trade. This time, it would be much more important spies.

January 31, 0745 Hours

Mrs. Zelenkov had never worn such fine clothes. She ran her hand over the smooth felt of her new coat and gathered a silk scarf around her neck. Her son looked handsome in his leather pants and knee stockings. Sergei seemed a little uncomfortable in his new businessman's suit and hat. They were a fine looking family ready to begin a fine new life.

The train ride had been stressful. At every stop she had wanted to pull back a curtain and see what was happening but Sergei would not allow it. The train car was elegantly paneled in walnut with leather and brass furniture. There was bread and cheese on silver platters along with heavy crystal decanters of wine. It would have been a delight if not for the fear of travelling through Soviet territory, now become a dangerous place for a defector.

A steward knocked and announced they had arrived at their destination, the city of Lienz in the British Zone. Sergei helped her disembark the train and called to a porter who loaded their bags and led them through clouds of locomotive steam to find a taxi stand. They walked arm in arm and laughed. For the first time, she allowed herself to think they might be safe.

At the pickup point, a young man with cold-reddened cheeks held a chalk board with the scrawled name 'Johann Sweitzer.' Mrs. Zelenkov put a hand to her mouth to hide her grin.

"That's you Sergei. That's you, your new name."

He grinned back at her and said, "And you are Frau Sweitzer."

Turning to the sign holder, he said, "Yes, I am Herr Sweitzer." The boy made a half bow and removed his cap.

"Sir, I have a car for you and a message also."

Sergei took the envelope and tore it open to find a telegram. He unfolded and read the teletype printed letters. She looked over his shoulder. "Pass to Tyrol closed- stop. Driver will take you to Malsburg-stop. New development- stop. Klein and friends near Salzburg- stop. Contact me when possible- stop. Signed, Dev- stop."

"What does it mean?" asked the new Frau Sweitzer.

Sergei folded the telegram and gave her a look that seemed full of false confidence. "We will be spending the night in a small mountain village. The passes into Tyrol are snowed in. So," he forced a smile, "We will make this a vacation, a small winter vacation."

January 28, 0945 Hours

James Cole twisted a doorbell that tinkled like the little bell on his Western Union delivery bicycle. He took a deep breath when Sherry answered wearing a plain housecoat and a soft smile. She looked tired but largely recovered. Her apartment was dark and a bit musty. She closed the door after him and hesitated slightly.

"Get you a coffee?"

"Yes please. How are you feeling?"

She took a pot from the stove and poured two steaming cups, then paused for a moment and spoke to the cups. "I hope you were not upset by last night... but I do not apologize." She turned to face him. "I meant what I said."

Cole stammered a bit. He was in uncharted territory, human emotions. "To be honest, I don't know how to react. You caused an unaccustomed flood of emotion, pleasant but alien."

"Alien, how so?" She sat with her elbows on the table holding her cup in both hands and blowing away the steam.

He shifted in his chair. "My relations with women have always been clumsy. I'm afraid I'll disappoint you... and I don't think I could stand that."

She sipped thoughtful and patient before answering. "I have known you for more than five months. That's not a lifetime but in that time we've shared a lifetime's worth of adventures. I've seen you under incredible stress and seen how you deal with people. I admire you. When you walk into a room, I feel as though everything is going to be all right. You make me feel as though I'm all right. I don't ever want to lose that feeling."

Cole realized he wasn't breathing. "Sherry, I'm afraid. I care about you too much to let you see the real me. I'm not even sure there is a real me." He looked out a frosty window and saw nothing. "On our first raid I shot a German guard in the head. It was cold-blooded execution. Later, Cynthia Ryan asked me how it felt and I just told her it was simply the expedient thing to do. What I really wanted to say was that I don't know how it felt."

He paused, gathering courage. "I don't know how it felt, because it wasn't me. It was Tyron Power, a GI Joe war hero that I was playing who shot that man. All my accomplishments, all my deeds were really done by some actor or figure I was portraying. Without my roles, I am just an empty shell of a man. I'm afraid of large groups because the more people there are, the more likely someone will see through my performance to the failed actor standing naked on the stage."

Sherry considered. "I don't believe you. You give names to your roles but they're always you. I think the only person you're trying to fool is you. Tell me about your life and why you feel you need a mask to hide your successes."

Cole sat back and relaxed just a bit. He could be a storyteller. "I don't remember my earliest years. I ran away from a drunk and brutal father when I was six. For the next three years I lived on the street as a beggar and thief. It was the depression and the streets teemed with abandoned children. I was big for my age and got a night job in the garment district at nine. I slept in the factory attic but I was able to attend school in the daytime."

He formed a smile as he remembered. "At twelve, I was walking to school when I saw a bunch of hooligans harassing a kid. He was a wimpy crybaby but they had ganged up on him and that wasn't right. I jumped in and whipped the whole bunch. Then I walked the kid home. His name was Harvey, Harvey Feldon."

Sherry looked interested. Cole kept on, "He lived in a big house. To me, it seemed a castle. His mother was a fierce old biddy with wild waving arms that could have scared the devil. When she saw her bloody son, she thought I had done it and tried to chase me off by shaking her fists. The boy tugged at her skirt and screamed for her to stop. Finally, she listened and called me back. When she found out I was homeless, she told me I could stay in their servant quarters if I agreed to be Harvey's body guard. I went to school with him and also worked as a telegram delivery boy in the afternoon. I stayed for eight years but I was never part of the family."

He felt he needed to explain. "They were Jewish and I was goy, an infidel. They were always polite but I lived and ate separately, avoiding the main house. I was an alien, unclean and unwanted. They spoke German in the house, even to their servants. That's where I learned the language. If you listen closely, you'll hear my slight Bavarian accent. They were originally from Nuremburg."

"That must have been lonely," said Sherry.

"Oh, I don't know. I had a roof and good food and I felt valuable as long as I did my bodyguard duties. Harvey was a friend of sorts. He was always embarrassed to have me around his Jewish friends so I held back unless there was trouble. Alone together, sometimes he would talk of his hopes and dreams but I was just a listener. He didn't care what I thought."

Cole's face seemed to warm. "But then, there were the movies."

"The movies?" Sherry said.

"Yes, the Saturday movies. We always went to the Saturday movies. There, in the dark with that magic beam of light on the screen, I could fade into the characters I saw. They were heroes and great men. I yearned to be just like them. Later, in my room, I acted out the parts."

"So then, how did you go to college?"

"The old woman—her name was Molly Feldon—called me in just before graduation and gave me a lecture. She criticized me for never dating but understood my hesitation since I had poor clothes and not much money. I think she felt a little guilty that she had supported me in such a meager state. Anyway, she knew I was an avid reader and reasonably smart so she arranged for me to attend the New York University with the full tuition and dormitory costs covered. She even found me a job as a stage hand for the school's theater troupe."

He breathed a deep satisfied breath. "I found myself there, or more accurately, I lost myself there in the theater. It was a magic, make believe world where you could be anything. I worked with the actors, rehearsed with the actors, read for the actors, but I didn't do shows. To walk onto the stage before a sea of expectant faces was paralyzing. The instructors said I had talent but I had to get over the stage fright. I never did."

"More coffee?" His untouched cup had grown cold.

"No, that's okay. When the war began, I enlisted. As a fluent German speaking actor, I was perfect for the spy game. On my first mission from Britain to France, my plane was shot down, killing the pilots. I was injured and the German officer's uniform I wore was soaked with blood. I had black oil stains on my pants from crawling out of the wreckage. It was a perfect costume, a battle hero's outfit. I wandered from German unit to unit demanding help. They would snap to, salute and offer me aid. I would then kill them."

He looked at Sherry's face but saw no condemnation. "I found a communication center and walked in as though I owned it. The commander was an obsequious lieutenant and I was dressed as a captain. I took over the place and put him to work concentrating his equipment close together, telling him it would be easier to protect. Then I rigged a bomb, took off in a staff car and blew the place to pieces. My next mission... well, you get the idea. That's how I came to be a major in intelligence."

Now it was Sherry's turn. "That was the war. That's what needed to be done. You were a hero. You're still a hero. The things you have done here were so bold I couldn't believe it."

"But it wasn't me. It was John Wayne or Randolph Scott or somebody."

"Ridiculous, it was you. You just use those actors to pattern your actions. You were the one thinking on your feet, taking the risks, making the decisions. They were just images. You were the hero. Stop demeaning what you've done. It's you, not them, I saw in my dreams. It's you, not them, I want to spend my life with."

James Cole felt his fingertips tremble. This was real, no role to play. His voice faded. "You do remember that I'm married."

Sherry straightened and leveled a hard look at him. "Yes, and you have to fix that. I know your wife and I know you and we both know that the two of you don't belong together. She is not the woman for you, I am." Her voice sounded tough.

Cole looked at her for a second and then they both broke into laughter. He chuckled, "Are you always going to be so shy?"

She put a hand on his, "Are you?"

CHAPTER SIX-FEBRUARY

February 1, 1500 Hours

Deb Cole paced nervously in the bitter wind. Finally, she gathered her courage and climbed the stone stairway to Colonel Mather's row house to bang the large iron knocker. She turned away, but stopped, took a deep breath and went back to knock harder.

The door opened and Frau Huntzof stood facing her former employer. They both hesitated, deciding how to act. Then Deb brushed by her into the parlor. There, she spun and clutched her purse almost defensively. "Please tell Mrs. Mather that I am here to see her."

Charlotte hesitated before raising her eyebrows and making a small, condescending smile. Without comment, she left. Deb muttered and paced like a cat until she heard the lady's voice.

"Oh hello dear, how are you?" Deb was struck to see her wearing a formal dress with a pearl necklace and matching earrings even in early afternoon. Mrs. Mather put her hands together as though ready to pray. It was an indulgent gesture of a powerful lady meeting an underling.

The words rushed out of Deb. "I'm so sorry to trouble you, Ma'am but I find myself in a predicament. They have taken away my house and I have no place to live. I'm in a hotel, but it's just temporary. I would greatly appreciate any help you and your husband might give to find me a home. I feel so lost in this foreign land."

Mrs. Mather smiled. It was a sweet but obviously insincere gesture. "Why Deborah, that's just awful. I didn't know anything about this. In fact, I haven't seen you or your husband since the night of the grand ball. You certainly seemed to have a good time then. So tell me, why has your husband not taken care of this?"

Deb stretched her neck as though straightening a kink. "We are going through a bad patch. He's in a different hotel."

"Nonetheless, dear, it is his responsibility. Eugene has no input to the Housing Office. They're in a whole different division. It would be improper for him to intervene. Now, tell me about this bad patch. Is it serious? If so, that can be a real difficulty. It's very important that you remedy any problems."

Deb tried to hold back but tears bubbled out of her. She started to embrace Mrs. Mather but the older woman recoiled. Deb gasped and whimpered. "I just want my house back. I don't really care about James. All he does is work. But I want my house, my beautiful house." She stamped a foot like a two year old.

"Anger will not help, my dear. You must reconcile and soon. An Army dependent wife must be under her husband's control in occupied Austria."

The older lady's tone softened. "Listen, they all behave badly sometimes. It's just the cross we all carry. Take him back and ignore his little infidelities. You'll live. You may not get your mansion back but you'll soon have a suitable house and a suitable life. That's just the way it is. Now run along and find your husband. Get him to call the Housing Office. It will all be fine."

Deb saw no help would be found here. She made a small, numb headshake and turned to the door. Frau Huntzov let her out with only a hint of amusement.

1800 Hours

Dinner at the Mather's was at six sharp regardless of what else was happening in the world. The colonel was dour, as usual. He poked at his meal and held up a piece of toast demanding, "Is this supposed to be bread? This is barely a cracker."

Frau Huntzov was just ladling out soup. She answered, "You know there is a bread crisis in this town. All crops in Austria were destroyed in the war. Now winter is come and there is no wheat. Your toast is made from some sort of ground nut meal and I had to bribe the baker to get that. It's tasty enough."

Mather sneered. "I suppose. An early winter storm seriously cut crop yields in Canada and the US. Russia, of course has no crops to speak of. Wheat futures are…" He realized that no one was listening so, with an even deeper scowl, he went back to eating.

For a time, the silence was broken only by the sounds of china and silver. Then Mather wiped his lips and looked thoughtful. "I had a most interesting lunch with Colonel Bukinev. He knows a great deal about our errant CIC Detachment. He actually knew every member by name."

Mather stretched arms onto the table with silverware in his hands. His face morphed into a tight little smile. "He thinks Cole has been seduced by a fanatic band of warmongers who just can't accept that the war is over. He calls them terrorists. He says Cole is a lunatic driven by bloodlust."

Mrs. Mather chewed and replied in an offhand way. "That seems a bit harsh. I think you should consider the source."

"Of course, but he knows so much about them it makes me wonder. He said Cole was seen drunk on his ear out in front of the American Bar in the company of an unknown man, probably his contact in their little secret organization. Bukinev knew tidbits about others. The Captain Roland who is such a good translator—our Russian friend thinks he is a homosexual. If that's true, I'll drum him out in a heartbeat."

"Again Eugene, I don't think you can rely on a Russian for information about your own people. It's really little more than gossip."

"Yes, you're right. It really is gossip. He said their female lieutenant—I don't remember her name—is loose, with a real eye for the men." Mather chuckled. "He even called Mrs. Cole a whore."

Mrs. Mather looked struck. She put a napkin to her mouth and looked away. "Good Lord," she blurted. "I hoped you wouldn't hear anything like that." There was a long pause before she continued. "Deborah was here today. She said James has left her and the Housing Office has taken away their house."

"That mansion? Maybe the housing people just came to their senses and realized that a major had no business in such a home, particularly while we live in this dump. But tell me, why did he leave her?"

Mrs. Mather chose her words precisely, "She didn't say but when I advised her to patch things up and ignore his indiscretions, I got the distinct impression that he might not be the one who strayed."

"So Cole's wife is alone here in Austria. That's a violation of Occupation Regulations and of my personal orders." He sucked something in his teeth and seemed to find that news amusing.

"Now Eugene, don't do anything rash. There are lives involved, a family to consider."

He just smiled and sipped his coffee.

February 3, 1200 Hours

The train exhaled huge clouds of steam as it built pressure. James Cole faced Deb and tried to be civil. "It's a sleeper car. You're booked straight through to Bremerhaven, Germany. A USO representative will meet the train as you arrive. They will give you a ride to the ship. I purchased a ticket on the USS America in a first class cabin. "

She looked at him with a cold stare. "You think you're rid of me but you have no idea. When I get home I'm going to get a lawyer and take everything from you. I'll get your salary, your belongings and your retirement. I'll leave you nothing."

He shrugged. "Deb, I'm being kicked out of the Army. They call it a RIF, reduction in force. I'll be taking a boat home on April the first. I'll have no salary. You know I don't own anything and I won't have a retirement. In this envelope you'll find official orders, your tickets and enough cash to last you at least six months. Spend it wisely. I'll send more when I can." He grimaced. "Deb, I'm sorry things didn't work out but don't be bitter. It's time to move on."

She crossed her arms bunching up her heavy wool coat. "I never even liked you. I don't know why I married you." She looked at her shoes. "I do thank you for my house. I loved my house. I took three full rolls of film so I can have pictures made. I will always remember my wonderful house." She turned away but stopped. "And the ball, I will never forget the grand ball." Her voice broke as she fought tears. "Thank you." And with that, she climbed three steps into her train car without another look.

She was gone. Cole wasn't sure what he felt. He was happy to see her go but with her, part of his life was being erased.

Feb 4, 0817 Hours

The meeting was tense. Cole stopped pacing to give the Detachment members seated around the conference table a tough but lovable Spencer Tracey look. He leaned onto the table. "We told the Russians we had a high ranking KGB officer to trade for Phyllis but we don't. Soviet Major Zelenkov has escaped our custody. We intended to use the murderous son of a bitch as barter and then let the Russians do what they do to spies who get captured. Now, with nothing to trade, we must get creative."

Lieutenant Cynthia Ryan chirped in as she so often did. "Sir, I don't see how creativity will help us. I mean, it was great what you did to rescue Sherry White, but what do we possibly have to trade for this political guy. It sounds as though it'll take a lot since he's such a big timer. Are we maybe going to do another raid?"

Cole was still Spencer Tracy. He made a wry smile and let his eyebrows pop for a second. "A raid is out of the question. We don't know where he's being held but we can be sure there are layers of troops surrounding him. No, we must use deception. We need a fake Russian major, any volunteers?"

Everyone at the table unconsciously pulled back into their seats. Cole let his smile linger. "Okay, here are pictures of our guy, Major Sergei Zelenkov. He's quite a handsome fellow. Just ask Lieutenant Ryan."

For once, Cynthia Ryan looked almost embarrassed enough to blush as she recalled their FKK encounter with the naked Russian. Cole savored the moment and went on. "All right then, it's decided. Roland will be our volunteer. He'll dye his hair and get a uniform made. He's taller and paler than Zelenkov but, from a distance, he'll do."

Roland's neck stiffened and his eyes began searching as though someone at the table might rescue him.

Cole went on, "Now, we don't intend to let Roland get close enough for the Ruskies to make a positive ID. We have to create such a disturbance it will disrupt the exchange so we can get Phyllis back without losing our decoy. Any ideas to save Roland's butt... any?"

Cole waited patiently. The crowd set to grumbling and looking at each other. Belcher finally made a pained face and held out an open hand. "How about a riot?"

1330 Hours

Billy Connors arrived on schedule and Major Cole skipped down the stairs slapping his gloved hands together. "I love the cold, don't you, Billy? It makes you feel alive. It makes you feel as though anything is possible. On a day like this, a man should be able to dismiss his demons and bring out his angels."

Billy, the driver, looked suspicious. He knew Cole well enough to know the man didn't make speeches without a reason. The major clamored into the back seat tucking his wool coat after him.

"Just drive, we're going to talk." Billy pulled out onto the busy Ringstrasse. Cole smiled. Billy Connors had good reason to be worried. He was clearly a suspect in Zelenkov's escape. Perhaps he was thinking that no one ever got shot in such a public place.

Cole watched the scenery pass. It was a brilliant, clear day but well below freezing. He began talking to the window. "It's cold outside. The people are suffering. Look at them, they don't have proper clothes or shoes and, even worse, they don't have food."

He leaned over the seat with his face almost touching Billy's ear. "What are we going to do about that, Billy? What are we going to do?"

1500 Hours

After dropping Major Cole off, Billy Connors made some phone calls and then crossed the bridge into the Soviet Zone. He had been there so often the Soviet guards all knew him on sight and waved his car through their checkpoint. He turned down a small street into the bomb-devastated part of town where he did most of his black market business.

He wasn't happy about this meeting. First of all, he wasn't going to make any money from the deal. Even worse, he was taking a personal risk. That's not the way he liked to do business. He was about to hustle his most important business contacts but what could he do? Major Cole was not a man to be crossed.

In an abandoned warehouse, four men with bad attitudes, bad suits and bad haircuts sat waiting. They shared a common look of surly impatience and mistrust behind a table covered with a shabby cloth. Billy knew, under that table, weapons were almost certainly pointed at him. This was going to be a tough sell.

He took a deep breath and started with his usual cheery tone, "Good morning gentlemen, have I got a deal for you? All you have to do is spread some rumors and get me some names. You'll each make a thousand and with absolutely no risk to you." He kept his bright smile but Billy's collar felt damp despite the chill. The men stared back at him with cold, dark eyes. No one responded.

February 4, 1050 Hours

Cole inspected the fake Russian uniform. Roland's formerly blonde hair now looked like a bad black shoeshine. Little details didn't matter. No one was going to see the imitation Major Zelenkov up close. He patted Roland's chest. "You could fool me." The tall captain forced a smile but his eyes were wide as a trapped rabbit's. Cole sounded confident, almost sincere. "I'm sure this is going to work. I'm positive."

Roland answered without humor, "I'll bet the Russians felt the same way when they attacked our building."

Cole just shrugged and thumped Roland on the chest again. "Just be a good Russian, stiff, chin up and shoulders back. You'll be fine." Then he turned back to the empty bridge. The Russian entourage was late, as usual. "Just don't be too late," he muttered to himself.

He paced with hands behind his back looking very much like an oversized Napoleon anticipating Waterloo. He had put a lot of faith in Billy Connors, not really a man deserving much faith. Eleven o'clock came and went. The streets were quiet, not a car or pedestrian. There weren't even any damned pigeons. The very air went completely silent. Eleven twenty, nothing stirred. Finally, at eleven thirty two, the Russian caravan rolled up to their side of the bridge.

"Hurry," Cole mumbled through his teeth, "We're running out of time."

The Russians milled about wasting precious minutes. At eleven forty two, Cole saw a man in a dark suit among the distant crowd. Everyone else was in uniform. That must be Phyllis. He turned to his team and shouted, "Bring the prisoner forward." The Americans made a show of pushing the Russian-uniformed Roland out onto the bridge. His hands were loosely tied in front. Belcher placed the round hat with a blue KGB band on Roland's head and cocked it just as Sergei Zelenkov did.

It was almost noon and sun beat down from a cloudless sky to make the frigid bridge seem tolerable. There was little movement among the Russians. From a side street, distant shouts could be heard but they were still far off.

Cole turned to Belcher, "Push him. Make him start walking, but slowly. He has to walk slowly, very slowly."

Roland gulped air and took his first small steps. Everyone else stepped back to make sure the Russians could see him moving. Shouts from the street behind were growing more frequent. Across the bridge, there seemed to be some confusion among the Russians. Phyllis was being shoved around and lectured by a finger pointing officer. Cole was dying inside.

At twelve eighteen, Phyllis was finally thrust onto the bridge but fell to his knees. "Get up," Cole whispered, "Get up." And slowly the man in a suit did rise. Clumsy and slow, he struggled but he did get up. Once standing, he staggered a bit as Russian troops taunted him. With unsteady steps, the man began to move. Roland was halfway to the crest of the bridge. "Faster, move faster you lazy Swiss fool," Cole shouted in frustration.

Phyllis stumbled along. His hands were bound and, as he came closer, it was obvious he had been badly beaten. Roland came to the crest of the bridge and halted. Phyllis was still 50 meters away from him. Without warning, crowds began streaming out of an alley behind Cole. Several agitators yelled in German, "Take the bridge." It was a food riot, one of many throughout the city demanding the Allies increase supplies of basic foods like bread and milk. Billy Connors had done his job and arranged a full scale riot.

Cole screamed, "Everyone, move—now." The soldiers guarding the American side of the bridge climbed into trucks and sped away from the mob. Detachment members peeled off uniform coats and hats to reveal white shirts with Red Cross armbands. They mixed with the surging crowd. Actually, they had no choice. The throng became a sea of angry arms and bodies in churning motion that swept all of them along.

Roland threw off his ropes and broke into a dead run towards the Russian side. As he came beside Phyllis, he turned and almost tackled the faltering diplomat. The Russians watched in confusion but, before they could act, the entire bridge was overtaken by a crowd that flowed toward them like waters of a burst dam.

Roland wrapped his arms around the bloody hapless spy and shielded him until met by the Detachment team with a folding stretcher. They quickly loaded Phyllis and hustled him back off the bridge fighting every inch of the way and screaming in German, "wounded man, out of the way." There were shots somewhere but they seemed far off.

The team fought their way against the flow of rioters until reaching the one remaining Army truck at the bridge entrance. Demonstrators had already climbed over it and smashed windows. Belcher fought them as he pulled back a canvas cover revealing huge Red Cross markings. Despite the angry crowd, Phyllis was loaded into the truck and the team drove off yelling in German, "Out of the way, wounded on board."

Cole sat in back with the rescued man. "Welcome home, Sir. I hope your injuries are not serious." Blood streamed from matted white hair down onto his face. He began to sob.

"I am so sorry. I told them everything."

1550 Hours

They rushed Phyllis to the Detachment building where a Medic stood waiting. The old man was still crying, still shaking his head. Even on the stretcher, he tugged pitifully at Cole's sleeve and whispered as he was carried up the entry steps.

"I tried to be strong and resist. When that failed, I tried to lie. I am so sorry. I finally gave them names and told them of our operations. Now they know about Paperclip, Syracuse, Renard and Ramona. They know it all. You must get our agents out. You must protect them. You must."

Cole tried to calm the man. Once inside, the Medic stuck a tranquilizing shot into a pale arm and told everyone they would have to wait until the patient was stable. Cole relinquished his hold on the stretcher and watched the Medic transfer Phyllis to a makeshift bed.

Belcher leaned to Cole sounding concerned. "All those names, do you know what they mean?" Cole shook his head. Mrs. Parks stood quietly in the doorway. She joined the two men and glanced all around to see who might overhear.

Seeing no one, she whispered, "They are OSS Operation code names. Paperclip is the effort to get German scientists to America. We have all been part of it but none of us know the full scope. Syracuse is Phyllis' program to infiltrate the new Austrian government. I don't know about the other two."

"Damn," Cole clenched a fist. "So much going on, much more than I suspected. I, or rather we, have been out risking our necks without really knowing much about the big picture. Does Aalpeter know of all these operations?"

Mrs. Parks made an awkward little shrug. "I don't know, actually. It is the nature of intelligence that action groups are compartmentalized and work without knowledge of one another. It's vital for security even if it leads to redundant, even conflicting, effort. I don't fully understand where Aalpeter falls in the whole mess. I do know that our effort spans several national agencies and even other Allied forces."

They were distracted by shouts from the hall. "Stop, wait, you can't go in there. Major Cole, there are men…" Lieutenant Ryan's voice was shrill.

The door flew open and three men in civilian overcoats blew into the room. Cole had his pistol out and was just sinking into a crouch when the youngest man spoke. "Put that damned thing away. I'm Sterling Carson and I'm here to conduct the debrief. You don't need to know who I represent except to know that Ambassador Winters sent me and General Berringer has approved my handling the debriefing."

He was young, smooth-faced and confident in the way of rich boys from old money. He scanned the Detachment people pausing to look at Cole's shirt, still wet with Phyllis' blood. He had to tilt his chin up into the much taller Cole's face. "You must be the commander. You, and you alone, will be allowed to sit in. You don't really have the clearances to be there but we don't want you thinking we're doing anything behind your back."

He spoke to the Medic. "You're done. Wheel the man into the interrogation room now." The Medic started to protest but Carson had already turned back to Cole. "You and I will be the interrogators. My two men will be in the observation room taking notes. Don't make a fuss. Time is already against us. I fear that people are going to die, good people just like you and your detachment. We need to start right now."

Cole hesitated for a moment and then looked to Ryan, Belcher and Mrs. Parks. After a thoughtful pause he pointed and told Carson. "I want her in the debrief."

The young man glared at Mrs. Parks. "She's British MI-6 you know?" Then, with a wave, he conceded. "She can take notes with my men in the observation room. Now stop quibbling. Let's get going."

Phyllis had been cleaned up and sported a fresh bandage over the split in his forehead but he was still a train wreck. They poured him into a chair where he sagged like a potato sack. The young interrogator launched right in.

"I represent the CIG. What does the princess wear?"

Phyllis answered absently, "Pink underwear." He raised his eyes. "Does it snow in Prague?"

"I don't know. I'm from Schenectady."

The old man seemed satisfied. "Very well, I'm Phyllis and I'm ready."

Carson began, "Yes, I'm Geronimo. Where were you interrogated, and by whom?"

"I believe I was taken to a minor palace near Gmund. I think it was called Schloss Heidren. I was held in an upstairs bedroom with guards always outside my door. There were three interrogators who worked in shifts. They were all military. I'm sure of that even though they always wore simple smocks with no markings." He smiled weakly. "But their boots were Soviet Army. They spoke with well-educated Muscovite accents and were familiar with current psychological principles and techniques of coercive persuasion."

"Were you tortured and how?"

"Of course. They used electric shock, physical stress by binding and hanging, near suffocation and naturally, sleep and food deprivation."

Cole was amazed that the two men spoke casually as though discussing baseball or the economy, not brutal torture. He chimed in. "What made you break?"

Phyllis hesitated for the first time. "They put a tourniquet on my testicles and then hung me upside down from a rope. I could only relieve the pressure by supporting myself on fingertips against the floor. I hung there for no more than a few minutes with arms stretched below me. I thought I was prepared to die but, it seems, not to stand such pain. Once they let me down I gave up all resistance."

Carson snapped back. "What did you tell them?"

Now Phyllis began his list. "I told them that my name was actually Christian Weiss, born in Austria but was now a naturalized American. My parents are dead but my wife and children still live in Vienna. They promised not to harm my family. I explained the current state of confusion in the American Intelligence organizations and told them that despite the conflict, several programs of the deactivated OSS have continued under the Pond group."

"Did they ask for specifics?"

"Oh yes, and I gave them all they wanted. I told them of Operations Overcast and Paperclip, the effort to get German scientists away from the Soviets. I said that our JIOA continues to operate outside President Truman's directives and has, so far, rounded up almost a thousand scientists and engineers. These men, representing the world's greatest physicists and engineers, have either been kept in Germany or shipped to the US. I told them specifically of our local efforts by Majors Cole and Aalpeter. They were already familiar with both men."

James couldn't contain himself. "I am James Cole."

Phyllis, or Herr Weiss, made a quick acknowledgement, "I regret to tell you that, from their questions, I infer that they believe you to be the man who assassinated one of their KGB men, the same Soviet major who killed Lushka. They spoke of that man with, what I took to be, a mix of fear and admiration. As for you Major Cole, to use an American metaphor, they now think of you as the fastest gun in a town filled with gunfighters. You should be very careful."

Carson added. "We knew Aalpeter was compromised and we've moved him to Munich. As for Cole, I suppose he will have to go as well."

"Not until I have my scientists safely on their way to America," said Cole.

Carson made a condescending frown. "We'll discuss that later. Now Mr. Weiss, what about your program, Syracuse?

How much do they know about our infiltration of the Austrian government?"

Phyllis, or Weiss, clouded and began to cry. Through his sobs he blurted, "I gave up everyone... Rudolf Shenk, Willy Brecht, Kurt Hertburg, Helge Madgestein... I told everything. Some of these men are probably already dead."

Carson sat back, his face pinched with obvious distress. "Do they know about the pipeline?" Phyllis nodded but could not speak. "Shit," said Carson. "We've lost our underground movement leaders and any chance to outmaneuver the Soviets in the new parliament."

Phyllis was near collapse. "I also told them about Devereaux and his betrayal."

Cole perked up. "What about Devereaux?"

"We thought he was a double agent for us. It turns out he was actually just working for himself." Phyllis sighed, "I feel sure the Russians will take care of him. The other members of the Operation Renard must be pulled out as discretely as possible. French Secret Intelligence Service does not yet know how deeply we have infiltrated them. Once exposed, they will be targets for assassination or blackmail."

Phyllis' voice faded, his head fell to his chest and he drooped deep in his chair. Carson yelled, "Medic." He turned to Cole, "You must get those scientists of yours moving. I don't care how you do it but get it done. We're out of time now that we've just lost our contacts in the Austrian government."

Carson started to walk out but stopped and gave a quick smirk. "And, by the way Hernando, we have plans for you." Then, he and his companions were gone with clicking heels and stern looks.

Belcher stood beside Cole and watched the men go. "What the hell is CIG?"

Cole shook his head. "I don't know that and I don't know what to do next."

February 4, 1300 Hours

Major General Berringer sucked on a cigar and loomed over the staff assembled around a conference table. "The Staff Judge Advocate has just informed me that we have a serious problem. We authorized dependent women and children to travel here before we had any legal agreements in place to cover them. Now, the new Austrian government has advised us it is not inclined to rush through any special provisions. They insist that the dependent civilians will be treated under Austrian laws with none of the exemptions or protections from prosecution afforded to military members of the Occupation."

A barrel chested colonel shook his head from side to side. "Sir, that's just absurd. We occupy this piss ant country. We should decide what they can do."

The giant Berringer chewed his cigar. "I agree George, but unfortunately we've already signed an initial Four-Power Status of Forces agreement that grants the Austrians all judicial responsibility not spelled out in the document. Nobody thought about dependents." The big general rolled back, his huge body spilling over the chair arms.

Another colonel looked troubled. "Our Military Police still have authority over the local police. I don't really see the problem."

Berringer took the cigar from his mouth. "Suppose your wife wanders onto the wrong street and gets picked up by a Soviet patrol. We don't have any agreements to get her back. Even if she were detained by the British or French it could be a problem. We'd be forced to go to the State Department for every incident, even a traffic ticket. Anyway, State demands that we get rid of all families of American Occupation Force members below the rank of colonel immediately. Even the remaining wives of colonels and above will be restricted to their homes unless accompanied by a protective detail."

Heads shook all around the table. Someone said, "After all the hoops we jumped through to get these women sent over here and all the disruption to their lives, now we're going to ship them home. They're not going to like this at all."

"It gets worse," said Berringer fingering his cigar. "Because this was an unprogrammed expense, they won't be authorized travel on commercial ocean liners. They'll be going by military ship, probably those cramped Liberty Ships taking our soldiers home. It's just not a good situation but that's where we are. Any questions?"

"Yes sir," someone chimed. "How long do we have to implement this policy?"

Berringer made a bulldog face. "We weren't given a time certain. I would say we should plan to have them gone by April, May at the latest. In the meantime, emphasize the potential problem to all officers and have them keep their wives and children off the street. We need a very low profile for our wives and kiddies. Any incident will shoot right up the chain of command. Okay, that's it. Go spread the bad news."

The crowd broke up with a lot of head shaking. As Berringer walked out, his aide whispered, "Sir, I haven't seen any messages from the State Department."

"There aren't any. That was a ruse. We have a reliable report that the Russians are using American officer's wives as espionage sources. So we've announced that we're sending them all home. That will allow us to pick out the most likely ones and boot them. It will take six months or more to get agreements worked out. In the meantime we'll have our bad girls taken care of and we can bring the others back. Start with G-2 Intelligence and have the division chiefs make a list of all assigned officer's wives in-country. Then have them do an evaluation of the women's loyalty. We need to find out who is a Russian agent and who is just a wife."

February 6, 0906 Hours

Everyone in the detachment knew Cole had been identified for RIF and would be kicked out shortly. Roland, the best German translator in the unit, had already been transferred to a small unit in Southern Germany. McMahan was sent to the CIC detachment in Salzburg.

Somehow, Colonel Mather seemed to have gained power and was still intent on destroying the unit. The assignments of Roland and McMahan were just the beginning. He had already announced Captain Charley Woods as the next Detachment commander after Cole's departure. That was a disaster in the making.

James Cole arrived late at the office and was met by a serious looking Mrs. Parks. She took his arm and whispered. "Mason needs to speak to you immediately. Here is the phone number. He'll only be there for an hour. It is an international call and you can't use our phones. You'll have to book it."

Cole took the note and crumbled it in his hand. What could Aalpeter or Mason or whatever, possibly want? What else could possibly go wrong? He thanked Mrs. Parks and left immediately for the Astoria Hotel. There Lidia, the desk clerk, took the number, spent several minutes shouting into a massive "J" shaped headset and then scribbled a number and presented it to James. She was always curt but efficient.

"The operator says that international trunk lines are not too busy right now. It should only be a few minutes. Here is your reservation number. I'll call you when the connection goes through. As you know, the booths are there to the left."

James poured himself a cup of coffee from an oversized Samovar and took a seat in the lobby. He liked this place. He had never before taken the time to study its intricate wood carvings and gold gilded statues. There was a remarkable scent, the smell of history. Wood and brass, cigar smoke and snuff, furniture polish and perfumes all mixed, just traces of human presence. Lidia leaned over the hotel front desk and motioned. "Booth three, please."

James squeezed into the claustrophobic phone booth and listened to static and hissing background noise on the line. Finally, he heard a ring-ring, followed by a crisp German voice.

"Herr Major Aalpeter, please," James asked.

The man replied, "Moment," and was immediately replaced by a breathless voice.

"James, thank God you got through. Everything is falling apart. Truman has created a new Central Intelligence Group, the CIG, but he's staffed it with old school military people. They think field operations, or any clandestine ops, are dirty and unbecoming a great nation. God forbid we would ever kill an enemy who wasn't in uniform or fight an undeclared war."

Our support from the Senate Un-American Activities group has sparked a backlash opposition group of senators touting 'Peace for all time.' They are anti-military, pro-Soviet and determined to rid the government of what they call 'reactionaries.' They are hunting down anyone with an OSS or anti-Soviet association. Berringer has already been fired. Mather's boss, Hunnicut, is being transferred. They're going down the list. I'm sure your head will soon be on the block."

Cole made a half chuckle. "I've already been RIFed. I'll be a civilian by April."

"I'm sorry but it could be much worse. Listen, I have some very important things for you. First, the new Austrian government is too mired down in its internal squabbles to work your scientists' travel authorizations before the fake visas expire. There is, however, someone who can help you. Countess Gertrud Von Stein lives in Salzburg, Number 3 Franz Joseph Strasse. She can pull strings. You must go in person and tell her I sent you." As an afterthought, he added, "And give my regards to Piet. I hope he is sober."

Cole wrote the address. "I have that. What else?"

"The money could be both of our downfalls. Under no circumstances can you reveal that you have that box of money. There's probably two or three million American dollars' worth of various currencies. It was stolen from Nazis but never reported to Allied treasure recovery teams. If they find it they will charge us with theft. Use it as you must. I trust you."

Cole gave that a quick thought. "I'll do my best. You know I would never take any for myself."

Aalpeter laughed, "Yeh, you're much too Boy Scout for that. I'm afraid I have been somewhat less scrupulous." He changed the subject. Do you know there is a witch hunt going on for an American officer's wife who's passing information to the Soviets?"

"No, I only know my wife has been sent back to the States."

Aalpeter shot back, "She is certainly not the one. Go see Charlotte Huntsov. I have a hunch she has information you can use."

Cole was taken aback. "Charlotte, my old housekeeper that I thought was a Russian spy but turned out to be informing for Mather?"

"Yes, but she's much more than a housekeeper. Use a code word of 'Eifel' to identify yourself. She will authenticate with the words 'granite stone.' She has a wealth of information."

"Okay and I need to ask about Sherry White."

Aalpeter hesitated, "What about her? She belongs to you now. Use her as you see fit."

"Yes but what about her status? I know she is paid through some Swiss bank."

"Oh yes, I made that arrangement. Tell you what, the contract has no expiration date. As far as I'm concerned she can draw that pay when she's sitting in a rocking chair in some old folks home."

Cole waited but the phone was silent for an uncomfortably long time before Aalpeter spoke. "James, I am proud to have worked with you. I wish you good luck. It seems that some of my past indiscretions are about to come back and haunt me." He took a breath. "I am going dark."

With that, the line went dead. James replaced the headset and spoke out loud. "Going dark, what could Aalpeter have done? What have I have done that Mather or someone like him could dredge up?"

2205 Hours

James took the evening train to Salzburg. Alone in his compartment, he had unaccustomed time to think. Rather than waste that time grousing about his personal situation, he took out a pad of lined paper and began to make notes. Somehow, he thought, all of the chaos of the last few months had to fit together.

On the left, he listed all his people: Mrs. Parks, Sherry, Belcher, Ryan, Roland and the rest. These were the good guys—he hoped. In the center, he listed other Americans involved in the scientists' rescue: Aalpeter, Mather, Winters, Berringer. He couldn't think of others. Then the Germans: Honig (sort of German), Rolf, Gint... there must be more. He added Devereaux as an honorary German. Finally—the page was getting crowded—he listed the Russians: Zelenkov, Lushka, Svetlana, Bukinev; who else?

He began drawing lines to connect the players. Soon his paper was a spider web. He tore off the page and began to list the players involved in each operation. His pad was filling but he found little insight. The one constant seemed to be Devereaux, popping up everywhere but remaining a ghost. Through the night he scribbled until jolted by the train's braking.

He stepped off the train and took in the air of Mozart's hometown just at sunrise. It seemed perfectly preserved from centuries past. Morning light illuminated a great castle looming over the city. Beneath the castle, velvet shadows flowed down a mountain slope to end at a maze of ornate buildings and churches with snow-sparkled roofs. He was tired but took the time to appreciate the spectacle of golden light and soft shadows. It was a fairytale setting.

His taxi wound through snow-packed medieval streets to Franz Joseph Street. Number three was a minor palace with onion-top towers and sculpted archways, all solemn and stately under a thick mantle of snow.

James Cole trooped through unshoveled snow to a massive front door and banged a brass knocker. A tiny woman dressed in a black maid's apron and cap cracked the door open a few inches. She said nothing but stood with a questioning look.

"Major Cole to see the Countess Von Stein."

The maid was barely taller than Cole's belt buckle but she was not intimidated. "You are too early. The Countess does not rise for another hour."

Cole tried to look distressed. "I have no transportation. May I wait inside?"

The little woman pursed her lips and considered before she opened the door and pointed to two chairs in the foyer. "Here only. I will tell the Countess you are waiting. Please do not damage anything."

"Thank you, the name was Major James..."

"I remember. I will call you. Please mind your wet shoes." She slid the doors into the main house closed and left him alone in a marble and polished wood entryway hardly larger than a closet. A small viewing port the size of a fist slid open. He saw eyes, a man's eyes. The opening slid shut.

In time, a wiry man in a red silk smoking jacket came in and sat in the chair opposite James. He stared in silence.

"Hello, I am James Cole."

The man ignored Cole's outstretched hand. "You are American but you speak German. What do you want? Why are you here?"

"I wish to speak to the Countess and only to the Countess. It is important."

"Many things are important. What is your important thing?"

"Again, I must speak directly with the Countess."

"Wait," said the small man, and he was gone.

Cole made a pile of coat, briefcase, hat, gloves and a small leather folder. The maid startled him when she opened a door and pointed with an open hand. She continued watching as though he were a thief as he brushed by her.

Beyond the anteroom, the main entryway opened to a wide curved marble staircase illuminated by light that shown like pillars from above. At the top of that staircase, a woman in a white linen pants suit stood holding a foot-long-cigarette holder. She wore a sweeping hairdo, wide padded shoulders and the haughty look of royalty. He didn't know if he had ever seen a more striking woman. He fought a strong urge to bow.

"English, German or French?" she asked in English.

He stood tall. "English or German would be fine. I don't speak French."

"Then it's German. My English is much improved but I am still more comfortable with German. Now, who are you and what do you want?" Her voice had a sultry authority.

"I am American Army Major James Cole. I have an urgent request for you from Major Horatio Aalpeter."

She took a draw on her cigarette holder and shook her head as she exhaled. The smoke made a snakelike pattern. "I am not familiar with anyone of that name. Is it Dutch?"

Cole flustered for a moment and then remembered something. "I am not sure but he also said to give his regards to Piet and hopes he is sober."

The man in a red smoking jacket surprised Cole as he rushed in and stood alert as a hawk. The Countess tilted her head as though unsure what she just heard. "This Aalpeter man, describe him."

"He is short and thick like a sack of flour stuffed into a suit. He wears round wire glasses and smokes both pipe and cigar.

He loves Jaegermeister schnapps and often inspects the glass lovingly before downing it."

Suddenly her demeanor changed completely. "Jimmie, you have brought news of Jimmie. How is he? Oh Piet, this man has come from Jimmie." She clicked her way down the stairs in impossibly high heels and gave James a quick kiss on both cheeks. The man in a red jacket relaxed and smiled. The Countess sat and patted the empty seat beside.

"Come and tell me, how is my good friend?"

Cole was caught off guard. The Countess entwined her arm in his and looked at him with wide brown eyes. He cleared his throat and phrased his answer carefully. "He has gone out of sight for a time. There is confusion in the American Army about how to deal with intelligence operators after the war."

She didn't seem surprised. Drawing on her cigarette holder, she said, "He'll be all right. The man is a cat with many lives. But whatever made him choose such a silly name? Aalpeter, it sounds like a joke."

James was uncomfortable in her grasp. "I hope you are correct about him being all right." Then to business, "I have a group of German scientists in a house outside Salzburg. They have American visas but cannot get Austrian movement authorization to cross into Italy. Can you help?"

The Countess released his arm and sat back. "Do you have names and papers for these men?"

"Yes, of course. I have them in my satchel in your hallway."

The Countess turned and snapped her fingers. The maid made a slight bow and went to recover his leather folder. Turning back, Countess Von Stein said, "This will be no problem. I have some small influence in the government. So come and have coffee and breakfast." She released his arm and stood to look all around. She inhaled deeply, "Everything I have, I owe to that funny little man." Then snapping her eyes to lock onto his, she said, "I would do anything for Jimmie, anything, and so,

I shall do anything for you." James stood awkwardly, almost embarrassed.

Breakfast was sweet buns and sausages accompanied by an array of cheeses. She sipped coffee but barely ate.

"You know, Jimmie came to me a year before the war ended. The Nazis were everywhere. He didn't care. He raided a tunnel where they stored gold and jewelry stolen from Jews and others. He stole tons of treasure from right under the Nazis' nose. Much he kept for the US Army but he shared a good amount with me and Piet and a few others. At first I was sickened by the idea of profiting from the misery of so many but he convinced me that it was necessary to rebuild our country."

Cole sipped his coffee. "He is a persuasive man."

Before his second cup, the maid returned with a folded note on a silver tray. The Countess opened it with one hand, nodded and placed it back on the tray. She looked at the maid, "Champagne for our guest." Then back to James, "Your request is approved indefinitely for everyone on your list." She smiled as though satisfied with herself. "I told you I had some small influence." Piet, the man in the smoking jacket, laughed and they spent the day telling stories about the man they called Jimmie.

February 6, 1630 Hours

James Cole felt excitement surge through him. He was so close to the end of his scientists' adventure. Mrs. Parks answered the phone with her normal cool tone. He gave her specific instructions to go to his desk and remove one of the drawers. Behind the false back she would find a small bundle of money. She was to go immediately to the post office and wire transfer 10,000 Reichsmarks to the Salzburg post office.

He had to share the news, had to tell someone. "I have travel authorization for our lost boys. Once I receive that money I'll hire a bus and move them from Annaburg, to the nearest train.

They should be out of Austria in days. They're going to make it. We're going to get them out safely."

She congratulated him, hung up and then followed his instructions. Before heading out to the Post Office she paused to inspect a map of Austria on the wall. Tracing her finger southeast of Salzburg she found the tiny town of Annaburg. So the scientists were about to be saved. She smiled and made a mental note.

February 7, 0900 Hours

The bus driver was shouting in German, "No, no, the snow is too deep. This is my best bus but the snow is so deep." He held a flat palm just above his waist to illustrate the depth. "We cannot go today."

"Tomorrow then?" Cole asked with a tightness developing in his stomach. The driver shook his head angrily.

"Not tomorrow, maybe not for a week, maybe more. It is February and the mountain passes are closed. No one can go to the mountains and Annaburg is high in the mountains. You must wait, I think until March."

Cole paced angrily in the snow covered parking lot. There must be a way but even the Countess couldn't help him change the weather. Then he had a thought and trudged off leaving the bus driver shouting, "Hello, hello, I have not been paid."

Captain Mercer had managed the scientists since they arrived. He seemed a sharp enough young man. Cole barged into his office without bothering to shake the snow off his overcoat and boots. The captain snapped to attention.

"Halftracks, do you have access to tracked vehicles that can make it through snow?"

Captain Mercer hesitated. "Perhaps, there are hundreds of left over vehicles still stored here. I'm sure some of them are tracks. I don't know about their condition and I don't know if we have drivers."

Cole leaned on the desk and shouted. "Find out, man. My visas are about to expire and I can't get new ones. We must move your charges out in the next few days. I'll drive one and you can drive another. We have to get this done."

Mercer relaxed a bit to smile and raise a finger in the air. "Just give me a minute."

February 7, 1550 Hours

Professor Vogleman sipped hot tea and looked through a frosty window. The whole world seemed lost in a single shade of white as endless snowfield merged with empty sky. No color, form or texture broke the monotony except for a distant solitary figure no larger than an ant stomping his way through the hard crust snow. He cast no shadow under a sallow overcast and left no mark except tracks that traced his path back almost to infinity.

"I hope the poor creature makes it here before frostbite does him in." Others gathered to watch the struggle. They squinted, adjusted glasses on noses and pressed forward fogging the window. "We should go out and help him," someone said. There was no response. Life was boring with little to do in the chalet. They had been snowed in for almost a week and any diversion was welcome, but not a venture into the deep drifts.

It took almost an hour before the man finally made it to their door. There, he stomped his boots and shook thick snow off his long fur coat. Vogleman and the other scientists helped him in and set him before the fire. His body shivered and chattered, cold radiating from his very core. They brought tea and blankets which he accepted while suppressing coughs and minor tremors.

"Whatever are you doing out in this weather?" asked Vogleman in German.

The man cupped his mug. "I was travelling from Lienz to Salzburg but the snow came too hard and my car slid off the road. I waited but no one came. Finally, I must choose, freeze to death in the car or walk. Here I am. Where am I?"

Vogleman chuckled softly. "You are near the village of Annaburg, 30 kilometers southeast of Salzburg. Our telephone is not working and we have no electricity but we have plenty of firewood and food. You will be safe here until the weather improves. Please, what is your name?"

"Johann Sweitzer. I am working in Switzerland but I have family in Austria. I was coming to look for them now that the war is over. Thank you for your hospitality. I hope I will not impose too long."

Vogleman waved a dismissive hand. "It matters little. We are here waiting for visas to leave for America but the process is very slow. You are welcome as long as you need to stay. Tell me now, how are your feet. You must remove your boots and dry your socks."

February 8

On his second day in the chalet Johann Sweitzer became more sociable. He met everyone and inquired about their lives. It seemed a natural thing. He appeared awed by the academic achievements of the distinguished scientists but, without electricity, the socializing ended early. A steward lit a few candles in the hallways but otherwise the whole place went dark at sunset.

When it was silent throughout, Johann walked lightly in stocking feet to Dr. Max Klein's room and eased the door open. The doctor snored like some huge beast. Johann moved cautiously in the darkness until he was close enough to feel Klein's breath and then shook the sleeping man's shoulder.

With a snort, Klein awoke. "Vas? Who is it? What do you want?"

"Be calm, my doctor. I wish to speak with you. First, you must know that we have found your wife Elsa. She is living with a relative near Berlin in Russian territory. She is well and will remain so if you cooperate."

"Cooperate? Cooperate with whom? What do you want?"

Johann spoke slowly, "You have made a point of telling everyone that you were a minor worker in the laboratory, a designer of experiments and a keeper of statistics. This is not true is it, my doctor?"

Klein was silent, gathering his featherbed cover up to his neck as though that might protect him. After a long wait, he sighed and spoke with a tinge of bitterness. "All they speak of is Einstein and Heisenberg. No one has ever heard my name. Those men were at big universities. I labored at the Kaiser Wilhelm Institute, alone, unknown and unappreciated."

"You are too modest, doctor. You were a member of the Uranverein, the Nazi Uranium Club. You were held in high esteem by the others. Dopel, Pose, and Zimmer all say you were the most important. What did you do that made you the most important?"

Klein moved nervously in his bed, thrashing and fighting his bedcovers. After another long silence he spoke. "Well, it doesn't matter anymore so I might as well tell you. I developed a simple, reliable means to initiate the nuclear reaction. I made a nuclear trigger superior to the one used by Americans. If Germany had not fallen, we would have built bombs to destroy whole cities. We were ready to make the world tremble."

"And now, sir, you must continue your work. I will bring you and your wife to a safe place where you can work. You will be treated as a hero with a grand house and money."

"No. Never. I hear a Slavic accent in your speech. You are Russian, yes?"

"Yes doctor, my name is actually Sergei Zelenkov and I represent the future. You can choose to be part of that future or you... and your wife... can perish with the Nazi past."

Klein's voice grew small. "Why must my wife die? She is not involved."

Sergei did his best to sound compassionate even to this unrepentant Nazi. "This is the way we do things. Help us and we reward you. Turn against us and all memory of you, your family and your accomplishments will be wiped away as though they never existed."

Klein's answer was almost venomous. "I will never serve the Russians. I am a loyal German, a proud German. I am sorry to bring suffering to my wife but I will die gladly for the Fatherland." His voice grew louder. "I am German. Long live Germany. Heil, Germany, heil."

Sergei let out a sigh of disappointment. He felt around in the darkness until he took hold of the doctor. Then, yanking him from the bed, Sergei found his throat. With a grunting heave, he lifted Klein's head and slammed it hard against the wall. Then, cocking the unconscious man's head back, inserted a pill into his gaping mouth, pushed the jaw closed and waited for a swallow. In less than a minute the scientist's body went completely limp.

No one had responded to the noise in Klein's room. Sergei listened, heard nothing and then dragged Klein out by the shoulders. Through the hall, down stairs and into the foyer, the man's feet bumped along. There, Sergei had assembled a featherbed and a great pile of blankets. He tied Klein into a bundle and then rolled him up in a large canvas tarp that was cinched tight with thin ropes leaving only a small breathing space.

He tied a tow rope to one end and strapped the whole package onto a pair of skis stolen from the chalet. It was clumsy work in the dark. Once Sergei finished wrapping his mummy, he donned his own winter gear. Everything ready, he dragged Klein out into the cold, put on his own skis and began their journey into an icy void.

This was an unpleasant task. Sergei didn't want to be there. He wanted to begin his new life in earnest. But that must wait. He still had obligations from his old life and Sergei

Zelenkov was a man who met his obligations... no matter the consequences.

1400 Hours

The tracked vehicles he found were drivable and large enough to carry ten passengers each. That was the good news. The bad news was that these vehicles were open to the weather and the weather was becoming fierce. Winds were forecast to gust over thirty miles an hour with heavy snow.

Mercer's solution was simple. He rigged a canvas tent in the bed of each truck and found kerosene heaters. That, along with a warehouse load of blankets might be enough to keep the old men from freezing. Cole didn't have to drive. They found plenty of motor pool drivers who reluctantly agreed to go out into a blizzard. By early afternoon a convoy of four bizarre looking tents on tracks began a painfully slow climb up into the Austrian Alps.

Cole rode in the first vehicle. The tent covered the passenger bed but the driver's cockpit was separate with only a small canvas convertible type top that was fine for rain but did nothing for cold. Worse, there was no heater. Gloves, hats, scarves and blankets were the only protection for the driver and his passenger. Ice quickly coated the windshield demanding they stop every mile or so to scrape.

In short, it was miserable. Cole wore a set of aviator's goggles and scanned out the side window to help the driver find what traces they could of the road. The bus driver was right. Just a few miles outside Salzburg the snow drifted up to four feet. To make it even more challenging, the road wound precariously up into the mountain with steep drop-offs. Driving in the dark was going to be impossible. By six it was time to stop. Cole saw a building and they pulled up to a barn, whose he had no idea.

Gathering everyone inside, he set up a schedule so someone would always be awake to monitor a kerosene heater. They huddled, grateful there were no livestock, but then, a few cows might make excellent bed warmers. Through the night, wind whistled through the barn and rattled doors. James Cole imagined the drifts becoming deeper. For sure, the temperature was dropping.

He tried to sleep but his feet stung from the cold even after he wrapped them in blankets. He was not alone shivering in the dark. No one slept more than an hour or two. Well before sunrise, they were up building a fire in a bucket to try making coffee. Cole slid the barn door open a bit and faced a smooth wall of snow easily as high as his head. His whole body sagged.

Mercer came to stand beside him. "Holy shit," he almost whispered. "How're we gonna get through that?" Cole seemed paralyzed.

Then another door banged open and one of the drivers stomped in carrying an armful of firewood. "Don't give that snowdrift no never mind," he tolled in a cheery voice. "The wind has done blowed away a bunch of the snow but it piled up against this here barn. I'm thinking it'll be smoother sailing today."

He was right. Much of the road had been blown clear by the night wind. Despair gave way to elation but there were still problems. One of the vehicles wouldn't start. They cranked the starter, jumped the battery and even trickled fresh gas into the carburetor. No use, it was dead. Cole paced and finally gave the order, "We'll go with three. We can still cram them all in. It won't be comfortable but it we'll manage."

February 9, 0640 Hours

Every muscle and joint strained as Sergei tromped through snow deeper than his boots. The gray hint of sunrise brought no warmth and did little to ease the dull ache of relentless cold. The skis had not worked. They bogged down with the weight of his clumsy load and dug too deep. Through the long night, Klein had not stirred. Wrapped in layers and tied at both ends, the man looked like a great gray banana being pulled on a string. Now walking, Sergei had to lift his leg high with each step and the effort was wearing him down.

He considered taking a break to make sure his captive was still alive but was afraid to do so. If he stopped, he might not have the willpower to start again. No, better to trudge on. Every step was a step closer. Every breath was one less that could freeze his lungs. He pressed on, bent forward at the waist, both hands entwined in the tow rope behind his back.

Sergei huffed clouds of steam and scanned the whiteness all around. It was hard to stay oriented in the pale void. No sun, no shadow and no landmarks to guide him, he could be going in circles. All he could do was glance back to be sure his tracks were staying in a straight line. Just one foot before the other; endless steps, endless pain, he trudged on.

Finally a gray shape began to take form ahead. A small collection of buildings, it grew sharper with every step. He hadn't been aware that falling snow was swirling around him. He hadn't noticed his eyebrows and the scarf over his mouth becoming crusted into snowballs. One step, one step, one step more; the buildings became a village.

He was 100 meters from the closest structure when he heard a vehicle's engine and a Jeep emerged from the curtain of snow. Sergei was so depleted he barely registered the men who held his arms and took the rope from his hands. They helped him into the back seat of the covered Jeep where he immediately passed out. Even unconscious, his violent shaking continued.

Sometime later, Sergei lurched awake and looked frantically around. Every muscle ached and his head throbbed. A hand touched his shoulder and he looked up to see Devereaux standing over him.

The Frenchman spoke in broken Russian. "You did well, my friend. Doctor Klein has a bit of frostbite but otherwise, he will be fine. His wife is already on a train through the Soviet Sectors of Germany and Austria and then into Switzerland. From there, it will be an easy trip to France where the doctor will join her along with Finklestein and other German scientists. Together they will work on a French Atomic Bomb."

Sergei made a jerky nod and a hint of a smile. He accepted a cup of strong coffee and realized he was dehydrated. Devereaux continued, "With your help, Comrade Sergei Ilyich Zelenkov, the French will regain pride and once again take their place in the world. Once we sweep aside the conservative Gaullists, Communism will bloom in our great nation."

Sergei tried to straighten up but the effort made him groan. "Monsieur Devereaux, you must also remember that Honig made great sacrifices for us. He allowed himself to be captured by the Americans and then traded for some minor worker, a secretary or something."

"Yes, of course." Devereaux seemed embarrassed by his omission. "Yes, yes, that is true. Once in Russian hands, he managed to get the occupation leaders to allow him travel into Soviet occupied Germany. There, he contacted Klein's wife and made the arrangements you spoke of for her move to France. Honig has already distinguished himself. He is helping create a new State Security group called Stazi."

Devereaux grew serious "Honig is a hero, but it was you who has made the great sacrifices. You have given up your homeland and your career. Your family has been thrust into a strange land and a strange culture. For you, life will never be the same."

Sergei sipped his coffee. His voice was hoarse as though damaged. "I kept my promises. I have done no harm to my homeland or the cause of Communism. When I received your message about the scientists' location I came at once. Comrade Devereaux, I have met my obligations."

The Frenchman rubbed his hands and seemed uneasy. "My friend, I am afraid I must give you some unpleasant news. The money the Americans gave you, all but the Austrian Schillings which are difficult to spend, it's all phony. When we tried to make deposits, the Swiss bankers confiscated it. To complicate life more, the apartment the Americans gave you in Geneva had only a one month lease. The United Nations, where you were to be employed, has never heard of you. It seems the Americans never meant for you to actually go free."

Sergei gave no indication of emotion. He just stared at the flickering fireplace and sipped. There would be time. He could be patient. He was a man who always met his obligations and now he had an obligation to the Americans who had lied to him.

February 9, 1530 Hours

The Innkeeper was a thick man with leather knee britches and a matching embroidered vest, the very postcard image of a Tyrolean mountain man. Muscled and greasy, he looked as though he could lift an ox while whistling a happy tune. Sleeves rolled above his elbows, he was busy washing beer glasses and joking with the Frenchmen when he heard the distant sound of engines. With a deep scowl, he walked to a hand blown glass window and rubbed the frost away.

Devereaux stared over his shoulder. "Whose are they? Can you tell?"

The Austrian shrugged. "Difficult to say until they are closer but we are in the American Zone. Any military vehicle is likely to be theirs."

Devereaux swore a stream of French and tried to push past the burly man who didn't budge. "Monsieur, I suggest you take your sick friend and go to your rooms. Keep out of sight until I tell you it is safe."

The Frenchman didn't like to be told what to do but he had no better idea. He shouted to his men, "*Allez, allez,* get the Russian to one of the rooms and keep him quiet. Pierre, you go park the Jeeps behind the Inn. Try not to leave obvious tracks. Let's go."

The Austrian Innkeeper went back to washing his glasses. Devereaux climbed steps to a loft and crouched where he had a clear view of the main area. There, in his cramped nook far from the fireplace warmth, he felt cold seeping into his sleeves and collar. His bare hands and face seemed to shrink from the chill as he took out a pistol, gathered his coat and hunkered down to wait. The engines came closer.

They stopped and six American soldiers came noisily through the door. They stomped feet and slapped their arms. He could see their frosted coats steaming in the warmth of the fire. One stood a head taller than the others. When he took off his knit cap, Devereaux saw it was Major Cole and swore under his breath.

Cole and the soldiers stayed at the Inn for almost an hour drinking coffee and hot wine. They laughed. The Americans are always laughing. Cole seemed to be asking the Innkeeper for directions and the Austrian pointed and made agreeable gestures. Finally, Cole took out a roll of bills and paid. The Austrian bowed repeatedly, obviously pleased by such a large sum. Damned Americans, they always had too much money.

After they left, Devereaux came out of hiding and became a drill sergeant. Shouting to his men, he ordered the Jeeps warmed up and sent two men to bundle Sergei Zelenkov in warm blankets.

"We must go today. I had hoped we could wait for better weather but now, we have no choice. We will drive in the tracks left by the American's vehicles. Maybe the snow will not be so bad. Hurry, we must be well down the mountain before darkness."

1730 Hours

As the American tracked vehicles approached, long blue shadows already stretched across the endless Alpine landscape now slowly fading to dull twilight gray. Looming high on a hill, one lone building stood guarding the mountain pass. It was a Bavarian style house, larger than most with gingerbread carving on the balcony and trim. Large stones on the roof guarded against mountain storms.

The three military vehicles pulled in and Cole leaped from the lead truck. Professor Vogleman, wearing only a sweater against the cold, rushed out to meet them. He grabbed Cole and hugged him without embarrassment. The old man bubbled with excitement. "Oh my good major, if only you had come yesterday. Our friend Professor Klein was kidnapped by a man named Sweitzer. I hope he survives. They went out into the storm last night."

"Sweitzer," said Cole. "Johann Sweitzer, I should never have trusted that Russian."

"Russian you say, I thought I heard a hint of an accent. So now, what will become of us?"

Cole tried to put their upcoming adventure in a positive light. "We will have everyone dress in their warmest clothes. These vehicles are not comfortable but they go well through the snow. In the morning, we head for Radstadt, just 20 kilometers away. The trains are still running there. You will ride to Innsbruck and on to Genoa, Italy. I hope you have all your paperwork to go with these freshly signed Austrian transit authorizations. In Genoa, you board a United States ocean liner for a week-long trip in luxury. In New York, you will be met and escorted to fine quarters. Your families will join you soon."

Vogleman seemed elated. "Come," he said, "and tell the others. They will rejoice."

As they walked to the door Vogleman looked back at the three open bed tracked vehicles with concern but said nothing.

February 10

Cole went with the convoy to Radstadt and made sure they boarded the right train. Captain Mercer agreed to continue on, babysitting them to the Italian border. With an overwhelming rush of relief, Cole caught a train back to Vienna. Once comfortably seated in his compartment, he let all the tension drain out of him and fell back into a deep trance-like sleep.

He awoke with a snort to face a young Russian soldier demanding in almost unintelligible German, "Papier, papier." Cole fumbled, still groggy and produced a set of orders and his gray card. The Russian studied them intently. Cole was sure the boy soldier couldn't read. "ID," demanded the soldier in a harsh tone. Cole produced his military ID card and handed it to the would-be tough guy who compared the name letter-by-letter to the orders. Unable to find a discrepancy, the soldier tossed everything back into Cole's lap and turned away.

Cole gathered his papers and took stock. He hadn't shaved or bathed for days. No wonder he didn't impress his Russian friend. He stretched and yawned. What day was it? Where was he? Obviously he was entering the Soviet Zone. That was good. It meant he was just a couple of hours from Vienna.

Arriving at the downtown train station, he felt oddly at home. The smells, the sounds, the feel; this was a foreign land filled with danger and yet this was where he belonged. Even more than the States, this was his place, at least until the first of April when he would become a civilian.

Back in his hotel room he tried to make a plan. With the scientists safely on their way everything else seemed trivial. He thought of Aalpeter, or Jimmie or any of his other names. The last thing Aalpeter said was to see Frau Huntzov. That could wait. He needed to catch up on the sleep he had missed over the last four days.

February 11, 0700 Hours

Morning came with brilliant clear skies and the comforting cacophony of the city at work. Cole rolled up his slotted shades and cranked open the window. He closed his eyes in the sunlight and took in the smells of the city. Damp stone buildings had a distinct odor that mixed with diesel exhaust and the ever present scent of coffee and freshly baked pastry. He realized that this had become his city. More than New York or anyplace else, he felt at home in Vienna and it made him smile.

He cleaned up and took a taxi to Mather's house. There, he rang and waited feeling full of energy and enthusiasm, just glad to be alive. The door opened and he removed his hat.

"Gunten Morgen, Frau Huntsov."

She raised her eyebrows and answered in English. "Please do not call me Frau. I am not German."

"Forgive me. I meant no offense." He wore a boyish grin. "Major Aalpeter told me to visit you." He made a show of looking around. Then, with a sly wink, "The iron work on these stairs reminds me of the Eifel Tower. The Eifel Tower, do you know it?"

Her face clouded in caution. "The iron is fine but it needs a granite stone base."

"So we understand each other," said Cole. "May we speak?"

She opened the door and led him to the kitchen. "We can talk here. Mrs. Mather is a stranger to the kitchen or to any kind of work. She would, however, like to share a little of her wine with you."

He grinned. "That seems very generous of her. Please, may we speak in Russian, just in case there are ears listening?"

She looked more relaxed than he had ever seen her as she took out a bottle of Italian wine, poured and began to speak Russian, "I forget you are a linguist, Major. Neither of the Mather's can speak a single word other than English. Actually, they don't speak English all that well."

"Let me see," he pondered out loud, "you speak English, German, and Russian… any others?"

"Czech, Serbian and French, I have an ear for languages."

"Indeed you do. Tell me, what brought you here. I'm sure it wasn't the Cossack story you told Sherry White when you were pretending to be my maid."

She feigned indignation. "I was not pretending. I was a good maid for you and that wife of yours. Anyone else would have quit in a week. Anyway, I worked for the OSS during the war. A man named Robert Brown hired me to infiltrate the Austrian resistance. The war ended and I went to work for Aalpeter who was then known as Trasker. He told Colonel Mather that I would spy on you but really, it was Mather I was supposed to be watching. My story about my working for the Russians was, as you said, just a diversion."

"The wine is excellent. My compliments to you, and to the lady who paid for it." They laughed and clinked glasses. He turned serious. "There is a suspicion that some American officer's wife is passing secrets. Do you have any ideas about that?"

Charlotte Huntzov downed her wine and inspected the crystal glass. "Yes, you are drinking her wine."

Cole's face went blank. He studied Charlotte's eyes and found no reason to doubt. "Tell me more."

She leaned forward with a gossip's grin. "I have been waiting for someone to contact me so I could tell my story. Since Aalpeter disappeared, I've had no one. Now, I will tell you. Colonel Alexi Bukinev is a fine talker, smooth as a snake's skin. He even speaks English with an American accent."

Cole nodded. "Yes, he was at New York University while I was there."

She was anxious to get back to her tale. "And he uses that fluency to seduce his American friends, the colonel figuratively, the wife literally."

"You're joking. She sleeps with Bukinev?"

"Every Thursday she goes 'shopping.' Actually I do all the shopping. She and Bukinev go to a hotel. I can't blame her too much. If I were married to Eugene Mather, I'd probably sleep with the trash man out of desperation. I don't know just how much she tells the Russian but I do know that Colonel Mather freely discusses his work at home. She's much smarter than he."

Cole's mind was churning. "The hotel, is it always the same one?"

"No, it's always different. I make the reservations. It would bring too much attention if she went into the Soviet Sector and even worse if a Russian colonel made a reservation in the American Sector. Usually, I wind up checking out hotels and quietly making the reservation for her. They arrive separately, spend two hours and leave separately. She's much more relaxed Thursday nights than any other time."

Cole was shaking his head. "Has she ever used the Astoria Hotel?"

Charlotte Huntzov poured another round and thought. "Not that I remember, certainly not recently."

Now he made a devious smile. "Can you tell her that next Thursday you have a room for her at the Astoria, number 708?"

"Yes, I'm sure I can do that." She sipped and wiped her lips. "There is something else. Do you know the Russian woman who was married to Colonel Lushka before he disappeared?"

"I have heard of her. She is supposed to be a very large but incredibly beautiful and very aggressive."

"Beautiful to you maybe, I think she is a beast. She is sleeping with your Captain Woods. They trade secrets and she always gets the better of him. He is the one who negotiated the swap of your Swiss diplomat. He is also the one who told them about your woman, Sherry White. Whatever happened to her? I liked that woman. She would be a better match for you than that tiny shrew you have."

Cole took a deep breath. His stomach tightened and he forced himself to remain calm. "Deb has gone back to America. We're getting a divorce. I do intend to pursue Sherry White."

"And good for you." Charlotte seemed genuinely pleased. "So now, my major, do you know how I will be paid now that Aalpeter is gone? I don't intend to live on a maid's wages."

He was distracted as he answered. "I'll make sure your payments continue for at least a few more months. But tell me, how do you know about the affair between Captain Woods and the Soviet woman?"

She beamed. "You forget I am a trained agent. While the Russian colonel and Mrs. Mather were wrestling in the hotel bedrooms, I would often sneak into their outer rooms and go through Bukinev's valise. He had a combination lock but it was easy to pick. He bragged that the woman called Svetlana had Woods completely under her control. He gave her everything she asked. In turn, she gave him bits of information with little value to Aalpeter."

"Aalpeter, what does he have to do with this?"

"Woods reports directly to Aalpeter. I thought you knew this."

James Cole felt anger building in his belly.

February 14

Without Sergeant Richardson, it took some doing to get the projector setup and working properly. But by Thursday morning it was ready and so was the plan. Lidia knew to give the colonel's wife the key to 708 without question and then to call Major Cole when it was returned. The film lab was on standby.

By Friday morning the 8-millimeter film was developed and in the can. Cole intended to review it but he just couldn't bring himself to watch. It seemed like cheap voyeurism. He was, of course, taking a chance in bringing a movie to the headquarters without even checking it out… but he went anyway. With a wink at Fraulein Gint, he took a breath and walked boldly into Mather's office.

"What in hell are you doing here? I didn't send for you…"

Cole stood at attention and spoke evenly. "I have found the American wife who is spying on us." He stood waiting, eyes straight ahead. There was a long silence while Mather considered.

"All right, so who is it, and how do you know this?"

Cole took the film canister from under his arm and slid it across Mather's desk using two fingers. The colonel drew back as though it were radioactive. "What's this? Who is on it?"

Cole said nothing. He simply stood. Finally, Mather took the small round case and gingerly pried it open. He removed the reel and began to unspool it. Holding the film up to the light, he squinted and seemed confused. "I can't tell who's in this little pornographic flick. Do you know?"

"It's your wife, Sir, your wife and Colonel Bukinev in the Hotel Astoria. They meet weekly for their trysts."

Mather recoiled as though struck by a physical object. He raised an impotent fist as though ready to attack a man twice his size. The desk between them prevented any violence but Mather raged, shaking his fist and shrieking like a chirping bird.

"Liar, you are a cowardly liar. You think you can degrade my wife with these lies? You have always been my enemy, my nemesis. I hate you. I hate you. I will see you dead. Do you hear? I will see you dead."

Mather seemed suddenly aware that the normally noisy building had fallen silent. His shouting halted all work in the surrounding offices as people stood and listened. Secretaries covered their mouths. Military men gaped. They were used to Mather's tirades but not death threats.

The skinny colonel continued hissing with only slightly reduced volume. "Get out. Get out now and consider yourself under house arrest. I'll review this film and decide on your punishment."

Cole stood his ground trying hard not to enjoy the moment. "There are copies. If you resign I will not bring charges of treason. In the meantime, don't make any rash statements. They might be used against you at your court martial." The tall major saluted and turned away, moving with slow deliberation.

Mather remained standing over his desk in unfocused shock and anger. Cole paused in the midst of an office of zombies. With a cheerful tone he said loudly, "Carry on, you still have jobs to do." And they did, resuming their beehive activity. Now James Cole could relish his moment of victory but what would come next? How would this work out? What exactly would Mather do?

February 18, 2245 Hours

James Cole collapsed into his office chair and ran both hands over his hair. His shoulder holster jammed against the chair and jabbed him in the ribs. He shifted, snapped off the holster and tossed it a drawer before he sank back drained.

Now what? His Army career was over. He had no real civilian skills. His wife had not yet filed for divorce. His detachment was slipping away like sand between his fingers. Thank God he had Sherry. She was the rock he could cling to. She was... He turned to the sound of a footstep. It was almost eleven at night. There should be no one else in the building except perhaps Mrs. Parks who seemed always to be here doing research or something.

James Cole cocked his head and listened. He heard nothing but he did smell something, something strange, an animal smell. It took a minute for his mind to sort it out. It was bear, like a bearskin rug or a bearskin coat. Sergei Zelenkov had a bearskin coat. Cole was just reaching for the gun in his drawer when he saw the figure standing in shadow. Both he and the shadow man froze. Cole's hand inched toward the pistol in his drawer but before he reached it, a gun's report echoed through the darkened building. Startled, he flinched and that hesitation cost him a precious second.

The second shot splintered his desktop showering Cole with a cloud of wood chips. He clawed for his pistol just as the third shot hit him and hit him bad. He felt a sharp chill in his ribs, a chest wound, a sucking chest wound. He had seen chest wounds. He probably wouldn't be conscious for long.

Cole tried to steady himself against the desk but he had no strength. Twisting out of his chair, he went down like dead weight slamming the floor. He didn't really feel pain but every breath sounded like a steam engine's exhaust. Despite the weakness, his vision was still surprisingly clear. From under his desk, he could see boots, well-worn Russian boots. His right hand was trapped under his body. He worked that hand straining for his backup revolver in a back pocket holster.

Sergei limped around the desk looking mean and dirty in his matted fur coat. He pointed his large revolver at James's head but seeing how helpless the American was, hesitated and relaxed. His voice was raspy as he spoke in Russian.

"So, American, it is your time. You lied to me, tricked me, and even humiliated me. This I cannot forgive. I kept my word to you but you gave me false money, no job and no home." He flashed a joyless grin across frostbite-withered lips. "Now, my family is lost. They have no country. I have no country. You took everything from me."

Cole coughed blood. "Not true. Money… house in Geneva… all good, all yours. Others handled job." He paused to spit and caught his breath. Talking was taking too much effort. "Prisoner swap used actor not you. You could have lived… in comfort in… in Switzerland." The words required too much. He pressed his face against a floor wet from his blood.

"You lie. Bastard, you lie." Sergei brought his gun to bear. But then a woman's voice distracted him with a shout.

"Stop." Mrs. Parks had pulled a small pearl handled automatic from a leg holster under her skirt. She stood stiff-armed with a steady aim. The Russian spit and spun on her. Cool as if on a firing range, she rippled three shots into him. Sergei dropped straight down, head making a thunk and gun clattering on the floor. Mrs. Parks stepped forward, kicked the

Russian's lifeless body and reached over him to retrieve his revolver.

With a toss of her hair, she said, "Well, that's it for this blighter. It was a good triple, one to the trunk, one to the chest and one to the head. He won't be getting up. And, as for you, my good major, I'm truly sorry to see you go but I think this man has done the job I would have eventually been forced to do."

James Cole dribbled blood out his nose but he was still breathing and he could still see. What he could not do is speak more than a grunt. His right hand continued working its way toward his pocket holster but he let his fingers rest there while he gathered strength.

Mrs. Parks leaned over to lift Cole's face and stare into his eyes. They were still clear. "You're quite a tough bugger aren't you? That shot would have already killed most men. Still, I can be patient. You don't have long. I do regret this. I really do, but it's necessary don't you know. You were simply getting too close to our little French connection."

She stared to some far-away image. "There's a Communist movement blossoming there. Jolly Old England will be next. I will be perfectly positioned to work from inside the SIS to make that happen. Everything is falling nicely in place, except," she paused, "for you, dear boy. But you will quickly die and take your stories with you."

She reached for the phone but kept her gun on the fading Cole. Dialing with one finger, she put the phone to her ear and spoke German in her curt English accent. "Yes, I wish to report a shooting. Two men are dead. Yes, 37 Richertsgasse. Please hurry."

Her call done, she looked down with a gentle face, almost compassionate. Then she pointed her small pistol at the wall and fired three more times until it was empty. "There we go. Now we'll just put this little gun in your hand. No bullets though, we don't want you to get any crazy ideas in your final moments. It will look as though you shot Major Zelenkov after he ambushed you. You'll be a bloody hero. They might even give you a parade."

Cole groaned as she took his left hand and placed her gun in his palm. She paused. "No, you're right handed. It wouldn't do at all to have them find you with this empty gun in the wrong hand. I am sorry it's not a more masculine weapon. Now, do be a good boy and roll over for me, will you?"

She took his shoulder and pushed with both hands until his bulky frame yielded and he flopped onto his back. A horrible gasping noise escaped partly from his throat and partly from his leaking chest wound. His quivering lips parted but he could not speak. The movement had almost freed his right hand. Cole worked his fingers around the handle of his revolver.

Then, with one excruciating effort, he wrenched his arm free and raised the gun with its barrel pointed at Mrs. Parks. She looked confused. The damned thing was upside down and still in its square pocket holster. He wiggled a finger into the trigger guard and squeezed with everything he had. The explosion blew the holster open like a lily in bloom. Even inverted, the shot found its target.

Mrs. Parks jumped. "Oh dear God." Her face fell. "Bloody hell, I'm done for," she exclaimed as her hand felt her belly and found it damp. Now she wailed like an abandoned bride. "I shall not live to see my beautiful new world. I can only pray it will come to pass. Someday, a world where everyone has dignity, value... purpose..." Her voice was fading. She leaned against the wall, began to wobble, went down on one knee and then slid down the wall. Her final words were barely audible. "At least Devereaux will..."

Cole fell back. His pistol fell under his desk, out of sight. The world became a distant gray echo.

The ambulance crew would later report that it appeared the American major returned fire at the Russian who had shot him along with an unidentified female English administrative worker.

February 22, 1100 Hours

Slowly he became aware of light. It was bright, reflecting off white tile until it hurt his eyes. He was on his back staring up into the light, but it wasn't at the end of any tunnel. He wasn't dead. Instead he smelled alcohol and pine cleaner, hospital smells. He turned his head and an electric pain shot down his neck and through his chest which was wrapped tight like a German baby in swaddling clothes. Only very slowly did he begin to take in his surroundings.

James Cole lay on a white metal bed in a white room surrounded by white people in white clothes and white shoes. A white curtain isolated him from the world. There were white blankets, white sheets: he hoped he hadn't bled on any of it.

There was talking but the voices seemed distant. The language was German with an Austrian accent. This must be a civilian hospital. The speakers' tone was relaxed, not emergency room chatter. It took a while for him to understand. They were discussing payment for his treatment. That was a good sign. He would rather be a deadbeat than a dead... anything else.

Then a familiar voice, it was Sherry and she was running to him. He smiled. If this was a dream, he liked it. But it was no dream. She took his hand and pressed it to her face where warm tears dampened his palm. He noted this with the strange dissociation of a spectator. She talked to him in English. He had to focus as though trying to interpret.

He could almost feel a veil around him, separating him from the rest of the world. Voices became clearer as he focused. Sherry was sobbing. He smiled and spoke in a hoarse voice. "Hi pretty girl. What brings you here?"

She wrapped her arms around him and the pain made him squeal. She immediately backed off and wiped her face with the back of her hand. "I'm so sorry. I'm just glad you're alive. The operation was a success and they say your prognosis is good, at least pretty good."

He still showed no emotion. "You know I've never been shot before. It was always the other guy. Guess it was just my turn." He smiled but it was a vacant, staring smile that faded as he drifted back into unconsciousness.

February 23, 2130 Hours

The handsome Frenchman followed signs to track number three at the Salzburg train platform. He was returning to France but in fine style. Using the money the Americans had so generously provided to Sergei Zelenkov, Monsieur Devereaux had outfitted himself in a fine new outfit. While he hated capitalism, he loved the things it produced.

The station was almost deserted and he felt quite at ease and twisted his handlebar moustache and let his guard down. A group of rough looking men joined him. One of them stood to his left and eyed him up and down. The man spoke in lower-class German. "What a fine coat, sir. It is mohair with a fox fur collar, no? And your hat, it looks like a Berliner, no? Also very fine shoes, Italian I think." He smiled with rotten teeth.

Devereaux prepared to defend himself as a second man moved silently to his right. A third came up behind and tipped the fine hat off his head. Devereaux reflexively reached out to catch his expensive new hat just as the man smacked his skull with a blackjack. Devereaux collapsed but the men by his sides caught his limp body to prevent his clothes from being soiled on the dirty floor.

Quickly they stripped off his coat, suit, shoes and watch. One pulled up his undershirt and announced with a grin, "Money belt, he has a money belt." They stripped him completely and began to laugh wildly as they fanned colorful bills of many nations' currency.

"So, my fancy Frenchman, the Werewolf underground thanks you for your contribution to the Nazi cause." They gathered his clothes and then, after looking up and down the station platform, rolled the unconscious man's near naked body off the platform and onto the track. Laughing and admiring their loot, the thugs raced upstairs and onto the street. One of them put on the hat and cavorted, playing the part of a high rolling dandy.

The evening train to Paris chugged into the station belching steam and coal smoke. There were no passengers waiting and no one noticed the slight bump as the train came to a crunching stop.

February 28, 0715 Hours

James Cole awoke with a start. He tried to sit up but pain hit him like an electric shock. Leaning back, he scanned his hospital room. Despite the pain, he felt a clarity he had never known. Sherry White lay sprawled on a corner chair and he smiled to see her. He called, "Wake up sleepy girl." She stirred, stretched and then bolted to his side.

"You're awake. How're you feeling?"

"Now that I see you, I feel great."

She brushed unruly curls from her eyes. "I must look a mess. I've been here in the chair for three days."

He smiled and it was a gentle smile. "No, with the sunlight on your face you look beautiful, like an angel."

She almost blushed. "So who is that talking, Clark Gable?"

"Nope, it's just me. Somehow I don't think I'm going to need all my Hollywood personas so much, at least not as long as I have you."

CHAPTER SEVEN

March 6, 1400 Hours

His recovery seemed slow. The chest wound was healing but Cole had very little energy and plenty of pain. Strangely, he felt confident, even happy. His scientists were safe in America. His divorce papers arrived. He only had a few loose ends left to tie up. Oh sure, there was the getting kicked out of the Army thing, but he had survived worse.

Sherry came every day and so did many of the other detachment people. One sunny morning Cynthia Ryan came bouncing in with a bunch of yellow flowers in a milk bottle. She had always been a little cheerleader.

After a perfunctory greeting, Ryan turned to Sherry. "You know, I had a real thing for this big guy at first and I was really jealous when I saw how he looked at you. I might still be, at least a little." She made a sideways glance at Cole and let out a teenaged sigh. "But really, I have to say that you two are going to be a swell couple. You're tops, certainly not like the Mathers."

Cole cut in, "What about the Mathers?"

"Well," Cynthia Ryan chose her words carefully. "Nobody wanted to share bad news when you seemed kind of fragile but you're looking pretty good now."

"Thanks so much for the diagnosis, now what about the Mathers?"

Ryan's face twisted as she searched for words. Finally she gave up and just blurted, "He killed her and tried to kill himself. Apparently he wasn't a very good shot. Mrs. Huntzov said he fired five bullets into his wife last Thursday night. With the one left, he shot himself in the head but it didn't kill him, just took off part of his face."

Cole tried to sit up in bed. "Where is he? Has he told anyone why he killed her?"

"He's up in Munich in the big military hospital. He can't speak. They think it's brain damage." Ryan shook her head. "It's sad. I feel so bad for the poor woman. Her funeral is tomorrow. We're all going, even Belcher who doesn't believe in funerals."

Cole fell back against his pillow, looked pensive as he shook his head. After a moment, he faced Sherry and said, "I want you to call the KGB office and formally invite Colonel Alexi Bukinev to the funeral." Then, as an afterthought, "And tell him to bring Commander Svetlana Borsky."

Sherry frowned deep. "All right, but on whose behalf am I inviting two Russians to an American woman's funeral?"

"Mine, I want them to know these two people are dead and I want them to know that I know the reason." His voice sounded suddenly thin, almost bitter.

Ryan hesitated but finally asked Cole the obvious question. "What do you know about this and how could you possibly know it? You've been here in the hospital for more than a week. How could you know anything about the Mathers?"

Cole made his sinister little smirk. "It's my job to know things. And while you're at it, make sure Charley Woods knows I made these invitations." Then, another afterthought, "And tell him something else. Tell him it's time for him to resign before he winds up floating in the Danube."

"Wow," Cynthia said, "That sounds harsh. Why do you want Charley to resign and who's going to toss him into the river?"

Cole only stared back. "He will know."

Sherry took his hand. "So you remain the man of mystery. Will we share some of these secrets at some point or will you always keep a part of you separate and dark?"

He gave the matter some serious thought before answering. "I have to work out a lot of things. I have never before had someone else in my life to consider. I'm just going to have to learn how to manage. For now, you should know that all these things are related and I'm not sharing more out of respect for the dead and the damaged."

"And how does that relate to Charley Woods?"

Cole leaned up on an elbow to level an unblinking stare at Cynthia Ryan. After a moment, she realized his meaning and said, "Oh well, yes, I gotta go. Great to see you doing so well, Boss. Take good care of him Sherry."

When she was gone he looked at Sherry and said, "Woods is the reason you were captured. He is the reason you were abused and humiliated. He is sleeping with a Soviet spy and passing her secrets. I invited the spy he worked with, Svetlana Borsky, to the funeral as a warning, just as I want Charley to be warned." More to himself than to Sherry, he mumbled, "Debts must be paid. Sergei Zelenkov knew that. He thought he was paying a debt when he shot me."

Sherry became noticeably distressed. "Please James, take time to heal. Don't do anything that will endanger your health or your future." She added softly, "our future."

March 7, 1500 Hours

The next day, Belcher burst into the room like a brass band. He grabbed the curtains and threw them open to the sun. "Afternoon Boss and may I be the first to say you really look like shit. The girls told me you were ready for a Rugby match. They lied."

Cole shifted uncomfortably in his bed. "They might have exaggerated just a bit. How was the funeral?"

"I guess the best word would be subdued. It's hard to say pleasant things about a lady whose old man put five slugs in her. Kind of makes you wonder what she did to provoke that much hate. Know what I mean?"

"Were there any Russians there?"

"No Boss, why would Russians go? Say, you know who else missed? Charley Woods didn't show. I can't believe that clown is going to try replacing you. Talk about sending a boy..."

"Dave, that will not happen. Charley Woods will never take over."

Belcher laughed. "You called me Dave. Since I've been here no one has ever called me anything but Belcher. I didn't think you even knew my full name."

They were both distracted by a commotion in the hall. Three men came walking so fast their civilian overcoats billowed behind them like superhero capes. Carson, the man who debriefed Phyllis, led as they stormed into Cole's room.

Carson ran his eyes over Cole's body, head to toe. "You going to survive well enough to go back to work and, if so, when?"

Cole made a shrug. "They say one more week here and then three weeks of gradual improvement. Not that it matters, I'm not going back to work. I'll be a civilian before that."

Carson leaned forward like a coach motivating a player. "Well, you won't go back to your old job but things are changing. I need to know if I can count on you."

Cole said nothing so Carson continued. "You've been out of the loop for a while so I'll bring you up to date. George Kenner, our man in Moscow, sent a long telegram to the Secretary of State who, in turn, gave it to President Truman. Kenner argued convincingly that protracted conflict with the Soviet Union is inevitable. The Soviets truly believe that the US is in the grip of monopolistic capitalists intent on world domination. Truman has reluctantly embraced a new policy of containment" He paused to let that sink in. "Just yesterday, Churchill made a speech about the Soviets."

Belcher had stepped out of the way but now chimed in. "I heard it. It was great." He made a gravelly voiced imitation of Winston Churchill complete with expansive arm gestures. "From Stettin in the Baltic to Trieste in the Adriatic, an iron curtain has descended across Europe…"

Carson sounded irritated. "Yes, thank you for that eloquent rendition. Now, here's the situation. The tide has turned and turned decisively as far as national intelligence is concerned. The CIG has been given new marching orders. They've created an Office of Special Operations and we're moving toward a new central intelligence agency under civilian control with broad responsibilities and autonomy. Here's how that affects you."

He turned to focus an intense look at Belcher. "How about you get a cup of coffee?" Belcher held up both hands in a mock submissive gesture and backed out of the room. Once he was gone, Carson turned back.

"I want you to start a civilian office here in Vienna. You pick the people you want. All I ask is that you select effective agents who can keep tabs on the Russians and protect our national interests. Can you do that?"

Cole's look of confusion slowly morphed into a confident stare. "Yes, I can handle it, but I can't say that I'll ever be completely whole again. There must be many men better suited, why me?"

Carson tilted his head. "There aren't many people I can trust and there is much to be done. The hot war has faded from prominence but a new 'cold war' is beginning and it's going to be hell. We have a special need for a special man."

Carson drew near. "We have hundreds of thousands of small arms left over from the war and enough ammunition to fight a sustained guerilla war if the Russians try to take over all of Austria. We intend to recruit, train and arm a secret army of Austrian nationalists. Will you help?"

Cole shook his head. "I just don't know. I'm sorry, but I just don't know."

March 8, 1730 Hours

The hospital, like most public buildings in Vienna, had broad marble steps with ornate iron railings. A century's worth of layered white paint reflected soft light onto ancient floor tiles worn smooth and gray. High ceilings echoed every sound and that had the curious effect of making you want to whisper. Sherry White passed an orderly pushing a gurney with a wobbly wheel and was tempted to put a finger to her lips to shush him.

There were no voices coming from Cole's room. That was a good thing. Fewer doctors usually meant fewer problems. She was surprised to find James Cole freshly shaved and dressed in civilian clothes standing by the bed in his room. She paused and allowed a concerned smile. It was the first time she had seen him in anything but hospital pajamas since the shooting. He was pale and, for such a large man, seemed fragile. His grin, however, was confident and strong.

He reached out to her and she took his hand not really knowing what to expect. She had spent a lot of time thinking about their relationship but there were so many unknowns. One thing was certain; her feelings for him were real. About that, she had no doubt. About their future, she had nothing but doubt... doubt, confusion and maybe even a little terror.

He cleared his throat as though making a speech. "Sherry, I have spent the night thinking and I've made a lot of decisions. First, I want to marry you. I want to marry you as soon as possible. I want us to find a house with trees and grass and flowers and I want to live there for a long time." He grinned and gestured with boyish enthusiasm. "Also, I want to start an orphanage. I want you to contact Billy Connors and tell him to buy the old school building in Shottenburg where we will create a home for abandoned Austrian children."

"An orphanage?" She felt a sudden rush of confused emotions. Certainly, she had contemplated marriage but there seemed so many obstacles—and what the devil was this orphanage idea? Where did that come from? She wasn't the type to run an orphanage. She wasn't even sure she was the type to have children. As his words sank in, she felt a rising anger in her chest. Well maybe not really anger, but irritation.

Her voice was sharp. "I guess I should be flattered that your proposal of marriage was number one on your list of things to do. As for the orphanage and a house in Vienna, it would have been nice to discuss before you made your decisions. It seems to me there are a few small problems in your plan."

Cole's smile waned. "I know, I know. But things are happening, and happening fast. Carson came yesterday and made me an offer. I don't know if I'll accept but it made me think and, after thinking, I know what I want.

He still held her hand as his eyes closed in on hers. "I know we should have talked first but I think that, in time, you'll agree that these are all good ideas, noble ideas. The one I'm most sure of is that I want to marry you and I will allow nothing to stand in the way. What I'm not completely sure, is whether you want to marry me."

He produced a small velvet box from his pocket and, with an awkward effort, opened it to reveal a ring. She was taken aback. "How in the world did you get that? You've been in this hospital for weeks." She let go of his hand and touched the box but did not take it. She was breathing through her teeth as she ran her free hand through her hair and shook her head as though saying no but, after a long silence, came back with a resolute voice.

"Yes, James Cole, I will marry you, but we have to talk about these other things. You're about to become an unemployed civilian. I don't know what my situation is. I certainly don't know if I want to become a caretaker for hundreds of orphaned children. That might be a very noble cause, but I don't know if it's my cause."

Cole's strength was fading. Seeing him falter, she took his arm to ease him back onto a chair. He laughed and it brought a wet cough. "I'm going to get better. I'm going to get stronger. I'm going to ask a lot of you. It will take me a long time to explain but I think that in the end you'll believe me when I tell you this is what we need to do."

1915 Hours

Charley Woods stumbled in from the storm. He was filthy and dripping. Two days of drunken rain-soaked wandering left him looking like a street beggar with clothes so dirty they weren't immediately recognizable as a uniform. Still, no one bothered him as he climbed the stairs to the second floor of the hospital where he saw Sherry White coming out of a room, Cole's room.

With a deep breath, he steadied himself and straightened to walk erect despite his drunken stare. A curious orderly watched, but seeing no obvious threat, went back to his crossword puzzle. Charley peered into Cole's room. The bed was empty. That confused him. He knew he wasn't thinking clearly, wasn't really sure why he was there. He was, however, sure that he was going to get Major Cole's attention.

Fumbling underneath his soggy uniform coat, Charley found the handle to his army issue .45 automatic. Hiding the gun beside his leg, he stepped into the room and called out, surprised by how childish he sounded. "Major Cole, come out, come out, wherever you are."

A voice came from a chair by the window. "I'm right here Charley but why the gun?"

Charley Woods' head bobbed and he slurred as he spoke. "I know you don't want me to run the detachment—doesn't matter.

I heard that you wanted me dead—doesn't matter either." He made a silly smile. "Cause it's you that needs to worry about being dead. You're not a major any...more and you don't have any power over me."

He displayed his gun as though it might have magical properties. Now his voice turned quiet as he looked at James Cole contorted uncomfortably in a small chair. "You can't hurt me anymore. You think I'm a traitor." He made an exaggerated head shake. "No. No. I was a spy, a good spy. I got a lot of information from the Ruskies. I did a lot of good. And the stuff I gave them—the stuff about the tunnel, the raid and the other—it didn't amount to a hill. But you still think I'm traitor."

Charley raised his gun using both hands trying to focus his aim in Cole's direction. But then he was distracted by running footsteps. He started to turn just as a screaming Sherry White leaped onto his back. The impact winded him and sent his gun flying. Sherry rode him to the ground hammering his head and shoulders with her fists, yelling, flailing and pounding the helpless drunk.

Charley covered his head with his hands and began a clumsy crab walk toward the door on elbows and knees. He was whining, might even have been crying, he wasn't sure. Sherry was still on his back, still hammering. He had to escape, had to claw his way free.

Once out in the hall, Sherry abandoned her attack and went back to grab the gun and protect Cole. Someone behind the central desk picked up a phone and dialed the police. Hospital staff gathered around to look at Charley stretched out on the floor. He was an American officer of the occupation and they were all Austrians. None dared interfere. They had lived too long under Nazi, Soviet and now Allied occupation.

Charley pulled himself to his feet using a door knob. Once standing, he straightened his coat and stretched his chin with an exaggerated sneer. Then, ignoring the crowd, he stumbled down the stairs and out into the pouring rain.

As he left, he could hear Sherry crying as she clutched Cole in shaking arms and kissed his forehead. She seemed unaware that she still held Charley's big gun in one hand. He heard her whisper, "I'll do whatever you want," she whispered," as long as you promise you'll never leave me."

1925 Hours

Colonel Bukinev stood beside a figure in black waiting under a store awning. A waterfall of runoff shielded them from the storm-drenched street. Even a crash of thunder was overpowered by the roar of wind and rain and traffic.

Charley came out looking lost, bewildered, overcome by the drenching rain. Bukinev opened his umbrella and put on his most American accent.

"Hey Charley, Charley Woods, over here—C'mon man, you're going to drown in this storm. Take my umbrella and I'll call us a cab." Bukinev held up his umbrella and motioned to come.

Charley hesitated. He knew he was drunk and couldn't trust his judgment. "Who… who's there? What do you want?" He backed away waving arms as if warding off a swarm of bees. He shouted above the torrential rain, "No, I don't need help. I'll be okay. Things always work out for me. I'm the good guy, the guy everybody likes." He beat on his chest for emphasis. "I get in trouble. I get in trouble a lot… but I always get out. I'm Ruly, do you understand? I'm Ruly, the guy who always comes out okay. You hear me, this'll be okay?"

Bukinev stepped into the downpour and shouted, "Of course you'll be okay Charley. After all, you're Ruly. But you have to get out of the rain or you'll get pneumonia. Here, take my umbrella." Bukinev walked into the downpour, put the umbrella in Charley's hand and eased him back toward the curb. "Now you stay right here. Don't move until I get us a cab. Okay Charley? Just stand right here."

Once he was sure Charley would obey, Bukinev stepped back and motioned as though hailing a cab. But it wasn't a cab that responded; it was a huge old German freight truck that pulled out from a dark side street accelerating noisily. It lurched through the flooded street leaving a rooster tail of spray that flashed in the reflected lights of traffic. Charley Woods stared at the oncoming truck lights as they bore down on him.

He let the umbrella fall, raised his face to pelting rain and stretched his arms wide as though pleading with the gods. The headlights were almost on him. He stood like a crucifix, stood and screamed, "I am Ruly. I am…"

The impact flattened him in an instant but the big truck continued on, snagging the body and dragging it along the curb before bouncing to a stop. The driver jumped out and did a very believable impression of a distraught man at an accident scene. Despite the rain, a small crowd of umbrellas gathered around the accident scene and the driver disappeared among them.

Bukinev retrieved the umbrella Charley dropped on the sidewalk. He opened it and stood with the sound of rain hammering on its fabric. The Russian wiped water off his face and leaned down to inspect Charley's body. An electric light swinging in the wind provided intermittent flashes of light on the scene. Charley's torso was pinned beneath the truck but one limp arm extended, snapping like a ribbon in the rushing current of gutter water. The man was dead, no doubt. Satisfied, Bukinev went back under the awning to the figure dressed in a black oilcloth coat and rain hat.

He had to shout to be heard, "I am sorry it had to end like this. I know you had begun to care about this man. His people thought him a fool but the truth was that he was actually quite a clever fellow. The reports he gave to Major Cole were simply the misinformation you gave him, largely useless. But, when he combined it with the files from the GRU girls, he was able to create a very accurate understanding of our penetration of the Austrian government."

Svetlana Borsky shook her head and water ran off the brim of her hat. "But we know what he reported."

Bukinev nodded, "We know what he reported to Major Cole, but his handler was actually some other major who worked in the Nazi art recovery group. The reports to that man, we believe, were much more thorough, much more damaging. We had to get rid of him before his handlers realized how much he really knew."

Svetlana Borsky looked up from her black rain visor, took in a deep breath and spoke in Russian, "He was the prettiest of them all. I underestimated him. He seemed like a fool but, it seems, I was the fool. He penetrated our organization more deeply than we ever suspected. I feel responsible."

Bukinev put his arm around his black coated companion and tried to sound fatherly even over the booming storm. "I'm sorry Comrade Borsky. I know you had come to care for the man but individuals must sometimes be sacrificed for the common good. You should go back to Moscow now. You can do great things there." She bowed her head but did not speak.

Bukinev gave her a perfunctory hug and they walked off together into the stormy darkness.

March 9, 1100 Hours

"We need to talk." Sherry sat down beside Cole's wheelchair.

He motioned at the wheelchair. "This is just a temporary thing while I'm going through rehabilitation. It's nothing to worry about."

"It's not the wheelchair that bothers me. First, why did Charley Woods come after you with a gun? And then there's this orphanage project. I spoke to the driver, Connors. He's a private you know, a potato peeling private who makes twenty dollars a month. When I told him about the school building you want to buy he didn't blink. Instead, he told me he would have a purchase agreement drawn up in two days along with three contractor bids for renovation. So tell me, Mister Cole, how do an unemployed former officer and an Army private negotiate to buy such a huge building? If I am going to be your wife, I need to know who the hell you are."

Cole took her hand. *"If* you are to be my wife?" After an uncomfortable pause, he spoke slowly. "Charley was always a volatile personality. I think he just let booze get to him. As for the rest, I have been planning how to tell you things. I will always have secrets, but not from you, not anymore. Billy Connors is my black market contact. He can get almost anything for a price. I have money. It's not my money. It was stolen by the Nazis but now I have it. I didn't take it but now I have it- a huge stash of money."

He checked her reaction and continued, "I swore that I would never use the money for my personal gain and I won't, but neither can I give it back. Just having it could earn me a life sentence in the Leavenworth Penitentiary. The orphanage seems a just use for the money, Nazi money for orphans of Nazi crimes."

She started to lean forward as if to hug him but he raised a hand. "There's much more. I have contacts. There is an Austrian Countess, a forger, politicians and many others. I intend to hire Mrs. Huntzov to run the orphanage while I spend my time covertly opposing the Russians. You see, they want to take over all of Austria. I have come to care about this country and I'll fight to save it. To that end, I intend to hire several former detachment people."

Sherry blinked and hesitated. "Wow, you intend to single-handedly save an entire country." She frowned and looked off into space. "Okay, you'll be David facing off with Goliath and just what is my role?"

Without a moment's hesitation, he answered. "I want you to be my wife. Everything else is secondary."

She seemed lost in thought for a time and then gave him a coy look. "Don't think for a minute that I'm staying out of this orphanage thing Mister Cole. We're a team now." She leaned back, more relaxed. "While we're at it, let's talk about who you really are. Colonel Mather called you a Republican stooge. I'm a registered Democrat. That might be a small problem."

He made a shrug. "To be honest, I've never registered to vote. All this political stuff—Republican, Democrat, Communist, capitalist—I don't put stock in any of it. If a government cares about its people, that's all that matters. The rest is just propaganda."

She seemed comfortable with that answer. "Okay, how about religion?"

Now he made a face. "Well, I hope this doesn't offend you but I'm not religious. I don't see much difference between religion and politics. History, economics, psychology, philosophy, I don't have strong opinions about them. When people think they alone possess absolute truth, then they are willing to kill."

She pressed him, "But you've killed."

He grappled with the question and was slow to respond. "Yes, I killed many... to prevent the other team from killing us." He looked at her. "That sounds like a contradiction doesn't it?"

She reached over and hugged him. "You are a man filled with contradictions but I'm still proud of you and I'm on your team."

CHAPTER EIGHT

April 11, 1500 Hours

James Cole healed faster than anyone expected. Things were quickly coming together, including his wedding. The small, quiet ceremony he and Sherry planned was not to be. The new orphanage became a cause for celebration in a city with little else to celebrate. Government officials, military figures and aid organization managers clamored to become associated with the home for war orphans.

Instead of one of Vienna's spectacular cathedrals, they decided to marry in a small war-damaged chapel. The austere, cramped venue quickly overflowed with a standup crowd that filled the aisles and spilled out to the gardens. Luckily, the weather was perfect for guests who strolled outside among the first blooms of the year. Everything was fresh, green and full of promise.

James Cole, now a civilian, wore a very European tuxedo and looked almost distinguished even as he towered over most guests. Sherry wore a tasteful and flattering tea length dress and small veil. They were a perfect couple in a perfect setting. In fact, they could have topped a wedding cake, but there was no cake at this ceremony.

The ceremony was brief and unremarkable. There was no reception. Cole said it was inappropriate to indulge in a feast when so many had to beg for food. This was exactly the right tone to bring contributions flowing. With so many apparent donors no one would have to ask where the money to rebuild the old school came from.

After the ceremony, James and Sherry Cole spent hours mingling with the high and mighty of Viennese life. Handshakes and introductions overwhelmed. Sherry, who spoke little German, stood apart from James and dealt mainly with the Americans and Russians, mostly senior Army officers. The American officers were uniformly apologetic about James's forced separation from the military and grateful not to face him directly.

To the handful of Russians, Sherry was cordial but restrained. Colonel Bukinev was the last. He was, as usual, flamboyantly suave. He bowed slightly, took Sherry's hand and kissed her knuckles. She forced a smile.

"My dear, you and your new husband are doing a wonderful thing. I promise you full cooperation from your Soviet allies. You speak our language and you know our culture. You will always be welcome in our areas. I guarantee it. We have many orphans who can benefit from your institution."

She was tentative. "We will, of course, help the poor children inside your zone but I must be honest, I did not enjoy your hospitality when I last visited there."

The Russian's blue eyes were as transparent as glass. His smile was not. "That was unfortunate but let me also be honest. You were a spy inside the Soviet Zone illegally eavesdropping on Russian military conversations. You are only alive today because of the compassion and kindness of your captors."

Sherry lifted her chin and tried to hide anger. "Did you know the man who shot my husband?"

If Bukinev was taken aback, it didn't show. "Yes, I knew him. It was a tragedy. He was a fine officer until he encountered your husband. Who could even dream that a Hero of the Soviet Union could defect and abandon his wife and son? Between you and me, I think being repeatedly humiliated by your husband must have driven him quite mad. I am so sorry."

He paused and leaned forward slightly. "Perhaps, at some point we might have coffee and I can properly express my regret."

Sherry sensed his meaning and tried hard not to laugh. "Sir, are you propositioning me?"

"Oh no, no, no. I simply meant to say that I hoped that we could be friends, that's all."

Her forced smile evaporated. "I understand you were 'friends' with Mrs. Mather. That didn't work out well for her."

Bukinev pursed his lips and stepped back, suddenly stiff and military. "Good luck to you and your husband, madam. I wish you a long and happy marriage untouched by tragedy."

As Bukinev left, Cynthia Ryan sidled up, "What was that all about?"

Sherry sipped her wine, "Just a Russian making a clumsy pass at me." She turned to Cynthia. "Say, you look adorable. I've never seen you in a dress before."

"And it will be a long time before you see me like this again. I hate feeling wind between my legs. I feel naked."

"Well, you didn't seem to mind that in the nudist colony with my husband."

Cynthia made a pained expression. "Touché, guess I'll never live that down. But hey, you got my guy. It didn't do me any good to show off my stuff for him. Now you have a great fellow and I'm still alone."

Sherry considered for a second. "You know you're not alone. Have you not noticed that no one ever says 'Belcher' without adding 'and Ryan'? You guys are a team. You finish his sentences and he always looks out for you. Admit it, you belong together."

"Belcher?" Cynthia scrunched her face. "He's like a big dumb lug, loveable but still a lug... and besides he's married."

Sherry shrugged. "He's not really married. His wife is living in New Jersey with another man. He hasn't divorced her but that's just so his son will continue to have military medical coverage. He's not dumb either. He has a degree in mechanical engineering."

"How do you know all that?"

Sherry leaned close. "Before she died, I worked closely with Mrs. Parks. She was a relentless investigator and she had a dossier on everyone in the detachment, even you."

"Me, what do you know about me?"

"Well, I know you married Air Corps Lieutenant Jerry Ryan while you worked in the code room at Upper Heyford, England. He died on his second B-17 mission and you joined the Army right after that."

"He was a great guy. I'll never find another like him."

"Don't be so sure. Look at Dave Belcher in a new way. Think it over and maybe you would both like to come and work for us."

Cynthia shook her head. "I don't see myself as a babysitter at an orphanage."

Sherry put her arm on Cynthia's shoulder. "Oh, don't worry, you wouldn't be babysitting. Dave Belcher has already signed up with us. Roland and Johnson are considering. You know McMahan is going to marry Fraulein Gint so we'll be able to get help from them. You would feel right at home."

1720 Hours

As the procession of well-wishers shook hands and clapped him on the back, Cole was careful not to offend. He needed contacts, patrons, donors and collaborators. Men lined up to speak to him and he spent time with each. Down the line, he was stunned to see a very familiar face, one he never expected to see again. The man was short and stout with a double-breasted suit and wire rimmed glasses. Neither gave any hint of recognition.

When it was his turn the man extended a hand. "Charles Conrad Collingsworth, pleased to meet you."

Cole shook hands and smiled politely. "Are you with the embassy, Mr. Collingsworth?"

"Oh no, I'm with the United Nations. I work with the DP Camps managing logistics. I'm new here in Vienna but looking forward to my stay. I hope I can be of some assistance to you."

Cole placed his hand in a pocket to deposit the folded piece of paper Collingsworth had slipped him in the handshake. He was sure it was contact instructions.

Collingsworth gave a nod and continued, "This orphanage thing is brilliant. You'll have so much access to so many resources. I wish you well and hope I can be a significant contributor."

Cole spoke softly, "You already have."

Collingsworth/Aalpeter/Mason/Trasker started to turn away but hesitated. "This orphanage idea is great, absolutely great." He looked around for eavesdroppers. "But remember, you're still in Vienna."

He moved on but Cole called after him, "It's a whole new world." But Collingsworth did not acknowledge.

James Cole shook hands with the next man in line and had a small epiphany. He was the center of attention in a huge crowd and it didn't bother him. Even more important, he wasn't playing any role. There just wasn't anyone else in the world he wanted to be. This was his own personal adventure and he needed no movie heroes to impersonate. This was his time. He took a deep breath and smelled flowers of the Viennese spring.

EPILOG

For nine years the US secretly trained Austrian resistance fighters called Militia-B Force. They were to be a sleeper force ready to fight any Soviet effort to take over all of Austria. But they were never needed. In 1955, the Soviet Union withdrew its Army without bloodshed.

There are no records of how many militia men were trained but we know that over 200,000 small arms were provided to them. Those guns were buried in fake coffins, some even had headstones. Others were stowed in cone-shaped containers under farmer's haystacks or built into walls as part of the post-war reconstruction. What became of all those guns is unknown.

Stalin got his A-bomb but not because of the captured German scientists. Communist spies in Britain, America and Austria provided all the information he needed. The French developed their own bomb but gave no credit to any German help.

The United States belatedly created the Central Intelligence Agency when the reality of the Cold War finally hit home. The new CIA was manned by a mix of politically connected bureaucrats and old wartime spies, oil and water.

Today, the Cold War is a distant memory and the thousands who died fighting it are largely forgotten but, without them, the world would be a very different place.

Vienna remains a vibrant crossroad for spies of many nations.